THE BEACH PARTY MYSTERY

HEADLINE HERO SERIES
BOOK 8

PETER BARTRAM

RED NOMAD studios

PRAISE FOR PETER BARTRAM'S HEADLINE HERO SERIES...

"I found myself quickly wrapped up in this and didn't want to put it down until it was done!" *Me & My Books*

"A fun read with humour throughout..." *Crime Thriller Hound*

"An excellent novel, full of twists and turns, plenty of action scenes, crackling dialogue - and a great sense of fun." *Fully Booked*

"A good page-turning murder mystery, with a likeable protagonist and great setting." *The Bookworm Chronicles*

"A highly enjoyable and well-crafted read, with a host of engaging characters." *Mrs Peabody Investigates*

"An amiable romp through the shady back streets of 1960s Brighton." *Simon Brett, Crime Writers' Association Diamond Dagger winner*

"A highly entertaining, involving mystery, narrated in a charming voice, with winning characters. Highly recommended." *In Search of the Classic Mystery Novel*

"Part adventure story, part politically incorrect comedy, this is a fast-moving and funny book. I would recommend it as a light and satisfying read." *Northern Reader*

"A romp of a read! Very funny and very British." *The Book Trail*

"Superbly crafted and as breezy as a stroll along the pier, this Brighton-based murder mystery is a delight." *Peter Lovesey, Crime Writers' Association Diamond Dagger winner*

"It read like a breath of fresh air and I can't wait for the next one." *Little Bookness Lane*

"By the end of page one, I knew I liked Colin Crampton and author Peter Bartram's breezy writing style." *Over My Dead Body*

"A little reminiscent of [Raymond] Chandler." *Bookwitch*

"A rather fun and well-written cozy mystery set in 1960s Brighton." *Northern Crime*

"The story is a real whodunit in the classic mould." **Crime author *M J Trow***

"A fast-paced mystery, superbly plotted, and kept me guessing right until the end." *Don't Tell Me the Moon Is Shining*

"Very highly recommended." *Midwest Book Review*

"One night I stayed up until nearly 2am thinking 'I'll just read one more chapter'. This is a huge recommendation from me." *Life of a Nerdish Mum*

"I highly recommend this book and the author. I will definitely be reading more of this series and his other books." *The Divine Write*

"Bartram skilfully delivers one of the most complex cozy mystery plots I've read in years." *Booklover Book Reviews*

THE BEACH PARTY MYSTERY

Headline Hero series

Book 8

Peter Bartram

Red Nomad Studios

Published by Red Nomad Studios, 2020

For contact details:
www.rednomadstudios.com
www.headlinehero.co.uk

Text copyright: Peter Bartram, 2020
Typesetting and cover design: Red Nomad Studios

ISBN: 979-8689870687

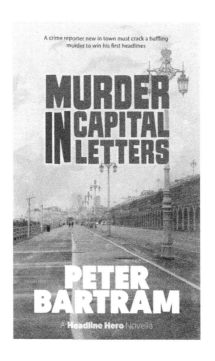

A crime reporter new in town must crack a baffling murder to win his first headlines.

Crime reporter Colin Crampton has been in Brighton only days before he stumbles on the body of a murdered antiques dealer. It's a great story but Colin must face down the cops and rival journos if he's to land his first scoop.

Claim your free copy by visiting the URL below:

https://www.headlinehero.co.uk/murder-in-capital-letters

ALSO BY PETER BARTRAM

My **Headline Hero Collections** are great value and include bonus
reads from **The Headline Hero Trilogy**!

Headline Hero Collection 1 - Books 1-3

Headline Hero Collection 2 - Books 4-6

Headline Hero Collection 3 - Books 7-9

HEADLINE HERO SERIES

Headline Murder

Stop Press Murder

Front Page Murder

The Tango School Mystery

The Mother's Day Mystery

The Comedy Club Mystery

The Poker Game Mystery

The Beach Party Mystery

The World Cup Mystery

The Family Tree Mystery

THE HEADLINE HERO TRILOGY

Murder in the Morning Edition

Murder in the Afternoon Extra

Murder in the Night Final

The Morning, Noon, and Night Trilogy Omnibus Edition

HEADLINE HERO FREE READS

PROLOGUE

April 1966.

Perry Turner picked up a record, glanced at the label, and flipped it onto the turntable.

The needle hissed as it hit the vinyl.

Turner cursed under his breath. Unprofessional. How long had he been in this disc jockey racket? Nearly a year. He should know by now.

At least he was good at the next bit.

He leaned in towards the microphone. So close, the muff tickled his lips.

He lowered his voice an octave so it sounded as smooth as molasses sliding over marble.

"And now for all you pop princes and princesses beginning another day's toil, here are the Mindbenders to help you on your way with *A Groovy Kind of Love*."

He muted the microphone and leaned back in his chair. He

smirked. Who'd have thought a one-time schoolboy swot with pimples would have the girls swooning whenever they heard his silky tones?

Well, okay, fair's fair. He'd had one letter from a 54-year-old school-dinner lady in Blatchington. She'd said her right leg went all wobbly when he'd introduced Dusty Springfield's *You Don't Have to Say You Love Me*.

Pity the silly old bat spoiled it. A week later she'd written in to say the wobbles hadn't been passion after all. The doc had told her she needed a hip replacement.

Still, no one could take away his biggest achievement.

Radio *Seabreeze*.

The idea had blossomed after Radio Caroline hit the airwaves in 1964. An unlicensed radio station the big-wigs at the BBC couldn't touch. It was broadcast from a ship moored outside the three-mile limit of Britain's territorial waters.

Perhaps he should run a pirate radio station, too.

He'd suggested the idea to his backers. They'd frowned at the notion at first. But then he'd explained his plan. And their lips had parted in wolf-like grins to reveal their grey teeth.

Besides, Turner knew in an instant that it would be a sure-fire way to make money.

More important, it was a way to win friends and influence people.

And one day – in some other place and some other time – Turner wanted to be that somebody whom others sought out as an influential friend.

But that was a dangerous thought.

Better kept a secret.

Turner had known it wouldn't be easy to make a mark with a new pirate radio station. Within months of Radio Caroline's first broadcast, there were close on a dozen others clustered around the coast of south-east England.

Besides, before he could join the fleet, he needed a ship. Not a posh liner like the Cunard's *Queen Mary*. Not one of those new oil tankers as long as a London street. He had to find a boat big enough to house all the equipment he'd need for a radio station – and with enough cabins to house the disc jockeys and crew.

He'd spent months searching the old boatyards of Britain until he'd found what he needed. A coaster in a dry dock in Hartlepool. It was a bit like the "dirty British coaster" John Masefield had written about in his poem. Although whether this coaster had ever butted through the Channel with a cargo of "Tyne coal, road rails, pig lead, firewood, iron-ware and cheap tin trays" he couldn't say.

It was called the *Sea Porter*. That would never do for a pirate radio ship. It carried an image of hunch-backed men sweating over heavy suitcases. So when the month-long restoration work on the coaster was completed, Turner privately broke a bottle of Georgian champagne over its stern.

And christened it *Seabreeze*.

Great name for a radio station, Turner had thought. Especially one that was going to be moored just over three miles off the coast of the English Channel outside Brighton.

His backers had grinned again. Especially when he'd had the idea of celebrating the radio station's first anniversary on the airwaves with a lavish party on Brighton beach.

The Mindbenders swung into their last chorus.

A groovy kind of love.

Turner glanced up at the studio clock. Seven minutes to nine. Just time for a couple more singles and an ad or two before Chunky took over at nine.

Who was he kidding?

Chunky – Charles Dunn, according to his birth certificate -

never took over at nine. The fat oaf would still be sleeping off last night's whisky.

Turner reached for another record and flipped it onto the turntable.

He leant in so close the mike muff tickled his nose. He raised his finger to stifle a sneeze.

The music started. Turner twiddled a knob to fade the disc.

"And next up, popsters, it's *Sha La La La Lee*, with The Small Faeces," he crooned.

Damn!

Turner grimaced. He hated making mistakes on air.

"You didn't hear that, popsters, I said, The Small Faces."

Turner pushed up the music's volume, and swore again. But, quietly, under his breath.

Charles Dunn shifted his eighteen-stone bulk on his bunk.

A tangle of sheets and blankets flopped onto the floor.

Dunn cursed, rolled over, and collapsed on top of them. His bulging belly wobbled like a shaken jelly. Dunn belched, tasted the peaty flavour of last night's whisky on his tongue.

He struggled to his feet and staggered a couple of steps to the washbasin and mirror on the other side of his cabin. He stared at the face in the mirror.

Christ, is that me?

He said "*aaaah*" and stuck out his tongue. The face in the mirror did the same. Dunn peered closer. The tongue looked as rough as a dosshouse doormat.

The eyes peering back at him were bloodshot. The nose flattened – the result of a drunken argument with a swing door. The cheeks sagged, the chin was flabby, the neck was stubby.

"The glamour of radio," Dunn said to the reflection in the mirror. "Thank my lucky bollocks there aren't any pictures."

Dunn reached for a shaving brush and soap and lathered up his chin. He opened a cut-throat razor and honed the blade a couple of times on a strop which hung beside the washbasin.

His hand shook as he positioned the razor underneath his chin.

"Now, don't do what dozens would have gladly done, given half the chance," he said.

His body stiffened and his hand stopped shaking. He ran the razor smoothly over his chin. The blade picked up the shaving soap.

Dunn wiped the soap off on a towel and continued shaving.

"It's a funny old life," he said to the half-shaved face. "There you are working in an office in London. The next minute you're a disc jockey on a ship."

Dunn grinned as he used the towel to wipe the remains of the soap from around his ears.

"You never know what life's going to deliver next," he said.

Still, he didn't miss the morning crush on the underground. Or the fog which came up the river in the evening. And he loved the seaside life of Brighton.

Pity he had to be careful about how he sampled it. He didn't want to run into one of his old customers. Not one who knew him from the past.

His secret would be out.

And that would never do.

* * *

Zena Lightheart's long blonde hair streamed in the wind as the powerful engine of the sleek motor cruiser roared up to full power.

Zena steered the rudder to the right. The cruiser left a foaming wake as it skirted the end of Palace Pier on Brighton's seafront. A gaggle of holidaymakers gawped over the railings at the end of the pier. They pointed at the cruiser and chattered excitedly.

"Okay, suckers," Zena murmured to herself. "Show's over. This little beauty is heading out to sea."

Zena's full lips parted in a tiny smile as she looked ahead at the hazy horizon. Or was it her eyes that were still hazy. From smoking a little too much weed last night.

Whatever!

If you had to leave the full flower-power experience in San Francisco, Brighton wasn't a bad place to pitch up, Zena thought. Most of them here got what it meant to be around at the dawn of the age of Aquarius.

And those that didn't could be written off as brain dead anyway.

Besides, Zena had her own reasons for coming to Brighton. But she was keeping those firmly to herself.

She aimed the cruiser at a point due south, just over the horizon. She didn't need a compass to chart the course. She'd made this run dozens of times already. When your radio station broadcasts from a ship out at sea, the mailman doesn't come calling. So Zena's early morning chore was to take the cruiser ashore and pick up the mail from the *poste restante* at Brighton Post Office.

Not that it was much of a chore on a morning like this. The sun slanted in from the east behind Seaford Head and projected little points of light onto the swell of the waves. A freshening breeze blew in from the south-east and white horses broke on the swell.

Zena looked at the bundle of letters next to her on the

bench. Must have been more than twenty today. Most of them would be requests to play a favourite song on somebody's birthday.

But the letter on top was something different. Not one of the little blue Basildon Bond envelopes the requests usually came in. This one was a full-sized white envelope. And the address had been typed in those big letters you got on fancy typewriters. And there was the correct stamp on it, too.

This will be the letter Perry's waiting for, Zena thought.

The cruiser bounced a little as the water became choppy. Some spray blew over Zena, soaking her tee-shirt – *Make Love Not War* – and leaving a damp patch on her jeans.

Zena laughed.

And pushed the cruiser even faster.

The rusty outline of the *Seabreeze* appeared minutes later.

Zena throttled back on the power and drew the cruiser alongside the accommodation ladder that ran down the port side of the boat, close to the stern.

She secured the cruiser to the accommodation ladder and grabbed the bundle of letters. She stepped onto the first rung of the ladder and hurried up.

The Kinks' *Dedicated Follower of Fashion* was playing over the ship's loudspeakers.

Turner had just stepped out of the studio as Zena reached the deck. Dunn climbed out of the companionway to start his set.

Zena held up the big letter. The one with the fancy typewriting.

"It's come," she said.

Turner smiled at Zena, then glared at Dunn.

Dunn shot a sneaky peek at Zena's wet tee-shirt, then scowled at Turner.

Zena waved at Turner, then stuck out her tongue at Dunn.

Each of them had a dangerous secret.

But none of them knew the secrets the others harboured.

And that was going to cause a lot of trouble.

ONE

June 1966.

Pete the Pickpocket stuffed the last piece of chocolate éclair into his mouth and licked the cream off his fingers.

He gobbled the pastry, swallowed hard, and said: "It's a bleeding liberty, Mr Crampton. Can't you do anything about it?"

I took a sip of my tea and said: "My by-line at the *Evening Chronicle* reads crime correspondent, not agony aunt."

We were sitting at a window table in Sally's Compact Tearoom. It was a tiny place with only three tables. Sally had set it up in the parlour of her terraced house in Sudeley Place, just opposite the Continentale cinema.

Pete examined his fingers to make sure they were free of cream. Those fingers were as nimble as a concert pianist's. He was a thin bloke with an instantly forgettable face and an untidy thatch of brown hair. He looked like thousands of other

9

young men. He was the kind of bloke you'd never notice by chance. Perfect cover for his trade.

I said: "Anyway, Pete, what's a bleeding liberty?"

"It's that London whiz mob. You know, dippers. Bernie Hunt's gang."

"What about them?"

"They're only threatening to take over my patch."

"You don't have a patch. You trawl up and down Western Road with occasional side visits to the magistrates' court when you're nicked."

"Yeah. Well, it's the principle of the thing, Mr Crampton. How would you like it if a team of scribblers moved in on the *Chronicle* and started writing stuff?"

"I'd take a day off. Besides, Hunt will only be coming for the beach party. He'll reckon that with thousands on the beach, there'll be pockets to pick."

Pete leaned across the table. "And he'd be right. This is my town – and I claim first dibs on the beach party dipping. They're going to have a stage with bands. There'll be a standing audience just as I like 'em."

"How's that?"

"Focused on something else. Eyes everywhere but on me, while my hand slides into their pocket or their handbag. It'll be like Christmas morning when I was a kid and I pulled pressies out of my Christmas stocking. And I don't want no London mob sticking their noses in."

Pete picked up his cup and slurped his tea.

We fell silent.

I glanced across the road at the Continentale cinema. Wondered how a building that started life as a congregational chapel ended up with a billboard outside showing a busty blonde nurse in a starched white uniform. The miniskirt was short enough to raise her patient's blood pressure. She was wearing black stockings. The buckles of her suspenders showed below the hem of her skirt.

The film was called *Naughty Night Nurse Does Her Rounds*.

A bloke with a ferret face and a grubby mackintosh sidled up to the billboard, took a furtive glance, then slipped into the cinema's foyer.

I switched my attention back to Pete. He stared moodily into his empty teacup.

I said: "You complain about Hunt's mob, but you came from London yourself when things got too hot for you."

Pete ran a finger round his plate to pick up a stray smear of cream. He sucked his finger while he thought about that.

"Yeah! Well, I had to quit the Big Smoke. I had a team but we all had to skedaddle a bit smartish after a stall job went arse over tit."

"Stall job? What's that supposed to mean?"

"One of the best scams. Sweet when we pulled it off. I worked it with Mairéad O'Kelly and Frankie the Fist. We had it down to a T. Mairéad would put on her extra tight jeans. Made her bum look like two ferrets fighting under a blanket when she walked. Anyway, she'd get in front of some sap who'd be fixated on it. He'd be trolling along a couple of feet behind her. Then she'd stop. Sudden like. Without warning. The sap would cannon into her. Freddie, who'd been following the mark, would bump into him. Freddie would start shouting at Mairéad for being such a dozy cow. She'd scream at Freddie for being a plonker and the poor sap was caught in the middle of the fight. I'd slide in like a peace-loving bloke who wanted to calm the row. But while it was going on, I'd be all over the sap's pockets and clean him out. I'd vamoose with the gear and when I was out of sight, Mairéad and Freddie would sling a couple more insults at each other and storm off in opposite directions. The sap would be so pleased he was out of it, he wouldn't even realise he'd been dipped."

I frowned. "A right little gang of Artful Dodgers, weren't you? Am I supposed to be impressed?"

"You would've been. But we picked the wrong mark."

"Had to happen."

"Yeah! An off-duty cop. Chief superintendent, would you believe? He knew every move in the book. And some. He let us start on the move, then tried to arrest us. Freddie put him down with a straight right to the jaw. We hoofed it like a stable of Derby winners. But we couldn't work in London no more."

"So you decided to give Brighton the benefits of your talents?"

"Seemed only fair," Pete said. "But what can you do about Hunt's mob moving in?"

I glanced out of the window at the Continentale. Now, a small man was studying the poster of the naughty night nurse. I switched back to Pete.

"What do you expect me to do?" I asked.

"Write an article exposing them."

"I can't do that unless they're convicted."

"But there must be something you can do."

I looked back at the bloke outside the Continentale. Something about the way he'd hunched his back over the poster reminded me of someone.

"Nothing," I said to Pete while I looked at the man.

"You might at least take an interest."

The man outside turned around and shot a shifty glance up and down the street.

I gasped.

It was Frank Figgis. My news editor.

He should be at work in his office. But as the thought crossed my mind, he hurried into the cinema.

"You seem more interested in what's going on out there than helping me," Pete said.

"Too right," I said.

"Ain't you even gonna buy me another chocolate éclair?"

"No."

"How about another tea?"

"No."

I stood up and moved towards the door.

"You might at least show a bit of sympathy," Pete shouted after me. "There'll come a time when you'll need my help."

I turned back. "When am I ever going to need to pick someone's pocket?" I said.

I hurried through the door.

It looked as though I was about to have an unscheduled meeting with Frank Figgis.

And the naughty night nurse.

* * *

An usherette shone a torch into my face and demanded: "Ticket."

I held up the stub and she switched the beam onto it.

She squinted at the ticket through horn-rimmed glasses.

"Sit anywhere," she said.

I blinked a couple of times as my eyes became accustomed to the gloom of the auditorium.

On the screen, the naughty night nurse I'd seen in the poster outside the cinema was at a table. She poured red liquid into a kidney dish.

I scanned the auditorium and searched for the familiar outline of the back of Figgis' head.

There were a dozen men scattered about the place. No

more than one to a row. As if each was afraid of catching something from the others.

Figgis was in the middle about ten rows back from the screen.

I crept down the aisle and edged into the row. I pulled down the seat and sat next to him.

I whispered: "I bet I know what happens next."

"What?" Figgis said absent-mindedly. He was riveted on the screen.

There was an uneasy silence. Then his body stiffened. And his head revolved slowly towards me. As though he didn't want to do it because he knew what he would find.

Even in the gloom I could see his eyes mist with confusion. Then glare with anger.

"What are doing here?" he hissed.

"I saw you come in. And fancied a date with the naughty night nurse. More to the point, what are you doing? You should be in the office."

"Slipped out for a couple hours. It's a quiet afternoon. Phil Bailey is filling in for me."

He relaxed a bit. But for less than five seconds.

"Now wait a minute," he said. "Look, this isn't what it seems. I can explain. You won't mention this around the office, will you?"

"Your secret's safe with me, Frank."

A bloke four rows behind us made a loud: "*Sssssh!*" It sounded like steam escaping from a busted pipe.

We ignored him.

Figgis said: "What do you mean, you know what's going to happen next?"

"She'll spill that red stuff over her uniform. Then she'll have to take it off."

Figgis grunted.

I said: "Are you having some kind of mid-life crisis?"

Figgis slumped lower in his seat. "I was fifty-nine last week. Next year it'll be the big six-oh. And then game over. And what have I got out of life? A smoker's cough and a pension I probably won't live long enough to collect."

"You're a young man for your age."

"This is supposed to be the Swinging Sixties. But none of it is swinging my way."

"*Sssssh!*"

We ignored him.

"It's all right for you," Figgis whispered.

"What do you mean?"

"That gorgeous dolly bird you hang around with. Plenty swinging your way."

"Don't let Shirley Goldsmith hear you call her a dolly bird if you value your manhood. She's a photographer's model, currently working on a fashion shoot in London. The Café Royal, no less."

On screen, the naughty night nurse tottered across the room carrying the brimming kidney dish.

"Couldn't Mrs Figgis help spice up your life a little?" I asked.

Figgis scratched his head. Pulled his Woodbines out of his pocket. The match flared in the darkness as he lit up.

He took a long drag on the cancer stick and blew out the smoke slowly. His body relaxed.

"I'm thinking of buying Mrs Figgis a baby-doll nightie," he said. "Every night the same. She climbs into a pair of PJs made out of army-surplus camouflage flannelette."

"Some men would find that alluring," I said.

"With reinforced gussets?"

"Ah! I see what you mean."

"And wrinkles."

"Well, Esme is getting on a bit. You have to expect a line or two."

"Wrinkles in the PJs. She boils them in bleach. It's like lying next to someone wearing corrugated cardboard."

"Perhaps you ought to try Esme with that baby-doll number. Tell her it'll keep her cool during these hot summer nights."

"*Sssssh!*"

Figgis' face flared with anger. He swung round and glared through the gloom at the hissing guy.

"Will you shut up, you old bag of wind?" he yelled.

There were strangled coughs and shuffling sounds around the auditorium. They sounded like nocturnal animals snuffling through undergrowth.

The other patrons weren't happy.

Especially as the naughty night nurse had overfilled the kidney dish and had it balanced precariously on one hand.

A lone torch beam swung from side to side as it came down the aisle. The light crept along the row until it reached us.

The usherette glared. "I think you two need to leave. Now. Or I'll call the manager."

I shrugged. "Come on, Frank."

He threw his Woodbine on the floor and stubbed it out with his foot.

On the screen, the kidney dish toppled sideways. The naughty night nurse spilt the red stuff right down the front of her uniform.

A tense expectancy hung over the auditorium while we shuffled along the row and walked up the aisle.

The bloke who sounded like the busted piston sneered at us. "Now you'll miss the best bit."

"I don't think so," I said. "Under that uniform she's

wearing wrinkled pyjamas in army-surplus camouflage flannelette."

* * *

I gave Figgis a lift back to the office in my MGB.

We didn't speak on the journey. There didn't seem to be any more to say. It was as though Figgis had felt able to unburden himself under cover of darkness. But now we were in the light, everything had returned to normal. Like master and man. With him as the master. And me in my usual muggins' role.

Phil Bailey looked surprised when we came through the swing doors of the newsroom together.

"Anything I should know about?" Figgis snapped at him.

"No. Quiet afternoon," Phil said. He glanced at the clock. "Only forty minutes to the final deadline of the day. Nothing big will break now."

I left them talking about a couple of stories that had come in from the Press Association.

I walked over to my desk and slumped down in my captain's chair.

I felt depressed. The afternoon hadn't turned out as I'd expected. Pete the Pickpocket wanted me to act as an accomplice. Figgis wanted me to help him catch the Swinging Sixties vibe.

Neither was going to happen.

My phone rang. I lifted the receiver.

A voice which reminded me of pigs snuffling windfall apples in an autumn orchard said: "If you move fast, you'll end the day on a big headline."

Ted Wilson, an honest 'tec – a collector's item in the Brighton police force – had a tip for me.

I said: "If it's got anything to do with pickpockets or naughty nurses, forget it."

Ted said: "I don't know what you're rabbiting about. But this has got to do with dead bodies. I'm with one in Embassy Court."

"The big block of flats on the seafront?"

"Yes. And you should know Tomkins has already alerted Houghton."

Detective Chief Superintendent Alec Tomkins loathed me on account of how I regularly exposed his bungled investigations in the *Chronicle*.

In revenge, he made sure he always tipped off Jim Houghton, the crime reporter on the rival *Evening Argus*, about any murder before I got to hear about it.

"I'll be with you in five minutes," I told Ted.

I picked up my notebook and raced for the door.

"What's the rush?" Figgis whispered as I flashed by him. "She'll have put that uniform back on by now."

TWO

I dodged my MGB past a taxi as I sped through the Old Steine towards the seafront.

The taxi driver had a pork pie face and yelled something obscene at me. I gave him a cheery wave.

But I wasn't feeling so cheery. My visit to the Continentale with Figgis had unsettled me. Figgis was right. He was getting older and one day he wouldn't be news editor of the *Chronicle* any more.

Who'd run the newsroom then? Not our hopeless editor Gerald Pope – His Holiness – who thought a front-page splash was a story about a drunk falling into Rottingdean Pond. It was a worry, but not the only one I had on my mind.

My tyres squealed on the hot tarmac as I sped the sports car I'd bought with a legacy from an uncle onto the seafront.

If Houghton had been tipped off about the murder at Embassy Court, he'd already be on his way. And the *Argus* only had forty minutes to deadline for its last edition of the day, too. If he beat me with a story in tonight's paper and I couldn't file mine in time, Figgis wouldn't be pleased.

The balance of power between Figgis and me had shifted in my favour inside the Continentale. But if Houghton scooped me, it would switch back again.

I manoeuvred the MGB into a narrow parking slot a few yards from Embassy Court's main entrance. I sprang out of the car. Normally, I'd take a moment to admire the clean lines of the curving balconies which made the building the finest example of art deco architecture on the south coast. But there was no time for art appreciation today.

As I stepped onto the pavement, Houghton limped around the corner and hurried inside.

Damn, the man had beaten me to it.

But in newspaper work, it's not always the reporter who's first on the scene who gets the scoop. It's the one who files the copy.

And with – I glanced at my watch – now only thirty-two minutes to deadline, that would depend on who found a free telephone first. Both Houghton and I would be banking we could phone our story through to a copy-taker in time for it to make the last edition.

There'd probably be a phone in the dead bloke's apartment. But the cops wouldn't let anyone – especially a couple of crafty journos – use that. Fingerprints. Evidence. And the fact it would be the ideal opportunity for Tomkins to make a free call and place a bet with his bookie.

No, I'd have to find a phone box and hope it was unoccupied.

Or make sure it was free for me to use. Which is not quite the same thing.

I scooted around the corner to the box in Western Street. It was the only one for two hundred yards in every direction. (When you're a reporter, and you know that finding a phone box is the key to calling in a story, you collect their locations like a train-spotter collects numbers.)

A couple of lads were playing hopscotch on the pavement nearby. One had a tangle of brown hair and pink cheeks. The wool on the left sleeve of his jumper had unravelled. The other had straight fair hair and a hole in his right shoe. I'd put them both at nine-years-old. Perhaps ten.

I shouted across the street at them. "Hey, do you want to make ten bob?"

They stopped their game and looked at me. A searching look as if to say "Is he for real or is he a nutter?"

The one with the unravelled sleeve said: "What do we have to do?"

The one with the holed shoe said: "Is that ten bob each or between us?"

I grinned. "Each if you can help at this telephone box."

Unravelled Sleeve crossed the road slowly. Holed Shoe swaggered over.

I said: "I'm going to make a reverse charge call in this phone box. A man will come on the other end of the line. I want you to go into the box and talk to him until I come back."

"What do we have to talk to him about?" Unravelled Sleeve asked.

"Anything you like. Football, cricket, television, hopscotch. Just talk to him about anything."

"What's the catch?" Holed Shoe asked.

"No catch. You just have keep talking to him until I get back. You let no one into the box, no matter what they tell you. Understand?"

The pair nodded.

"If you're still there when I come back in about half an hour. I'll give you each ten shillings."

"Cor," said Unravelled Sleeve.

"We could buy chips on the way home," said Holed Shoe.

"And Tizer," added Unravelled Sleeve.

I slipped into the phone box and called the copytakers' desk at the *Chronicle*.

Albert Claygate, chief copytaker, came on the line.

"Harlequin," I said.

"What?" Albert said.

"Code Harlequin," I repeated.

"Oh, Harlequin. That one. Who do I have to keep talking this time?"

"Two nine-year-old boys."

"Ten," Unravelled Sleeve said.

"Who's going first?" I said.

"Me," Holed Shoe said.

I handed him the phone and scooted across the road.

* * *

The cops had strung up a blue tape across the stairs leading to the upper floors of Embassy Court.

They'd posted a uniform plod to stop people sneaking under the tape.

I took the lift.

Brighton's cops never think of everything. Fortunately.

Ted had told me the murdered man was on the second floor. Flat number 27. It wasn't hard to identify the apartment. A couple of the forensics team were outside the front door doing something with a doormat.

I strolled up and said: "You won't get any footprints off that."

A forensic guy with mournful eyes looked up. "If you knew what we'd found on doormats, you'd never wipe your feet again."

I didn't wipe my feet. Instead, I pushed in through the door. I could hear raised voices coming from a room off to my left.

Ted yelled: "And I say you can't sit down there."

Jim Houghton said: "My leg's giving me gyp. If I don't sit down, I'll fall down."

I stuck my head round the door and said: "Don't count on me to pick you up."

Jim turned an evil eye on me and said: "How did you get up here?"

"Same way as you, I expect. In the lift."

I moved further into the room. "Where's the *corpus delicti*?" I asked.

"What?" Ted said.

"He means the stiff," Jim added.

"In the bedroom, back of the apartment," Ted said. "But you can't go in there. Tomkins is examining the body."

"He gets all the fun," I said. "Who's the unlucky devil?"

"One Claude Winterbottom," Ted said.

"With a name like that, he's well out of it," I said.

"Occupation?" Jim asked.

"Being dead," I said.

"Before that?" Jim grumbled.

Ted harrumphed. "Some kind of investment consultant as far as we can make out. But we're still looking into that."

"How did he die?" I asked.

"Bludgeoned," Ted said. "Around the head."

"What with?" Jim asked.

"We haven't found the murder weapon yet."

"But whoever did it, wiped the weapon clean with Winterbottom's handkerchief. Left the bloodied snot rag beside the body."

23

"Strange to have left that when he took the weapon with him," I said.

Ted shrugged.

"Which might mean he brought the weapon to do the job. Which would make this killing premeditated," I added.

"That's speculation," Ted said stuffily.

"Time of death?" Jim asked.

"The doc's still in there with Tomkins, but it seems likely it was some time last night."

"But only discovered this afternoon?" I asked.

"The hall porter used his house key to get in. He was worried as Winterbottom hadn't been down for his morning paper. *The Daily Telegraph*. Apparently, he enjoyed doing the crossword."

"And now he's become like a crossword clue," I said.

"What do you mean?" Ted asked.

"One down."

Ted rolled his eyes.

Jim glanced at his watch.

He thought he'd covered the move, but I'd seen him out of the corner of my eye. He was thinking about his deadline. Wanted to get his story into a front-page splash in tonight's last edition. Knew he needed to find a phone box fast.

Jim turned towards Ted. "No doubt there'll be a press briefing in the morning."

Ted nodded.

"I'll wait until then to pick up more details. Write it up for tomorrow's midday edition."

Like hell he would.

He was planning a dash to the nearest phone box now.

Jim said: "Evening all."

He sauntered from the room. All nonchalant like. But I heard his feet pick up speed in the corridor.

I allowed myself a sneaky grin.

In his hurry, Jim had left without asking an important question.

"Any idea about the motive?" I asked Ted.

Ted shrugged. "If we had some suspects, we might be able to find some motives. At the moment, we're drawing a blank."

"I'll call you in the morning," I said.

"Is there anything I can do to stop you?" Ted said.

"Probably not," I said.

Out in the street, I heard Jim yelling at Unravelled Sleeve and Holed Shoe.

The pair were still in the phone box when I stepped around the corner.

For a man with a gammy leg, Jim was doing a remarkable version of an Irish jig. He hopped around the box shaking his fists.

Unravelled Sleeve was on the phone. Holed Shoe had his face pressed to a window inside the box. He stuck out his tongue as Jim sashayed by.

I walked up to the box. Jim's face looked like a boiled beetroot. His hair had flopped over his forehead. Beads of sweat rolled down his temples. He bounced around and jumped up and down in front of me. His eyes loosed off a nuclear-powered hate glare in my direction. He opened his mouth to speak and a sound like a foghorn filled the street.

I said: "If you did that dance down the Palais on a Friday night, you'd be a shoo-in for a spot prize."

Jim stopped his jig. Breathed in deep. Wagged an angry finger at me. Then waved it at the phone box.

"These two are your stooges," he screamed. "I can't file my copy. Only five minutes left."

"Stay calm, Jim. I'm sure there's a simple explanation. They're probably just ringing their mum to say they'll be late home for tea."

I walked over to the box, opened the door, and winked at the pair.

I spoke loud enough for the two to hear. "If you're calling your mother could you wind up, so this old man can use the phone?"

Unravelled Sleeve winked at me.

He shouted down the phone: "I want fish fingers and baked beans for tea, Mum."

He dropped the phone so it dangled on its cord. The pair hustled out of the phone box.

Jim crowded in ready to barge inside ahead of me. He'd pulled a dog-eared notebook out of his pocket and held a pencil in his right hand.

He waved the pencil angrily at the boys. "I should tan your backsides," he shouted.

"Not with a pencil, grandad," Holed Shoe shouted.

He grabbed the pencil and raced down the street.

Jim looked like he was about to explode. He took off after Holed Shoe who waved the pencil in the air like a battle trophy.

He turned back and shook his fist at me. "This time you've gone too far, Crampton. I'll ruin you for this. Just see if I don't."

I gave him a cheery wave and watched Jim as he hobbled down the road.

I rummaged in my pocket for a couple of ten-shilling notes.

"One each," I said to Unravelled Sleeve as I handed them to him.

He nodded and headed off after Jim.

I slipped into the box, picked up the dangling phone, and held it to my ear.

"You still there, Albert?" I asked.

"You sound as though you've pulled a right scam this time, even for you."

"I'm ready to dictate copy," I said a bit po-faced after the excitement. "Take a par."

* * *

I stepped out of the phone box having dictated three hundred words of my finest prose.

Albert had said he'd send it straight up to the subs. I'd hit the deadline and in less than an hour, the paper with the story would hit the streets.

There was no sign of Jim. He'd probably disappeared to another phone box. Or to buy another pencil.

I stood in the warm sun and looked up at the sleek geometric lines of Embassy Court. I was tempted to slope off for a drink at Prinny's Pleasure. But there was more work to do.

I crossed the road to the entrance and pushed my way through the glass doors.

The hall porter was sitting at his desk in the foyer. He was an old bloke with a snowy thatch of hair and wrinkled face, like it had shrunk in the wash. He wore a brown uniform with some gold braiding round the collar and cuffs. His name badge read: Herbie Stubbs.

He was studying the morning's edition of *The Sporting Life*.

I strolled up and said: "Going's hard at Kempton Park tomorrow."

He said: "It's always hard to make money in this game."

"I was talking about the surface of the race track."

He looked up and frowned. "I knew what you were talking about."

I said: "So what's your tip for tomorrow?"

"Stay schtum while the rozzers are around."

"The wisdom of a philosopher."

"Keeps my lips buttoned around reporters, too."

"Not sure what Socrates said about them."

"Know thy enemy."

"I think that was Sun Tzu."

"Never knew the bloke."

We fell silent. Herbie concentrated on his paper.

I said: "Looks like I might have a busy day tomorrow. Won't have time to put a bet on."

"Shame."

"Don't suppose you'd put a quid on for me?"

"Which horse?"

"I'll leave it to you to make the selection." I made a point of shuffling uneasily from one foot to another. "Don't suppose you'd be able to pick up my winnings?"

"Might not be any."

"With you making the selection? Bound to pick an outsider that gallops home."

I put a pound note down on Herbie's desk. He looked at it, waggled his head from side to side, as though he were weighing the pros and cons of a big decision, then picked it up.

"When'll you collect the winnings?"

"Hard to say. I'm so busy. I'll probably forget, anyway. Terrible memory."

"Yeah! I heard that about reporters."

"Not like hall porters, eh? Got to have a good memory to remember all those tenants with their likes and foibles."

"You could say that."

"Claude Winterbottom have any?"

"Living, I'd say."

I grinned. "Apart from that?"

"Never took to the bloke. Always had his nose in the air. Thought he was better than other people. Certainly, the likes of me."

"What did he do?"

"Some kind of financial consultant, I think."

"Flush with cash, then?"

"Not so you'd notice. Even tried to borrow sixpence off me last week to buy a newspaper. No chance. I saw him once driving a flash car – Jaguar, I think, racing green colour with a removable tan hood – but he never parked it here. And he had a boat – motor cruiser, I think he called it – moored in Shoreham Harbour. Saw pictures of it in his apartment when I went up there a few months ago to fix a leaking tap."

"So he moved in elevated financial circles?"

"I don't know about that. He had some dodgy geezers turn up here to see him sometimes. None too friendly, some of them, either. I wouldn't have trusted him with the slip from my pay packet, let alone the hard-earned inside it."

"You don't know who any of these dodgy geezers were?"

"The kind I'd rather not know. But, wait a minute, there was one bloke who was a bit different from the rest. Some kind of God botherer."

"A clergyman?"

"No, not a vicar. More like one of those preacher types you see on street corners. Don't think he was Winterbottom's type. But, then, few were."

"You've not a good word to say about Winterbottom, then?" I asked.

"He wasn't like some of them. Give you a cheery 'good morning' on their way out. I'll say one thing for him, though. Always kept himself and his apartment tidy. Brought his rubbish down regular as clockwork once a week. All neatly tied up in an old brown paper laundry bag."

That had my attention.

"When did Winterbottom last bring the laundry bag down?"

"Would have been the morning before yesterday."

"What did he do with it?"

"Chucked it in one of the bins out the back, I expect."

I nodded thoughtfully at his racing paper.

"Good luck with the runners and riders," I said.

"Yeah! I could do with some."

I sauntered out of the lobby like a guy with nothing particular on his mind.

Like hell, I had.

If I were a religious type, I'd have offered up a silent prayer. Please make it that the bin men haven't collected the trash since Winterbottom deposited his laundry bag.

As I made my way to the back of Embassy Court, I hoped the cops hadn't started on their bin search yet. But they had enough to do without rifling through smelly rubbish. Nobody would be eager to remind Tomkins they had to be searched in case they ended up with the task.

Long shadows crept across the concrete in the yard at the back of the building. A dozen metal dustbins were marshalled in a line against the wall. I crept into the shadow and had a quick look around.

Nobody was about, but that didn't mean someone wouldn't suddenly appear with a bag of rubbish. I'd need to be quick. And it wasn't going to be easy. The residents obviously shared the bins, so Winterbottom's trash could be in any one of them.

I started at the first bin and had a good look inside. Most of the rubbish lay loose in the bin. I could safely discard it as

Winterbottom tied his in a laundry bag. So did some of the other residents. This was obviously the kind of place where you sent your shirts and your smalls off to Goacher's laundry once a week. They came back in a neat Goacher's bag and you used it to throw out your trash.

I found Winterbottom's bag in the seventh dustbin I searched.

It was obviously his because there were three empty envelopes addressed to him at the top of the bag. No letters, though.

I scanned the yard. Nobody about, but I couldn't be caught searching a dustbin. There was a small bicycle shed on the far side of the yard. There was a narrow gap behind the shed and a wall. Just enough room for me to squeeze in and do what I had to.

I upended the laundry bag and tipped the contents on the ground. There were empty tin cans, a few old teabags, some bits of soap, dirty cotton wool (*yeuk!*), and some scraps of paper. The paper scraps looked like they'd been torn from a larger sheet.

I gathered them all together. There were eight pieces in all. So Winterbottom had torn the letter in half. Then torn the halved pieces in half. And finally torn the halved half pieces into eighths. Within a minute I'd arranged them all on the ground to reassemble the page.

The letter came from a company called Crouchpenny Easy Loans. A slogan under the letterhead read: *Let's give you some cash for your stash.* The letter to Winterbottom wasn't so friendly.

Dear Mr Winterbottom,

When you came to see me nine months ago, you promised me that if I invested £5,000 in your Winterbottom Double Your Money Investment Fund, I would receive £416.13sh.4d interest a month, ensuring that I doubled my money in one year. You assured me this was possible because you invested the money in what you called the Dark Market, where irritants such as commissions and tax were skilfully avoided. To date, I have received only one interest payment which means that £3,333.6sh.8d is outstanding. If I do not receive payment by the end of this week, I will ask my lawyer to sue your balls off.

Yours truly
Manfred Crouchpenny.

* * *

Under the typewritten letter Crouchpenny had scrawled a PS: *Or I may come round and cut off your legs.*

I gathered the scraps together with the other rubbish and put it in the laundry bag. Then I replaced he bag in the dustbin.

You won't catch me purloining possible evidence. Besides, I already had exactly what I wanted.

THREE

I arrived back in the newsroom with plenty on my mind.

If the cops discovered the threatening letter from Manfred Crouchpenny, it would provide them with a prime suspect. Even a dimwit like Tomkins would surely order a search of the dustbins. It was routine police practice in case the killer had decided to be tidy and chuck his weapon of choice away.

So should I slip Ted Wilson a hint to give the old bins the once-over?

I gazed around the newsroom while I puzzled on that conundrum. Most of the desks were deserted. My fellow journos would be in the pub hoisting the first pint to their lips. But Phil Bailey rattled out a late piece on his old typewriter. Sally Martin rifled through a pile of press cuttings and headed off to the morgue. They knew to ignore me when I gazed at the ceiling. It meant I had a problem.

I switched my attention back to my Remington. I'd decided what to do. It was the cops' job to collect evidence, not mine. As long as I hadn't put any obstacles in their way, I could gather my information and they theirs.

In the morning, I'd find out more about this Crouchpenny and what his beef was with Winterbottom. Perhaps the cops would have already arrested Crouchpenny for Winterbottom's murder by then. But I didn't think so.

I could knock off for the night with a clear conscience. No more work for me.

And then the phone on my desk rang.

I lifted the receiver to my ear.

An agricultural voice which reminded me of seagulls following a plough said: "Since when did you start using child labour?"

Ted Wilson was having his little joke.

I said: "I don't know what you're talking about."

"Tomkins has found out how you used two kids to occupy the phone box. You'll be sending nippers up chimneys next."

"You can't get them these days."

"What, child sweeps?"

"No, chimneys. Everyone's switching to central heating."

"Yeah! The missus wants us to kick the coalscuttle into touch."

"No need to ask who told Tomkins," I said.

"Jim Houghton. They've both sloped off for a drink at the Regency Tavern."

That was bad news. It meant Tomkins would brief Jim Houghton on the investigation. Jim would get details I didn't have.

I asked: "Any big breakthrough in the investigation after I left?"

"Just routine. Usual door-to-door in the flats to see whether anybody had seen or heard anything," Ted said.

"And?"

"Most of them had heard their neighbours' TVs on too loud."

"Come on, Ted, there must've been something."

"Well, we do know that Winterbottom had at least three visitors during the evening – two men and a woman. Sketchy descriptions for the men – middle-aged suit and tie types, according to the residents who saw them. A better description for the woman. In her early sixties, dark hair tied back in a bun. Tweed skirt, sensible shoes. Of course, there could have been other visitors no one saw."

"But no names presumably?"

"You must be kidding. This early in our enquiries?"

"Have you searched the area?"

Crampton's cunning question, designed to tease out what had happened to the dustbins.

"Didn't seem a priority today, but we'll take a look around the corridors and corners tomorrow. Give the dustbins a quick once over."

So, I'd have the early morning to follow up the Crouchpenny connection before Mr Plod discovered Winterbottom's link to the easy loans man.

I said: "Not a nice job searching dustbins."

"I'll delegate it to the uniform branch."

"Doubt whether they'll find anything."

"Yeah! Empty whisky bottles and used condoms." Ted sounded subdued. "At least it reminds you that some people have a good time."

I said: "You're holding something back."

"How do you know?"

"Because you always sound a bit down when you do it. You're suppressing your natural generosity."

"An amateur psychologist is the last thing I need. But, yeah, there is one point – but this is on deep background. Agreed?"

Deep background meant I could know what it was to aid

my own investigation, but I wasn't to use the information in print. At least, not yet.

I said: "Agreed."

Ted cleared his throat. "There's just a hint that Winterbottom may have been supplementing his investment scams with a little blackmail. We've found one or two notes which appear to come from aggrieved victims."

"Any names?" I asked. "Silly question. Blackmail victims don't sign their letters. It just provides the blackmailer with more ammunition."

"Yeah, silly question. Haven't got time for any more."

The line went dead. I replaced the receiver. Stood up and headed for the door.

My phone rang again. I tried to pretend I hadn't heard it. Took three more steps towards the door. Turned back. Couldn't help myself.

Curiosity. It may have killed any number of cats, but it's made the careers of even more reporters.

I lifted the receiver to my ear.

A woman's shrill voice said: "Colin, I'm being followed. By a man."

My girlfriend Shirley Goldsmith sounded frightened.

In the background, I could hear the hubbub of people. Tramping feet. The sound of steam brakes. The garbled tones of a Tannoy announcement.

I'd worked it out before Shirl yelled: "I'm in a phone booth at Brighton station. The weirdo is over by the news stand pretending to read the *Evening Argus*."

"Must be a weirdo if he's chosen it over the *Chronicle*."

"Be serious, Colin. This guy has followed me all the way from London."

"From the Café Royal where you were doing the photoshoot?"

"Yeah! Looks like he was at some other meeting there. Spotted me in the lobby. Latched on to me when I left."

"Listen, this is what you do. Step out of the booth and make a point of looking for the sign to the ladies' loos. It's just above the steps that lead down under the station foyer. Hurry down them. He'll think you're spending a penny and wait at the top of the steps. But carry on through the tunnel at the bottom of the steps. That'll bring you out into Trafalgar Street. Should be enough to throw him off. From there, you can leg it round to Prinny's Pleasure. I'll meet you in the bar."

"You think that'll work?"

"Can't fail," I said.

The line went dead.

* * *

Shirley twisted on her bar stool in Prinny's Pleasure and sipped her Campari and soda.

Red for danger.

She whispered: "You said this couldn't fail. He's sitting over there."

I had a sip of my gin and tonic (one ice cube, two slices of lemon), and twisted round on my stool. "Where?"

"In the corner. On the bench between the table with the wonky leg and the stain on the carpet."

I spied the bloke as he hoisted a pint of lager and took a healthy swig. He wiped the foam from his lips with the back of his hand.

I hadn't spotted him when I'd hurried in. Hadn't even looked round. Prinny's Pleasure wasn't the kind of pub you looked round. The green flock wallpaper had turned grey. The mock chandeliers hung with cobwebs. The tables were stained with years of beer slops. The worn carpet squelched as you walked on it. The place smelt of stale beer.

Jeff Purkiss, the pub-keeper, was a thin bloke with a mop of tangled brown hair. He shaved with a blunt razor blade because he usually sported two or three spots of dried blood on his chin. Perhaps he did it deliberately to divert attention from the dirt under his fingernails. I found the place a useful dive to interview discreet contacts. There weren't usually any other customers.

Until tonight.

I took a closer look at the bloke as he had another swig of lager.

He had a lean and wiry frame, with long legs which stuck out. He had a narrow face with a small mouth and a nose that was a little too large for the rest of his features. He was wearing a denim jacket over tan slacks, blue shirt, no tie. I'd put his age at about thirty.

He didn't look like your average dirty old man in a raincoat.

But he didn't look like the kind of drinker who'd choose a hovel like Prinny's Pleasure when there were a dozen decent taverns within five minutes' walk.

I switched my attention back to Shirley. We'd been together now in an on-off sort of way for four years. We'd met when she was working her way around the world. She came from Australia. Sometimes talked about going back. But I hoped she'd stay.

Shirl's blonde hair was ruffled. Her face looked pale. And she had her worried eyes. She was wearing a pair of red bell-bottoms and a flimsy cream top which may once have been a handkerchief.

Not surprising she'd picked up a follower.

But why did the guy follow her into the pub? That would only draw attention to himself.

I said: "I'll tackle the guy in a minute, but tell me the full story."

Shirley sipped her Campari soda. She said: "Well, you know I've been booked for this two-day shoot with a Swinging Sixties theme."

"That's the Cool London photoshoot you talked about?"

"Sure. We're doing a lot of the shots out on the streets, but the photographer is using a room in the Café Royal for the indoor work. I noticed the bozo, earlier today. He was coming up the stairs at the Café Royal after me. He went into one of the rooms where some big pow-wow seemed to be going on. A film company, apparently. Planning their next blockbuster. Didn't think any more about it until the lunch-break. The bar at the Café Royal has more fancy mirrors than a tart's boudoir. I spotted in one that he was watching me from across the room."

"With his tongue hanging out of the side of his mouth, no doubt."

"You need to take this seriously, buster."

I nodded. "I do."

"Anyway, sometimes guys eyeball me. It happens. I can't help it if I'm drop-dead gorgeous."

"And modest with it," I added.

"Okay, smart-arse, listen up to the serious bit. I started catching sights of him on the way home. At Piccadilly tube station. On the Brighton Belle. At the station, when I called you. And now in the pub. Wasn't here when I arrived. I went straight into the ladies' khazi. When I came out – there he was. Supping his bevy in the corner."

"It's enough," I said. I drained my gin and tonic. "I'm going to ask the guy what his game is."

I slid off my bar stool and turned around. Looked at his

bench in the corner. The one between the table with the wonky leg and the stain on the carpet.

But the bench was unoccupied.

An empty glass stood on the table. The last streaks of foam ran down the inside of the glass.

Shirley's stalker had left.

I spun round to Shirley.

She gawped across the room. "I didn't see that."

"See what?"

"See him leave."

"He must have slunk out when he realised we were talking about him."

Shirley shrugged. "Now we'll never know who he was."

I signalled to Jeff. He was at the far end of the bar. He was wiping a grubby cloth round the rim of a glass.

He put down the cloth and glass, and sidled over.

I said: "That guy in the corner – ever seen him before?"

Jeff glanced vacantly around the room.

"What guy?"

"The guy who ordered a pint of lager and sat in the corner."

Jeff waggled his head from side to side as though he'd been asked to solve a baffling mathematical puzzle. Fermat's Last Theorem, perhaps.

He said: "You can't expect me to remember all my customers."

"You don't have any customers."

"You two are here."

"And so was a third person."

"Until a minute ago," Shirley chimed in.

Jeff's face lit up. Like he'd just solved Fermat's Last Theorem.

"Oh, the guy with the cut-glass accent."

"He had a posh voice?" Shirl asked. "I never heard him speak."

Jeff sniffed. "You were in the ladies' comfort room."

"Only ones who get comfort in there are the flies," Shirley said.

"We're getting off the point," I said. "What did he say?"

Jeff scratched his head. "He said, 'A pint of lager, please inn-keeper'."

"Anything else?"

"He said, 'What's the damage, mine host?' And I said, 'Ten pence...'"

"Thanks, Jeff. We're not interested in what you said."

Jeff pulled a sour face. "Please yourself. What's the problem, anyway?"

"The bozo was stalking me."

"Not surprised," Jeff said. "Did I ever tell you I was once stalked by a woman?"

I ignored Jeff and turned to Shirley.

"We're not going to find out any more about mystery man tonight," I said.

Jeff said: "Big girl, she was. For her age. Probably forty."

Shirley said to me: "I'm starving."

Jeff said: "One day I came round a corner and there she was. I just about-turned and ran. And you know what? She shouted after me, 'I want you'."

I said to Shirley: "Let's go and eat at Prompt Corner. Mystery man will never find you there."

Shirley grinned and kissed me on the cheek.

Jeff said: "And you know why she wanted me?"

"Not interested," I said.

"Because I was behind with my rent. She was a debt collector."

Shirley and I headed for the door.

41

Jeff shouted after us. "But I had the last laugh. Very persuasive, she was. Never had a debt collected like that before. If you come back, I'll tell you more."

We went out and closed the door behind us.

* * *

Later that night, I arrived back at my lodgings in a sombre mood.

My dinner with Shirley had been more subdued than usual. When she was on a modelling assignment she bubbled with fun. But the strange stalker had unsettled her. And me. I tried to persuade her that he was a harmless bloke. That it was probably a coincidence that she'd seen so much of him in one day. And that he would disappear from her life forever tomorrow. Just in case, I'd said I would meet her off the London train when she returned from her modelling shift tomorrow.

It didn't do much for Shirley.

Not surprising. It hadn't convinced me.

I rented the top floor of a five-storey house in Regency Square. The place had once been the residence of Hector and Beatrice Gribble. I'd never met Hector, but seen a picture of him. He had the beaten expression of a bloke who regards life as a bit of inconvenience between birth and eternity.

Some years ago, Hector had dropped off the perch. Faced with making ends meet, Beatrice had turned the place into a lodging house. As a landlady she made the lady governor of Holloway women's prison seem like the angel of mercy.

I inserted my key in the lock and turned it quietly. I don't know why I bothered. The front door squeaked on its hinges when you opened it. I'd asked the Widow – the tenant's secret nickname for Mrs Gribble – countless times to apply some much-needed oil but she'd brushed the pleas aside. I think she used the squeaks as an early-warning signal that a tenant was on the move.

In the hallway, a dim bulb cast a sepulchral gloom over the place. The hat stand held a trilby, a bowler and a straw hat with a hole in the crown. A print of Holman Hunt's *Light of the World* on the wall had slipped sideways in its frame.

The Widow shot out of her parlour. She was wearing a long pink dressing gown tied at the waist with a cord. She had pink slippers with pom-poms. She'd wrapped her hair in curlers and put a net over them. It looked like the kind of thing gardeners use to keep the birds off their raspberries.

She was holding a copy of the *Chronicle's* night final edition. My story about Winterbottom's murder was the front-page splash.

She said: "Oh, it's you Mr Crampton."

I said: "So you did take the optician's advice and get a new pair of glasses."

Normally, the Widow would puff out her cheeks at that. A sign I'd annoyed her.

Instead, she tried a grin. A row of grey teeth, like tombstones, appeared between pale lips.

She said: "You will have your little joke, Mr Crampton. The point is: I've got a question to ask you."

"If it's that one about paying my rent in advance, the answer's no."

"It's more complicated than that."

"Isn't it always?"

"I need to know whether it's possible to get money back from someone who's died."

"You could always try going through their pockets," I said. "But you'd have to get there before the body started to smell."

The Widow stamped her foot and a little flurry of dust fell from the Holman Hunt.

"Did someone who's died owe you money?" I asked.

"I'm not going into that now. Not while you're in one of your flippant moods."

She stomped back into her parlour and slammed the door.

"I'm always in one of my flippant moods," I said.

But, in fact, I wasn't. Winterbottom's death, Crouchpenny's letter, and Shirley's mystery follower had seen to that.

I climbed the stairs knowing that I was going to find it difficult to get to sleep.

FOUR

But sleep must have knitted up my "ravelled sleeve of care".

Because the first thing I saw after my head had hit the pillow was light filtering through my curtains.

And someone was hammering on my door.

Thump. Thump. Thump.

Was the place on fire?

I couldn't smell smoke. Or hear the crackle of flames.

I rubbed sleep from my eyes and levered myself up in bed.

Thump. Thump. Thump.

The door shuddered in its frame.

I shouted out: "Clear off, I'm asleep."

"It's Mrs Gribble," a voice behind the door shouted.

"In that case, I'm unconscious."

"This is no time for your little jokes, Mr Crampton."

"I agree. Come back in two hours and I'll have some bigger ones."

I slid back under the covers.

Thump. Thump. Thump.

"You don't understand. The police are here," the Widow yelled through the door.

"They can come back in two hours, too." I shouted.

"I don't think they will. You see..." The Widow's voice trailed off in a low moan. "...they've come to arrest me."

That had my attention. I sat upright so fast it was like my toes had caught fire.

A switch flipped in my brain. The neurons fired up.

"Arrest you? What for? Running a bawdy house?"

"This is a boarding house," the Widow yelled back. Her voice was shrill, an octave higher than usual. But coarse and scratchy. Like Maria Callas with laryngitis.

"Depends which way you look at it," I said.

"I have my pass key and I'm coming in."

The ultimate threat. Like Kennedy to Khrushchev. Remove your missiles from Cuba or I'll nuke your country.

If the Widow stormed in, she'd see my trousers thrown on the floor – all the more convenient to put them on in the morning. She'd spot my shirt artistically draped over the back of the chair. My underpants hanging from the light-fitting on the wall. The Widow had no idea how bachelors lived. And I was in no mood to provide her with an insight.

"Wait two minutes," I yelled. "I'm getting up."

I stumbled out of bed. Fumbled into my underwear. Stepped into the trousers. Rummaged the shirt around me. Hastily buttoned it. Slipped my socks on. Stepped into my shoes and tied the laces. Glanced in the mirror by my bed. I was ready to face the world.

I opened the door.

The Widow was on the landing hopping from foot to foot like there was a painful ruck in her knickers.

Outside someone put their finger on the doorbell and left it there. The bell shrilled in the hallway. On the lower floors, there were angry sounds. Other tenants grumbled as they stirred from their slumbers.

I said: "Who the hell is ringing that bell?"

"It's the police," the Widow whined. "They rang a moment ago. I opened the door and this great oaf in a greasy suit flashed a card at me and claimed he was a detective chief superintendent."

"Tomkins."

"I think that's his name. He said he'd come to arrest me. I asked to see his warrant card. He fiddled around his pockets but couldn't produce it, so I slammed the door on him."

That sounded like the Widow in action.

I asked: "What was the charge?"

"Murder."

My jaw hung slack.

I mean, I really thought it was going to fall off.

Downstairs, the bell stopped ringing. Silence descended on the house.

Then I laughed.

The Widow, a cold-blooded killer? Ridiculous.

She was maddening, infuriating, irritating, and a regular nosey parker who poked around in my room when I was out. But the idea she'd intentionally harm someone was fanciful.

As long as you avoided eating her rissoles you were safe.

I said: "Who the hell are you supposed to have killed?"

"Mr Winterbottom."

"What? Claude Winterbottom? The investment advisor? The one who was murdered last night?"

"That's what Tomkins said before I slammed the door on him."

Downstairs, the rusty hinge on the letterbox flap squeaked as someone opened it.

Tomkins shouted through. "Gribble, open this door. Don't make it worse by resisting arrest."

I said: "Did you even know Winterbottom?"

The Widow shifted uncomfortably. She looked down and studied a hole in the carpet.

"Yes," she said.

"How come?"

"I met him a year ago at the *thé dansant* at the Old Ship Hotel. He seemed a very respectable gentleman. Wore a pin-striped suit and a Brigade of Guards tie. We did the Veleta together. He wanted me to join him in the hokey-cokey, but I never put my whole self in on a first date."

"But you met him again?"

"The following week at the *thé dansant*. I was surprised he had a briefcase with him. I asked whether it contained sheet music for the dancing. He said it held papers that would have me tripping the light fantastic like the cat that got the cream."

Winterbottom evidently had a taste for mixed metaphors.

Downstairs, Tomkins yelled again through the letterbox. "Mrs Gribble, open this door or we'll break it down. *Ouch!* I've just caught my fingers in the flap."

I asked: "What were the papers?"

"They were what Claude – we were on first-name terms now – called a copper-bottomed, gold-plated investment opportunity. Apparently, there were bits of paper called pork belly futures. I didn't really understand it, but Claude explained. Apparently, you bought the futures and that meant when you wanted to buy the real pork bellies, they cost less than what you'd normally pay. So, then you sold the cheap pork bellies you'd bought for a huge profit and lived in the lap of luxury. At least, that's what Claude promised me."

"Like the cat who got the cream?"

"I said I normally bought my bacon from the Co-op, but

Claude said if I invested in his scheme, I could afford to order it from Fortnum & Mason. He was very persuasive."

"I bet. And let me guess the rest. You handed over your savings."

"All the money Hector had left for me in the Halifax Building Society. Two thousand pounds. Claude said I'd make a profit in six months and I could have the two thousand back at any time. But a few weeks ago, I needed the money to pay for the building work I had to arrange on the rooms at the back. I asked for my two thousand pounds. Claude keeps coming up with excuses why he can't pay. Something to do with liquid."

"Liquidity."

"That, too. But I needed my money."

Downstairs Tomkins yelled through the letterbox. "Two minutes for you to open the door or we'll bring in the enforcer."

The Widow shot me a worried look. "Who's the enforcer?"

"Not who, but what. It's like a battering ram."

The Widow turned towards the stairs. "I don't want the front door broken. That'll only be another expense."

"Before you face Tomkins, answer me one question."

"What?"

"Did you see Winterbottom yesterday evening?"

"I went to his flat in Embassy Court to insist he returned my money. He just fobbed me off. Something about pork bellies had fallen through the floor on the Chicago Mercantile Exchange.

"I told him the Exchange should keep the bellies out or get a stronger floor. He just laughed at me. Then I stormed out."

"And he was still alive when you left?"

"Worse luck," the Widow said.

She hurried down the first flight of stairs and shouted: "If you harm my door, detective chief superintendent, it'll be the last thing you do."

The Widow would find she had a lot to learn when dealing with the cops.

* * *

By the time I made it downstairs, the Widow had retreated to the kitchen.

She was standing by the Welsh dresser and waving a sink plunger at Tomkins.

The bold Tomkins had taken refuge behind the kitchen table. A couple of uniformed cops – a sergeant and a plod - cowered by the door.

Tomkins pointed at them. "You two – rush her. One from each side."

The sergeant said: "She's armed, guv."

"With a sink plunger?"

"There's a hell of a suction power in those things," the sergeant complained. "Could do a lot of damage in the wrong place."

The plod piped up: "If that got locked onto my meat and two veg, it would scupper my bedtime manoeuvres with the missus for weeks."

Tomkins rolled his eyes in despair.

The Widow said: "Three blokes and you couldn't assemble a decent man from their parts."

"That'll be enough of that talk," Tomkins snapped.

I said: "Wouldn't it be a good idea if we all calmed down and tried to sort out this misunderstanding?"

Tomkins swung round. I leant casually on the jamb in the doorway.

His eyes flared: "No newspapers. Get out."

I said: "I'm here as a tenant, not as the representative of the Fourth Estate."

"I don't care which estate you're in, this woman is coming with me."

"You've got to get that sink plunger off her first."

"An offensive weapon."

"Not half as offensive as bursting into a woman's house at seven o'clock in the morning and accusing her of murder," I said. "And without a shred of evidence."

"We have evidence," Tomkins said.

"What evidence?" the Widow shrieked.

"Letters."

I glanced at the Widow. The light of fire dimmed in her eyes. She lowered the plunger. Replaced it on the draining board.

"Are there letters?" I asked her.

"I wrote them when I was trying to get my money back," the Widow said. "I just wanted Mr Winterbottom to pay me what he owed."

"So normal business letters between a client and her investment manager," I said.

Tomkins smirked. "There's nothing normal about saying you'll kill someone."

I looked hard at the Widow. "Did you threaten to kill Winterbottom in the letters?"

The Widow stared morosely at the floor. "Not really."

Tomkins smirked: "We've got the evidence. Found the letters in a stack on his desk."

He pulled a small pile of blue envelopes from the inside pocket of his jacket. Took a letter out of the top envelope, unfolded it and read: "The way you've treated me, I wish I'd never met you at the *thé dansant*. I wish you were dead."

I said: "That's just a throw-away line. It's an expression of a hope, not a statement of intention to act."

Tomkins put the letter on the bottom of the pile and pulled out another. He said: "Blah, blah, blah... Here's the bit I was looking for... 'You've cheated me out of my husband Hector's savings. If he were alive today, he'd take his old service revolver and shoot you. I only wish I knew where it was...' Damning, I'd say. Any jury in the country would convict."

I said: "You've overlooked an important point, Sherlock. Winterbottom wasn't shot. He was bludgeoned with an unknown weapon."

Tomkins snarled. "Not elementary, my dear Crampton. Gribble, do you own a rolling pin?"

The Widow gave Tomkins a pitying look. "Of course. How do you think I roll out the pastry for my jam tarts?"

"I could just eat a jam tart," the plod said.

"Shut up," Tomkins said.

I said: "I suppose Winterbottom – a strong and active man - just stood there while an old and feeble woman bludgeoned him with the rolling pin she reserves for her jam tarts."

"Don't you call me old and feeble," the Widow said. "I could show you a thing or two."

"I'd rather not see your thing, especially if there are two of them," I said.

"That's enough," Tomkins yelled. "Gribble, where is that rolling pin?"

The Widow shot me an uneasy look. "As it happens, I spilt some black treacle on it last week. You can't get that stuff out, so I threw the rolling pin out. I was planning to buy a new one in Hannington's today."

Tomkins preened himself. He had a smirk like the grin on a Halloween pumpkin.

"I knew it," he said. "Threw away the murder weapon.

We'll never recover that. But we've got more than enough evidence anyway."

But it wasn't enough because Ted Wilson had told me the forensic team hadn't completed their search of the area. They were going to look in the dustbins today – where they'd find Manfred Crouchpenny's letter, kindly replaced by me.

When Ted's team discovered the letter, they'd have to concede Crouchpenny could be an alternative suspect. That would take the heat off the Widow. But it was too early for Ted's team to have searched the dustbins.

I said: "You've arrested Mrs Gribble before you've finished your search of Winterbottom's flat."

"We've got all we need there," Tomkins said.

"What about the surrounding area?" I asked. "The yard at the back of Embassy Court. And the dustbins. You might find evidence that points to another suspect."

"What other suspect? We already know who did it. I've told Ted Wilson to abandon the search."

That was bad. If the dustbins weren't going to be searched, the evidence of Crouchpenny's letter to Winterbottom would disappear with the next collection. I'd have to retrieve it before that happened. When I presented it to Tomkins – he wouldn't be able to ignore it. He'd have to release the Widow – at least on bail.

Tomkins pointed at the two plods. "Why haven't you put the bracelets on her?" he snapped.

"She's already wearing a gold bangle on her right wrist," the sergeant said.

"And a gold watch on her left - just like the one I bought my girlfriend from H Samuel," the constable added.

Tomkins slapped his hand to his forehead. "I meant handcuffs. Why do I always end up with the idiots?"

"Must be that likes attract," I said.

"Any more from you and I'll arrest you as an accomplice," Tomkins growled.

I turned to the Widow. "Best to go with them for now," I said. I gestured to the two uniforms. "You don't want these clodhoppers bringing you down in a rugby tackle."

The Widow gulped. A single tear rolled down her right cheek. Her shoulders slumped.

She turned to me. Her eyes were misted with tears. "What will I do about my tenants?"

"We'll struggle by," I said gently.

"And I'd just made some more rissoles last night."

"They'll keep."

The two cops stepped forward. She held out her arms and they put the handcuffs on.

She tried to shrug. But it's not easy in handcuffs. Instead, she took a lingering look around her kitchen, then allowed the cops to lead her to the door.

She turned at the door. "This is my final goodbye to Regency Square and everything I love about it," she said. "Now my savings are gone, I'll have to sell the house to pay my legal costs. I'm afraid I'll have to give you a month's notice, Mr Crampton. And my other tenants."

With a final glance over her shoulder, she shuffled from the room.

Tomkins glanced at his watch and smirked at me. "Not even eight o'clock and I've arrested a dangerous killer. That'll be a time record for solving a murder. The national newspapers will love me, Crampton. I'll be a household name."

"Yes," I said. "Like Dettol."

* * *

I ate a hurried breakfast in Marcello's – although I had little appetite for the poached eggs on toast.

The Widow's arrest had unsettled me. Yesterday, I was on the trail of an exclusive murder scoop. Today, Tomkins had scuppered that. He'd arrested the wrong person for the wrong reason. But it would be the story that led all the papers after the regular morning police press briefing.

The Widow hadn't done herself any favours when she'd entrusted Hector's savings to a conman. I had no doubt that Winterbottom was running an investment scam. The letter from Crouchpenny reinforced the evidence of the Widow's own experience. And I knew she wouldn't see a penny of her money back. Not unless Winterbottom had left some of the cash in a bank account that Tomkins uncovered. But I wasn't confident about that.

The circumstantial evidence against the Widow – her letters to Winterbottom – was strong. If they were read out in court, I could see a jury giving the Widow some old-fashioned looks. But they didn't prove she'd killed Winterbottom. Except that she'd admitted to me – and would tell the cops – she'd visited him on the night of his killing.

Ted Wilson had told me that one witness had seen a woman fitting Gribble's description at Embassy Court at, or close to, the time of Winterbottom's killing. That wouldn't look good either. Altogether, I was convinced Tomkins had got it wrong, but miscarriages of justice happen. And the more I thought about it, the more it seemed that this case had all the hallmarks of a potential guilty verdict.

Which meant that the Widow would be in jail. And I would be out of lodgings that suited me very well. Unless I could prove to Tomkins that the Widow was innocent.

And there was an obvious way to do that.

I had to collect the torn pieces of Crouchpenny's letter from the bins at the back of Embassy Court before the dustmen emptied them.

* * *

The tyres on my MGB squealed on the road as I stamped on the brake pedal and skidded the car into a parking space outside Embassy Court.

I leapt out of the car and raced into the backyard. The bins were all in a row. Just like they'd been yesterday.

Which was the one with the letter? It was the seventh one along. I hurried over. Yanked off the lid. Stood and gawped.

The bin was empty.

I put the lid back and tried the bin next to it, in case I'd made a mistake.

Empty, too.

I was about to lift the lid on the next bin, when Herbie Stubbs stepped into the yard.

"Hey, what are you up to?" He moved closer. "Oh, it's you."

"I'm just looking for something I dropped yesterday."

"You won't find that now. The bin men came at seven this morning."

He wandered across the yard.

I stood there feeling like I'd been given a present in a fancily wrapped box. I'd ripped off the paper and found the box was empty.

My one hope of persuading Tomkins to point the finger of suspicion at Crouchpenny had just vanished.

And the odds on the Widow spending a long time locked up, looked alarmingly short.

FIVE

The cop shop's briefing room was already busy by the time I walked in at five to nine.

A murder always encourages a good turnout. There were reporters from the nationals and a group from press agencies. There was a buzz of conversation as journos swapped stories about juicy murders they'd covered in the past.

Nobody took too much notice as I took a seat at the back. (I've never understood why journos head for the front. At the back you see who's taking an interest, who's making lots of notes, and who seems to be on good or bad terms with whom.)

Jim Houghton was over the other side of the room talking to John Connor, who ran a local news agency.

As soon as he spotted me, he left John in mid-sentence and limped over.

He was wearing an ancient tweed suit which missed a sleeve button. The trousers were crumpled. The jacket had a tear by the pocket flap. A blind man could tell when Jim was approaching. His suit gave off a heavy musk like he'd hung it overnight in a mushroom shed, rather than a wardrobe.

He leered over me. So close I could've mapped the filigree of lines which criss-crossed his face. A hank of greasy grey hair flopped over his forehead.

I turned my face away.

He said: "I'm not surprised you haven't the guts to look me in the eye."

I said: "I don't want you to see my eyes watering from the pong around here."

"So no remorse for your disgraceful behaviour at the telephone kiosk."

"Don't let it get to you, Jim. There are no phone boxes here."

"You haven't heard the last of this, Crampton. I've said I'll finish you. And I will."

"Don't bet on it."

Jim turned about sharply. The musk of the mushroom-shed tweed hit me right between the nostrils. I grabbed my handkerchief and smothered my face while Jim stalked over to his favoured seat in the front row.

Jim had left me with an uneasy feeling. And not just because of the smelly suit. I'd played tricks on him before. He'd been angry, but he'd got over it after a day or two. He'd accepted it was all part of the cut and thrust of journalism. Part of the great game of deadlines and headlines. After all, he'd tried his own scams on me.

But the phone box prank had clearly got to him. Perhaps it was his age. He'd be getting his pension book through the post in a couple of years. Perhaps there were younger bloods snapping at his heels at the *Argus*. Jim had said he'd finish me. Hyperbole? Perhaps. But this time I had an uneasy feeling he meant it.

I was musing on this when the door on the other side of the room opened and Tomkins marched in. He had a fat bundle of papers under his arm. He dropped them on the top table and sat down in his chair.

His eyes surveyed the room until he saw me. His gaze locked onto mine. His lips parted in a sinister grin. Like the one Boris Karloff used in the flicks when he played Frankenstein - and was about to tear someone's head off. Pretty scary if you were alone in the dark with only your popcorn for company. Although it would have been a lot less scary if you'd have known that Boris Karloff's real name was William Pratt.

Well, Tomkins was no Karloff in the sinister grin department. But he was definitely a prat.

He picked up a sheaf of papers and started to read his prepared statement. I didn't bother to take it down in Pitman's. I knew what he'd say. I knew he'd pin the killing on the Widow. I knew he'd mention the letters. And I knew he'd bend the truth just like he did in court. Which was why so many of his collars walked free after their briefs had cross-examined him.

So while Tomkins droned on, I drew a matchstick man every time he told a lie or half-truth. One stick for the man's body, two for his legs, two for his arms, and one for his head. By the time Tomkins sat down, I had two men and one without a head. Seventeen lies.

Tomkins called for questions. Three or four eager-beavers among the press agency guys shot their hands in the air. Jim Houghton didn't even bother, but Tomkins called him anyway.

There was an undercurrent of grumbles as the eager-beavers lowered their arms.

Jim lumbered to his feet. "Detective Chief Superintendent, you have told us that you've arrested the landlady of a boarding house."

Tomkins nodded.

"Can you tell us a little about the inhabitants of this so-called boarding house and what part any of them might have played in the events surrounding this serious crime?"

Jim looked over his shoulder and flashed me a malicious grin before he sat down.

So this was what Jim meant when he said he'd finish me. He'd try to implicate me in Gribble's alleged killing. Of course, after a while Tomkins would be told there wasn't enough evidence to charge her. But, by then, some of the mud chucked at the Widow would have stuck. And the stuff that missed her would have splattered me.

This was a stitch-up. Tomkins and Houghton had planned it between them.

I leapt to my feet. "Perhaps I can help as I am a resident of the respectable premises in question. Where, incidentally, other residents include the maintenance engineer in a sock factory, the chief packer at a surgical appliances warehouse, and a lady piano tuner, who happily has no need to practise her trade in her rooms."

Heads swivelled round to watch me.

At the front, Tomkins had stood up and was wagging his finger at me.

"Sit down, or I'll have you arrested," he screamed. His cheeks were flushed and a little dribble of spittle ran down his chin. I ignored him.

I said: "None of the residents were involved. However, Mrs Gribble, the lady Chief Superintendent Tomkins has arrested on a trumped-up charge of murder, sought my advice. She wanted to know whether she could keep Tomkins out as he hadn't brought his warrant card with him."

"Is that true?" one of the agency reporters yelled.

Tomkins looked like he'd swallowed a wasp.

I said: "As it turned out, I advised Mrs Gribble to let Mr Tomkins in so she could clear up any misunderstanding about this case. Instead of accepting her explanation, he arrested her on no evidence at all."

"I'd call the letters when she threatened to kill Winterbottom evidence," Jim chipped in.

"I'd call them ordinary business correspondence," I said.

"I'm ordering you both to shut up and sit down," Tomkins yelled.

Jim sat down like a good boy. But as I'm not a good boy when it comes to police press conferences, I didn't sit down.

Instead, I asked Tomkins a question. "Did you explore any other leads before you rushed to judgement and arrested Mrs Gribble?"

Tomkins glared at me. "There was a clear motive for murder in her letters."

"But there were lots of letters in Winterbottom's flat. Have you read them all? Perhaps another dissatisfied investor has also wanted to top him."

"We're making continuing enquiries," Tomkins spluttered.

"Shouldn't you make those enquiries before you arrest an innocent woman?"

"I know your game, Crampton. If Gribble ends up in Holloway, you're out on the street. No cosy rooms in Regency Square. You've got a stake in all this."

"My stake is to ensure an innocent woman walks free," I said.

"Very noble," Tomkins sneered. "And that ends this press briefing."

And with that he stalked from the room.

I snapped shut my notebook. I stood up and headed for the door. Henry Turpin, one of the stringers for the nationals, stepped in front of me. He had his notebook open and his pencil poised over it.

"What's it like lodging in the house of a killer?" he asked.

"Mrs Gribble isn't a killer," I said.

"But she might be convicted despite your efforts to proclaim her innocence."

"She'll be acquitted because there's no credible evidence against her. And, anyway, what's your game?"

"Just thought there might be an angle."

"What angle?"

"Journo risks it all to fight for doomed landlady angle."

Trish Spencer and Wilfred Alperton, two agency reporters, crowded around me.

"Yeah! I was thinking the same angle," Wilfred said.

"I'm looking at the love interest," Trish said. "Young journo risks his career to save his older secret love."

I shook my head. In exasperation. Not an emotion I usually experience. But this was going too far.

I said: "There is not a doomed landlady angle. There is definitely not a secret love story. And the only story that stands up is that Gribble is innocent."

"But you've got that story," Trish said. "We can't go back to our editors playing catch-up with you."

"Yeah! We need something different," Henry said.

"A fresh angle," Wilfred echoed.

I shook my head and left them swapping notes. I stepped through the door and headed into the street.

When I'd walked into the press briefing this morning, I'd thought the Widow was the one with the problem.

Now I realised I had a problem. And a big one, too.

* * *

I called in my copy from a telephone box down the street.

Then I headed for Marcello's – my second visit of the morning. I wanted time to think. The last thing I needed right now was Figgis on my back demanding to know how I planned to develop the story.

I stepped up to the counter and ordered a strong coffee. The breakfast rush was over, so there were plenty of free tables. I took one at the back. Marcello was a chatterbox when he wasn't busy. He was leaning on the counter. But after my experience at the press briefing, I was in no mood for gossip.

I took a sip of the steaming coffee and cursed myself for my folly at the press briefing. It had seemed right to ride into action as a knight-errant when Gribble was arrested. But now I realised I was a knight with no shield and a busted lance. I'd expected Tomkins to attack me. Few cop shop press briefings with Tomkins ended without some verbal sword-play. And I'd usually parry his thrusts.

But I should have realised how my fellow hacks would react. I'd beaten them to the punch with a scoop. And the only way for a rival reporter to get ahead is to rubbish the scoop. That's why they'd decided to treat me as their fresh angle on the story. When their stories hit the streets, Figgis would not be pleased. Neither would His Holiness. He thought it was bad taste to run stories about murder. So what he'd do if he saw other papers with stories that implicated one of his reporters didn't bear thinking about.

I took a gulp of my coffee. It had turned cold.

I desperately needed a way to convince Tomkins that the Widow wasn't the only suspect. If Tomkins had done his job and searched the dustbins at Embassy Court, he'd have found the evidence himself. I should have kept the pieces of the torn letter from Crouchpenny and handed them to Tomkins. But that would only have created fresh problems. He'd have charged me with interfering with a police investigation. I wouldn't have put it past him to charge me with ripping up the letter myself.

I couldn't even tell Tomkins that I'd seen the letter. He'd call me a liar.

The only way I could make the Crouchpenny link to Winterbottom an active feature of the police investigation was to forage for hard evidence.

I left the rest of my cold coffee, stood up, and walked over to the counter. Marcello was polishing the chrome on his espresso machine.

I said: "Got a telephone directory?"

Marcello turned. "Of course I have."

"Can I borrow it?"

"What for?"

"I need to look up my chiropodist's phone number."

"Should remember a number like that. Feet, you can't be too careful."

He rummaged under the counter and slapped the book down in front of me.

I took it to a spare table. Looked up Crouchpenny's office address. Returned the directory.

Marcello watched me closely as I left the café.

I made sure I limped like a guy with a painful corn on his big toe.

SIX

Crouchpenny Easy Loans operated from a grimy shopfront property in the London Road.

There was a dog-eared photo in the window. It showed a smiling woman holding a fistful of fivers. There was a speech bubble coming out of her mouth: "I've got more cash for my stash." She didn't look like the type who'd spend it wisely.

The front door had a metal grille over the window and one of those triple locks that are supposed to be unpickable. The doorframe had been reinforced with metal jambs.

It looked like Crouchpenny took his security seriously. For all I knew, there'd be a machine-gun nest in the foyer.

I pushed open the door, ready to duck if anyone opened fire.

I needn't have bothered. Instead of the machine-gun there was a beaten-up desk on the other side of the room. It stood on a square of wrinkled carpet with the corners turned up. There were in- and out-trays on the desk. Both were piled high with papers. A drift of documents had cascaded onto the desk.

A young woman with a bob of auburn hair was sitting

behind the desk. A tarnished nameplate balanced on the desk's edge. It read: "Vicky Trott. Receptionist."

Vicky was turning the pages of the midday edition of the *Evening Chronicle*. She looked up as I closed the door behind me. She had full lips that would have made a pretty smile if she hadn't been so bored. Nice hazel eyes, too, if they hadn't been giving me a hard stare.

As I crossed the room, she folded the paper and stuffed it into her desk drawer.

I said: "I'm looking for Manfred Crouchpenny."

Vicky closed the drawer and said: "Who isn't?"

"Popular, is he?"

"Not so you'd notice."

"Any idea where I can find him?"

"That's another question I get asked a lot."

"Got an answer?"

"Not at the moment. So unless you've come to repay money he's lent you, push off."

I shuffled uneasily and bowed my head like a bloke who'd been put in his place.

Then I lifted the piece of paper off the top of the in-tray and started to read it.

Vicky glared at me, stood up, and tried to snatch the paper back. She knocked over the out-tray and a shower of papers fluttered to the floor.

She said: "Give that back. All this stuff is confidential"

"No doubt that's why it's scattered over the desk and the floor instead of being locked in a filing cabinet," I said.

Vicky sat down heavily and said: "Stuff you."

I handed back the paper I'd been reading.

Vicky said: "Seen enough, nosey?"

"More than enough. Would I be right in thinking you're not happy in your work?"

"What's it to you?"

"I might be able to help."

"Yeah! And I've got a date with Sean Connery tonight."

I said: "You're looking for a new job."

Vicky's eyes glanced at her desk drawer. The drawer where she'd stuffed the *Chronicle*.

"Suppose I am?" she said.

"Found anything that suits?"

"Nah! But how do you know I'm job-hunting?"

"You had the *Chronicle* open at the situations vacant ads."

Vicky shrugged. "Don't know why I bother. I get the first edition of the paper every day, but by the time I ring for a job I like the look of, it's always gone."

"Suppose you saw the job ads before anyone else?"

"And how am I supposed to do that, smart-arse? I can't get out until my lunch break at midday. By then the paper's been in the newsagent's for an hour."

"I could get you proofs of the job ad pages in advance. Before they appeared in the paper. You'd have a start on any other applicant."

Vicky leaned back in her chair. Stretched out her legs. Kicked a few of the papers that had fallen on the floor out of the way.

She gave me the kind of wary look people do when they wonder whether someone's for real.

"You could do that?" she asked.

I nodded.

"How?" she said.

"Does that really matter? Do you bother what Crouch-penny does when a borrower is late with his repayments?"

Vicky pulled quite a pretty grimace. "I'd rather not."

"So why fuss where the job ad proofs come from?"

"I guess it doesn't matter. But what do you get out of it? I ain't taking any of my clothes off."

"You can dress yourself in *haute couture* for all I care. All I want to know is what Crouchpenny's relationship was with Claude Winterbottom."

"Frosty," Vicky said. "Crouchpenny met Winterbottom about six months ago. Winterbottom ran some sort of investment scam."

"How did you know it was a scam?"

"It was obvious. Winterbottom was one of those smarmy types who thinks he's better than anyone else. Thinks no one can resist him. Even tried it on with me. As though I'd give it out for a corpse."

"But his dubious charm worked on Crouchpenny?"

"Crouchpenny has as much class as a rat's bum. Thing is, he knows it. He'd like to have the smooth chat like the Winterbottom types. Thinks it would enable him to go legit, rather than handing out penny-ante loans to desperate types who have to sell their children to pay him back."

"And Crouchpenny invested in Winterbottom's scheme?" I asked.

"Five grand," Vicky said. "Winterbottom told him he'd double his money in a year. That's a laugh. He won't double it in a lifetime. Even if he lived to be a hundred."

"And now Crouchpenny wants his five thousand pounds back," I said.

"You're quick."

"Would Crouchpenny kill for his money?"

"The slob has a big mouth but a small willy. Not that I've seen anything I shouldn't."

"Just a turn of phrase?"

"Yeah! When it comes to getting physical, he has enough trouble moving his belly round a tight corner. When he wants to get tough, he calls in a couple of hard cases, Will Butt and Ivor Thumper."

"Are those guys for real?"

"You better believe it. Butt is a scrawny streak of malice who fights dirty. Thumper is a great bundle of muscle and bone. Thinks he's some gentleman prize fighter from the days of bare-knuckle punch-ups. You don't want to tangle with either of them. They drive around in a converted hearse. They think it makes them look more menacing."

I thought about that. Ted Wilson had told me that three figures had been seen visiting Winterbottom's apartment. None of them had Butt's or Thumper's description. Of course, they could have arrived unseen. From Vicky's description, they sounded like the types who'd regard beating a bloke to death as a good night out.

They sounded like a couple of guys to steer clear of.

I said: "Even for a loan shark like Crouchpenny, five big ones must've been a tidy stash to lose."

"Tell me about it. For days after he'd discovered he'd been scammed it was like a thunder cloud had blown in every time he walked into a room. He became obsessed about making the money back the only way he knows how."

"By finding more mugs for his not-so-easy loans?"

"Yeah! Trouble is most people around here may be skint, but they've had their fingers burned by Crouchpenny before. He had to look elsewhere for new suckers. Even tried advertising on that pirate radio station."

"*Seabreeze?*"

"That's the one. Didn't do much good. The funny thing was, though, after a couple of weeks he seemed to have found a new source of cash. Even paid my wages on time."

"Any idea where the money came from?" I asked.

Vicky shrugged. "He spends less time in the office. Goes out more. Where? Don't know. But he's a real tightwad."

"Careful with his cash?"

"Careful! He treats it like it was going out of fashion. Look at this lot."

Vicky pointed at a pile of forms on her desk.

"Every time Butt and Thumper drive that hearse, they have to fill in one of these chits with the date and time of the journey and the address of the place they visited."

"What's the point of that?"

"Old Big Belly says it's so he can claim tax relief on the running costs. Personally, I think it's so he can check up on what the two dimwits are up to. Anyways, it makes work for me. I have to file the damned things."

I said: "Where will I find Crouchpenny now?"

"He'll be in the Hare and Hounds until half-two. Then if the mood is on him, he'll have gone on to the Clancy for the afternoon."

I knew about the Clancy. It was a members-only drinking den. You joined it if you were a crook, a drunkard, or you'd lost interest in living.

I said: "Thanks for your help. I won't forget about the job ad proofs."

Vicky grinned. "Yeah! Like you're the one man in Brighton who never lets a girl down."

* * *

I stepped outside through the high-security door determined I wouldn't let Vicky down.

Not as far as the job ads were concerned.

But that was something for next week. Right now, my

mind was focused on the paper I'd been reading in the office. The paper I'd snatched off the top of Vicky's in-tray.

It had been a letter from one Arnold Digby who ran a garden shop selling plants, seeds, and other stuff for the green-fingered brigade. I hadn't had time to read the whole letter, but Digby had been complaining that he'd been troubled by Crouchpenny's "hired thugs" who'd threatened to "do him over". The drift of the letter – as far as I could make out in ten seconds – was that Digby was a couple of payments late on a loan he'd taken from Crouchpenny. He'd needed the loan because late frosts had killed off some seedlings he'd hoped to sell at a good profit.

The letter didn't say so, but I assumed the thugs had been Butt and Thumper, whom Vicky had mentioned.

So this was how Crouchpenny dealt with people who owed him money. No late-payment red bill in a brown envelope. No solicitors threatening court action in circumlocutory language. No summons, with the bailiffs to follow if you didn't pay up.

Instead, you ended up with a beating. And with more parts bruised than your self-esteem.

As I stepped out towards the Clancy club, I wondered whether Crouchpenny's thugs ever went further than a beating. Did they kill to order? The letter suggested Digby owed less than two hundred pounds. Perhaps that only warranted a roughing up. But if somebody – a crooked investment adviser, to take an example at random – owed five thousand pounds, perhaps that merited harsher action.

Of course, there's a problem about killing people who owe you money. Once they're dead, they don't have to settle the debt. But Crouchpenny sounded like the kind of hard case who might not think like that.

Perhaps he'd had five thousand pounds-worth of thrill just for knowing that Winterbottom was lying in a coffin.

I'd reached the Clancy club. And I hoped I was about to find out.

* * *

A fussy little man hurried up to me as I pushed through the swing doors into the Clancy club bar.

He had a thin face and a hangdog expression that would have made him a shoo-in if he'd chosen a career as an undertaker. He had a single strand of Brylcreemed hair combed over a bald pate. He was wearing a white mess jacket and black trousers.

He said: "I'm Simkins, club steward. Are you a member?"

I said: "My subscription's in the post. I'm looking for Manfred Crouchpenny."

Simkins' hangdog jaw sagged a bit. "Looking for a loan?"

"No, a gin and tonic. One ice cube, two slices of lemon."

Simkins brightened up a bit at the prospect of a cash sale. He sloped off behind the bar and busied himself serving the drink.

He put the glass on the bar and said: "That'll be one and ninepence."

I said: "Put it on Crouchpenny's account."

"I hope there's not going to be any trouble. The insurance company has said they'll withdraw our cover if any more furniture gets broken."

I looked around the place. The walls were covered in faded red flock wallpaper. The acorn pattern had faded on the worn carpet. There were a dozen small tables with those glass tops you see in cheap hotels. There was no sign of Crouchpenny anywhere.

I said: "They tell me Crouchpenny drinks here most afternoons."

"I couldn't say, sir," Simkins said. He picked up a clean glass and started to polish it.

"I don't see him anywhere."

"Mr Crouchpenny values his privacy."

"Except when people owe him money, I understand."

"I really couldn't say, sir."

"There seems to be a lot you couldn't say. Is there anything you can?"

Simkins gave me a pitying look and moved up to the other end of the bar. He'd decided a clean ashtray urgently needed emptying.

I took a good pull at my gin and tonic and wondered what to do if Crouchpenny had chosen to break his usual routine.

I'd decided to finish my drink and head back to the office when a door opened on the far side of the bar.

Two men pushed their way through. One a scrawny streak of malice. The other a bundle of muscle and bone.

Butt and Thumper.

They looked at me like they'd like to use my head as a football. Before they packed it into the nose-cone of a rocket and launched it into space.

I smiled back and raised my glass to them. They exchanged confused glances and hurried towards the exit.

As they passed me, I heard the scrawny streak of malice say: "Do you know the way?"

The bundle of muscle and bone said: "Sure. My grey-haired old granny used to live in Ditchling."

That had my attention.

But it would have to wait.

Because I'd bet a gallon of gin to the lemon in my glass that Crouchpenny was in the room the pair had just left. I picked up my glass and crossed the bar.

The pair of hard types had left the door ajar. I pushed through like I belonged in the place.

Crouchpenny was slumped on an old leather Chesterfield. His bum occupied about a third of the lengthy divan and his belly the rest of it. It moved sinuously as he breathed like a deep-sea monster would as it trawled the ocean depths in search of food.

He was wearing a grey worsted two-piece suit. It had huge trousers that you'd easily fit on the hind legs of an elephant.

I adopted my cheeriest tone and said: "Don't mind if I join you?"

Some bones crunched and some muscles creaked as Crouchpenny moved his head to get a better look at me. He had a huge forehead. (You could have drawn a map of the world on it.) Two cheeks bulged on each side his face and seemed to squeeze his lips together. But it was his eyes which dominated. They were hard and cunning with big eyelids that drooped insolently over them.

Crouchpenny's squeezed lips moved in a coquettish kind of way.

He said: "This is a private sitting room."

"I just saw a couple of refined gentlemen leave and assumed that, like a railway waiting room, it was open to all."

"The two who left are my associates. They were here at my invitation. You are not." He shifted on the Chesterfield and the belly flopped sideways.

I said: "I guess it must be nice to have a room where you can invite who you like. Did you ever invite Claude Winterbottom? Won't be able to now."

Crouchpenny's lips curled in a snarl. "That smarmy grifter wasn't welcome here. And who are you anyway?"

I crossed the room, parked my gin and tonic on a table, and pulled a card out of my pocket.

I flicked the card into Crouchpenny's lap. "Colin Crampton, *Evening Chronicle*."

"A newspaperman," Crouchpenny growled.

"You're quick," I said. "Let's see if you can be just as quick on this one. Why did you kill Winterbottom?"

"I rejoice the man is dead. I hope his body rots slowly to slime. It will be an improvement."

"That sounds like a confession."

"It sounds like the pleasure of revenge. But I didn't kill Winterbottom."

"He owed you five thousand pounds."

"He owed me ten thousand. He had promised to double my money. I planned to make him pay."

"And then the debt would be settled?"

"And then we would have to see."

I thought about that for a moment.

What if Crouchpenny had ordered Butt and Thumper to threaten Winterbottom with a beating? What if they'd been too enthusiastic? They'd struck me as a pair of low-lifes who enjoyed their work. What if they'd gone too far? What if they'd killed Winterbottom by accident? They'd still be guilty of murder. Manslaughter, at least. And if Crouchpenny was the man who'd given the order, he'd stand in the dock, too.

I said: "When people owe you money, you don't care how you get it back, do you?"

Crouchpenny flipped his hand dismissively. "I'm a businessman. I advance loans and live off the modest interest."

"Not modest. You charge rates double, treble or more than other lenders."

"I have expenses. But they don't include killing my customers. If you want to find Winterbottom's killer, you should look elsewhere. He had real enemies."

"Like whom?"

Crouchpenny's cunning eyes narrowed. "Why should I tell you?"

"Because if you do, I'll tell you something you ought to know."

A deep laugh, like a roll of thunder, rumbled up from Crouchpenny's chest. "'The rich rules over the poor, and the borrower is the slave of the lender.'"

"Your motto, I suppose?"

"Not mine. The Good Book. Proverbs, I believe. But don't ask me to quote chapter and verse."

"You don't strike me as the type who has his nose stuck in the *Bible*. More like Harold Robbins' *The Carpetbaggers*."

"I don't read books. I make them. Loan books."

"What's that supposed to mean?"

"Consider my comment a clue."

"To what?"

"To Winterbottom's killer."

I said: "So I'm looking for a Holy Joe type? Is that what you're saying?"

"Who can say what I'm saying?" Crouchpenny sniggered.

This conversation was going nowhere. Crouchpenny wasn't going to open up. It looked like he got his jollies from creating a man of mystery persona. I picked up my glass and drained my gin and tonic.

I said: "It's been a pleasure, Crouchpenny. I'll be back."

I turned towards the door.

Crouchpenny waved his hand. "You were going to tell me something I ought to know."

I held up my empty glass. "Yes. I've put this drink on your account."

I stepped through the door and closed it behind me.

SEVEN

I could have spent longer in verbal sword-play with Crouchpenny.

But an incident earlier in the Clancy's bar had caught my attention.

And it merited urgent action.

The incident was a snatch of conversation between Butt and Thumper as they'd walked past me.

Butt had said: *"Do you know the way?"*

Thumper had replied: *"Sure. My grey-haired old granny used to live in Ditchling."*

That had triggered an uneasy thought in my mind. About Arnold Digby's letter. The one I'd snatched from Vicky Trott's in-tray. Digby's garden centre was in Ditchling. The address was pride of place at the top of his headed notepaper.

Perhaps Butt and Thumper were on their way to Digby for a little debt collection. With extreme violence. If I caught them at it, I could threaten them with the police, unless... Unless they told me what they knew about Crouchpenny's operation. And, specifically, his relationship with Winterbottom.

The main question in my mind was whether I could reach Digby before they'd smashed his garden gnomes. Or him.

* * *

But there was no sign of the pair when I pulled the MGB onto a small parking lot outside Digby's place.

I switched off the engine, sat back, and let out a deep sigh. The needle on the speedometer had touched a hundred on the road out of Brighton. But I'd slowed down when I reached the outskirts of Ditchling. It was one of those picture-book places you find nestling in the Sussex countryside. There were ancient houses with oak beams and sagging roofs. There were moss-encrusted flint walls. There was an old-stone church and graveyard with weathered headstones. There was a village hall with a noticeboard. It carried news of scouts' picnics, Women's Institute keep-fit sessions, and parish council meetings.

Singer Vera Lynn lived in a comfortable house down one of the lanes. The troops had called her the "forces' sweetheart" during the war years. But I wouldn't be calling today to ask her to reprise her signature tune – *We'll Meet Again*. Perhaps another time.

Besides, I had an uncomfortable feeling I was about to meet Butt and Thumper again.

Digby's place was in a lane on the outskirts of the village. It occupied a small plot of land between a wisteria-clad cottage and a water pumping station. The place was surrounded by a half-hearted picket fence that wouldn't keep out an eighty-year-old on crutches. There was a painted sign which read Green Fingers. It didn't mention whether that was the name of the place or the physical condition of the owner.

I climbed out of the MGB and took a look around.

The lane was deserted. No customers, no passers-by. This

didn't look like the kind of place Digby would call a gold mine. But, then, I don't suppose a gold mine owner would call his place a garden centre. It was one of those bizarre thoughts that race through my mind when I get nervous.

I'd just realised that I'd hurried out here knowing there was likely to be a punch-up. Pity, I'd left my boxing gloves at home.

But in cases like this a sharp remark can often get you out of trouble. Take my word for it. You can give your antagonist a punch on the snout. But then you find you've splashed blood on your shirt. Much better to cut him dead with a sarcastic remark. Saves on laundry bills.

With this helpful thought in my mind, I strode through the gate into the garden centre.

I almost tripped over an untidy pile of fence posts to the side of the gate. In front of me, there was a long concrete walkway with side paths off to the right. The paths were lined with trestle tables loaded with potted plants. There were little patches of colour here and there where various varieties had burst into bloom. A splash of bright red geraniums. A drift of pink begonias. A mosaic pavement of pansies in purples and blues and yellows.

I could have enjoyed a couple of quiet minutes to take a closer look. But I had in mind that a pair of thugs were on their way to beat up the proprietor of the place.

There was an old-fashioned Nissen hut on the left side of the central path. It was one of those wartime constructions, often thrown up in a couple of days to house troops. It had whitewashed walls built out of concrete blocks and a curving roof made out of rusting corrugated iron. Not pretty, but functional.

The hut had a door in the middle. As I watched, the door opened and a man stepped out. He was a couple of inches short of six feet tall, had broad shoulders, and legs that were slightly bowed.

He saw me, gave a cheery wave, and headed in my direction.

He had a smiley open face with a broad forehead, prominent nose, and jutting chin. His eyes were a little too far apart. He had a thick thatch of dark brown hair which was combed back and rested on his collar. He was wearing a checked shirt and blue corduroy trousers.

He called out as he approached: "I'm Arnold Digby. Did I see you looking at the begonias?"

I said: "If you mean the *begonia coccinea*, a species of the genus of perennial flowering plants in the family *begoniaceae*, the answer is yes."

Digby grinned with pleasure. "Ah, a botanist after my own heart."

"No, just someone who can read the labels stuck on the sides of flowerpots."

I stepped forward and handed him a card. "Colin Crampton, *Evening Chronicle*."

Digby frowned. "I hope this isn't about advertising in those interminable gardening supplements you run. Last time, I took half a page and only sold a packet of beetroot seeds and a dibble."

I shook my head. "A couple of men are on their way to see you. They're not interested in beetroot seeds. And I'd keep them away from the dibbles. They might stick one where you'd least expect it."

Digby's eyes may have been too far apart, but they could get it together to give me a hard stare.

"Two men? What men?" he demanded.

"The kind who collect unpaid debts. With extreme violence."

Digby looked down at the ground. Kicked a stray clod of earth out of the way.

"Debts? I don't have debts."

"That's not what Manfred Crouchpenny says. But I can help you."

"How could you help me?"

"Crouchpenny's thugs rely on the power of fear. As well as the fist. But they can be frightened if you know how."

"You don't look like someone who could throw a punch."

"I rarely have to. Everyone is frightened by something. I knew an all-in wrestler. Twenty stone of solid muscle. Biceps like rugby footballs. Seventy-eight knockouts in the ring. Twice as many down his local when some smart-arse got lippy. Yet there was one thing that would have him run a mile."

"What?"

"A spider. Even an itsy-bitsy one who'd scurry for a hole in the woodwork if he'd so much as moved."

"Well, as it happens, this place is crawling with them."

"All-in wrestlers?"

"No, spiders."

Digby shot an anxious glance at the road. "If what you say is true, when do you expect these, er... gentlemen? And, more to the point, how can you frighten them off?"

"With the one thing they hate. Publicity. Debt collectors like to work in the shadows. They hate it if there's a chance their picture will appear in the paper. Largely because their picture is already on police files. And they don't want the cops taking an interest in their work."

Digby studied the floor again. Couldn't find any more earth to kick around. Looked up a bit sheepishly.

"As it happens, I did borrow some money from Crouch-penny a few months ago. It was those late frosts we had in

April. Killed off hundreds of seedlings I'd taken out of the greenhouse. Normally, I'd have sold the lot in the spring. But..."

His voice trailed off and he shook his head.

"And your takings dropped," I said. "So you thought you'd take up a loan just to tide you over."

Digby nodded.

"But the banks didn't want to know," I said.

"When do they?"

"Because they only like to lend money to people who don't need it."

"Tell me about it."

"So you went to an unauthorised lender."

"I was desperate," Digby pleaded. "Crouchpenny said I could extend the term of the loan if business was slow to pick up. But then, only two months later, he demanded five hundred pounds plus interest repaid immediately. Showed me some small print in the agreement. Lawyer-speak. 'Heretofore.' 'The party of the first part.' I couldn't understand it and I wasn't going to fork out for a lawyer to tell me what I already knew."

"That Crouchpenny wouldn't take no for an answer."

Digby nodded. He looked around the place. The kind of look people give when they're forced to leave a house they've lived in all their life. Sad but resigned.

"What should we do?" he asked.

I said: "We should go into your hut and I'll use your telephone to make a call."

"To the police?" he asked.

"No, they wouldn't be interested in your problem. This will be a call to someone with unique skills to help us out of this predicament."

* * *

Five minutes later, I replaced the telephone receiver and said: "And now we wait."

Digby shot me a worried look. "What happens if Crouchpenny's hard men turn up before help arrives?"

"Then we'll engage them in diverting conversation."

Digby looked at the ground again. But there was nothing to kick in here.

We were in the Nissen hut which he'd turned into a garden shop. There were forks and spades and Dutch hoes – just in case anyone from the Netherlands dropped by, I suppose. There were three kinds of trowel, pruning knives, secateurs, and twee gardening gloves in pink, blue or yellow. There were packets of seeds for carrots, and peas, and cauliflowers. There was a heap of terracotta flowerpots stacked up high like a chimney. And behind them a garden gnome with blue jacket, red trousers, and a yellow pom-pom bonnet. He had the kind of knowing sneer on his face which would have the daffodils drooping their heads in shame.

Some of the stuff had dust on it. Looked like not many garden lovers shopped here. It wasn't hard to see why. When it came to cash at the bank, Digby was up the Swannee in a leaking canoe.

He said: "If those thugs left before you, why aren't they here yet?"

I said: "Because they'll have stopped off on the way for a glass or two of Dutch courage."

"You mean they'll be drunk when they get here?"

"Types like Butt and Thumper aren't brave. They're a pair of cowards at heart. They like to smash stuff up because they can't understand it. It's their way of getting back at a world that's beyond their comprehension."

"So if they're rolling around from drink, you should be able to handle them."

I noticed he hadn't included himself in the handling party.

But I said: "If they were brave men, drunk would be easier to handle than sober. But when you're dealing with cowards, drunk is more dangerous. The booze makes them forget they're cowards and fuels the hidden hero in their souls."

Digby shrugged his shoulders like he disagreed with me, but didn't like to say so.

He said: "I don't think they'll come. I've probably got nothing to worry about."

Bang!

The door of the Nissen hut flew back on its hinges and crashed against the wall.

Butt and Thumper shouldered two-abreast into the place.

Their mouths were set in a determined scowl, but their eyes were glazed with drink.

They each carried a fence post from the pile I'd seen lying next to the entrance gate. The posts had been sharpened at one end to make it easier to hammer them into the ground.

They advanced into the hut carrying the posts like spears.

I sensed Digby move backwards and edge behind me.

I looked at Thumper and said: "The posts are ten bob each, but I can do you a discount on the fencing panels to go with them. And if you spend more than fifteen quid, you get a free garden gnome."

Butt said: "My Mum's always wanted a gnome."

Thumper said: "Shut up."

Butt looked at me and said. "Has it got a fishing line to dangle in a pond?"

I said: "No, but it's got a yellow pom-pom hat."

Thumper said: "Shut up."

Butt said: "I'd pay extra for the fishing line."

I said: "We'd have to order it in. Can you come back a week Friday?"

Butt looked enquiringly at Thumper.

Thumper said: "Shut up."

Butt said: "You're only jealous because you ain't got one."

"A gnome?"

"No, a mum."

Thumper dropped his fence post on the floor and said: "Watch your mouth. My Mum ran off with the tallyman when I were three. It weren't my fault."

Butt said: "Is the offer of the gnome still on if we bash the bloke hiding behind you?"

I shook my head. "Afraid not."

Butt looked at Thumper. "I suppose we'll have to get him anyway."

"First sensible thing you've said since you downed that third large scotch in the Serving Wench."

"If I can't have the gnome, I'll have some fun hitting that bloke hiding behind the other bloke," Butt said.

"Unless the hiding bloke has got the money." Thumper leaned sideways so he could see Digby behind me. "Have you got the spondulicks?"

A quavering voice behind me said: "You know I haven't. I told Crouchpenny that early repayment wasn't in the written agreement."

Butt said: "A punch up the bracket wasn't in the agreement but that's what you're getting if you ain't got the loot."

Thumper said: "Look, you pay up or we bash you. We ain't got more time to waste. We got deliveries to make to people who get very twitchy if they don't get what they want on time. People who pay up with no trouble."

The pair advanced three steps towards us. Like they were going into battle.

Digby stepped back into a pile of garden spades. They crashed to the ground.

Thumper said: "Butt's gonna whack Digby with the fence post. And I'm gonna do him with this cosh." He reached inside a pocket and whipped out a short wooden cosh with a leather strap. He wound the strap around his wrist.

He said: "This is made of real teak. It's hard wood. Digby will discover how hard if he doesn't pay up."

I said to Butt: "Suppose we give you the gnome as a down-payment."

Butt looked at Thumper. "You think the boss will go for that?"

"The boss don't like little people."

"Yeah! I guess so, him being twenty-three stone and everything."

Butt stepped forward and jabbed the fence post at me like a bayonet.

I grabbed the end, yanked it to the right, and shoved back.

Butt stumbled backwards and crashed into one of the trestle tables. It toppled over and he landed on top of it. Hundreds of seed packets skittered over the floor. Butt floundered around on them.

Digby screamed: "You're crushing my *solanum melongena* egg plant."

Butt yelled: "Sod your eggs. I've bruised my bum."

"It's the bright purple variety," Digby yelled.

"So's my bum now."

Thumper shrieked: "Shut up."

Butt scrambled up off the floor. Grabbed the fence post.

Thumper twirled the cosh around his wrist.

He nodded in a conspiratorial way at Butt. "Let's take one each. You go for the lippy one. I'll go for the bloke with the purple eggs."

Thumper gave his cosh a couple of practice swishes. "I'm gonna bury you with this." He moved threateningly on Digby.

Butt brandished his post. Kept the sharp end higher in the air to make it harder for me to grab. "I'm gonna run you through with this," he said.

This wasn't turning out like I'd hoped.

Digby said: "What do we do now?"

I said: "We back away from them."

"So much for your clever phone calls."

"We'll play for time."

"Time's run out for you two," Thumper said.

We backed up through the Nissen hut. Thumper and Butt crept forward step by cautious step.

There wasn't much we could do now.

The two of them glanced at one another. They were going to charge together.

I glanced down to my right.

I was standing next to the gnome. Up close, the expression on his face looked evil. Like he'd cast a spell on us.

Thumper and Butt shuffled their feet on the floor. Like a pair of bulls preparing to charge.

They moved forward. I seized the gnome by the scruff of his neck. Hoisted him up and swung him around my head. He was heavy. Felt like he'd pull my arm out of its socket.

Thumper and Butt were almost on us.

I let go of the gnome. He flew through the air with all the grace of a pregnant pig.

He smashed into Thumper and Butt as the two closed in for their attack.

The pair staggered back under the force of his weight. They crashed to the floor in a heap.

They sprawled on the ground. The least attractive *ménage à trois* you'll ever see. Two plug uglies and a gnome.

And then there was a bright flash of light.

Like the sun had winked and set off a flare.

For a moment, my eyes were blinded.

I looked beyond the source of the light.

Freddie Barkworth, the *Chronicle's* chief photographer, ejected a flash bulb from his camera.

Butt and Thumper pushed the gnome to one side. They scrambled to their feet. Shoved past Freddie as they raced for the door.

"You never said there'd be a cameraman," Butt yelled. "The boss ain't gonna like this."

"Shut up," Thumper screamed as the pair vanished through the door.

* * *

Arnold Digby slapped his hands together in a job-well-done gesture.

He said: "That's settled their hash."

I gave Freddie Barkworth an open-eyed look. "I was under the impression, we'd settled their hash," I said.

Freddie raised his camera and said to Digby. "I want a picture of you with the gnome."

We gathered around the little creature. He was lying on the ground, next to the garden spades.

Digby said: "You've damaged him. There's a crack in his cheek and chip on his nose."

I said: "From the look on his face, he should have a chip on his shoulder."

"That's not the point. You damaged him when you threw the little fellow."

"Necessary defence," I said. "Of you."

Digby knelt down next to the gnome. Pointed to a spot on the gnome's left knee where the paint had flaked off. "How am I going to cure damage like this?" he asked.

"You could try the National Elf Service," I said.

Digby groaned and cradled the gnome in his lap.

And at that moment, Freddie's flashgun fired again.

"I wasn't ready with my pose," Digby complained.

"That's what makes it a great newspaper photograph," Freddie said.

"With publicity like that, customers will flood in," I said.

Digby's face lit up. Not perhaps the full 100 watts. But enough to put a happy crease in his cheeks.

"Do you really think so?" he said.

"Publicity like that can't fail," I said.

EIGHT

I left Digby to collect up his seed packets and to complain about his damaged gnome to anyone who'd listen.

I phoned in my copy about the rumpus at Green Fingers from a phone box in Ditchling. The publicity would annoy Crouchpenny and make him more likely to talk the next time I tackled him. And when Freddie's picture of Butt and Thumper with the gnome appeared on the front page, the pair would probably quit town for a while. The cops would be on their case. And, anyway, who's going to hire hard men who roll around on the ground with a garden gnome? It's not nice.

I would normally have relaxed during the drive back to Brighton. I might have taken the route over Ditchling Beacon and enjoyed the view along the coast to Beachy Head.

But there was too much on my mind. So I took the main road back into town.

My quick-fire visits to Vicky Trott and the Clancy club – not to mention Green Fingers – had taken my mind off the morning's police press conference.

But as my adrenalin levels returned to normal – or as

normal as they ever get in my game – the worries flooded back. There was no doubt that Jim Houghton was out to embarrass me. And Alec Tomkins would happily fall over his flat feet to help out.

What I hadn't bargained for was my fellow journos taking up Houghton's cause. I'd been too wrapped up in my own scoop to appreciate they'd want one of their own. And the easiest one to hand was to rubbish mine – and me.

If I was roughed up in print, I could take it. Figgis would probably brush it aside with a couple of cynical barbs. But His Holiness wouldn't be so relaxed about it all. I sensed trouble.

And as the Patcham Pylons appeared ahead of me – signalling the Brighton boundary – I realised that wasn't my only worry.

Shirley was troubled about her stalker. So much, that I'd insisted I meet her off the train when she arrived back from her modelling job in London this evening.

I glanced at the clock on the MGB's dashboard. I had just ten minutes to reach the station.

I floored the accelerator and the MGB roared past the Pylons.

I parked in Trafalgar Street and legged it into the station with a minute to spare.

There was a crush of people pushing through the barriers off an earlier train. They had the tired faces – part tension, part relief – of people who are glad that another day's toil is over.

A burbled announcement from the Tannoy informed anyone who was interested that the London train was running seven minutes late. That gave me time to head over to the news stand. I hadn't yet seen the evening papers, but feared the worst.

I grabbed the *Evening Argus* and London *Evening News* and handed over a shilling.

I scurried to a quiet spot behind the news stand and looked at the *Argus'* front page. A headline screamed: REPORTER'S AID FOR MURDER SUSPECT LANDLADY.

Jim Houghton had excelled himself in malice. According to Jim, death stalked the Widow's boarding house. His evidence for this was that Hector, the Widow's late husband, had died in "unusual circumstances". (In fact, he'd pegged out while completing a 500-piece jigsaw puzzle of the Royal Pavilion – and who wouldn't?)

The Widow's apartments were a place "for transient workers with no desire to put down roots in Brighton". (In other words, people who expected to get on in life.) I was "a reporter who'd interfered in police investigations to the annoyance of senior officers". (Yes, I'd solved cases which had baffled Tomkins.)

And, finally, I had a relationship with the Widow "which went beyond that normal for a landlord and tenant". (Too right! I had to sort out her disasters just to make life tolerable.) But it wasn't difficult to see what Jim was implying.

I tossed the *Argus* in a nearby bin and turned to the *Evening News*. It wasn't quite as obvious as the *Argus*. But the drift of the piece was that a journalist tenant had ridden to the rescue of his landlady who was on a murder rap that cops expected to stick. So much for Fleet Street's finest.

As I folded up the *News*, a whistle announced the arrival of the London train.

I hurried over to the platform's gate.

The brakes on the Brighton Belle let out a deep sigh as the carriages came to a halt. The doors opened at once and two hundred city types, back from the office, flooded onto the platform. It was like an invasion of the zombies. All wearing grey suits, black laced shoes, and bowler hats.

I caught a glimpse of Shirley halfway down the train. She'd kitted herself out in a canary yellow two-piece suit with pencil skirt and matching pillbox hat.

She pushed her way through the grey suits towards the ticket barrier. She had a smile on her face and a skip in her step.

She came through the barrier and straight into my arms. She plonked the kind of lingering kiss on my lips I felt I could save up for a rainy day.

She said: "He's gone."

"The stalker?"

"Yeah! Haven't seen the creep all day."

"So the problem is over?"

"I guess so."

"Let's go and have a drink."

Shirley licked her lips and kissed me again. "I thought you'd never ask," she said.

* * *

But when we walked into Prinny's Pleasure five minutes later, it was plain the problem had come back.

Stalker was sitting in the corner nursing a pint of lager just like the night before. Same wiry frame. Same long legs. Same narrow face.

The previous evening he'd worn a denim jacket. Now he had one of those safari jobs with more pockets than a shoplifter's overcoat.

Shirley grabbed my arm. I hustled her over to the bar.

I said: "I'm going to tackle him."

"Get me a drink first," Shirley said. "I need it."

Jeff ambled up and said: "Business is looking up."

I nodded towards the corner. "You're attracting the wrong kind of customer."

"Better than no kind of customer."

I ordered a gin and tonic and a Campari soda for Shirley.

She still clung to my arm.

Jeff poured the drinks and put them on the bar.

As he did so, two fingers tapped lightly on my shoulder. It felt like a small bird had landed.

I turned around. The stalker was standing behind us.

I heard Shirley gasp and she gripped my arm harder.

The stalker's lips twisted into the kind of lop-sided grin I might have found endearing in other circumstances.

He said: "I feel I should have introduced myself earlier."

I said: "I feel you should have found a different pub to drink in. Like one in John O'Groats."

"Oh dear, I see I've played this situation badly."

"Your first mistake was tangling with me."

"No, buster, your first mistake was following me," Shirley chipped in. "Are you some kind of pervert? Do you get off from spying on girls?"

"Yes, that is to say, no," he burbled.

"What's that supposed to mean?" I asked.

"Perhaps I ought to introduce myself properly."

"Perhaps you ought to push off," I said.

"No," Shirley said. "Let's get the guy's name. Then we can call the cops."

The stalker rummaged in his pockets pulled out a card. Handed it to me.

The card read: "Curtis Grainger. Casting director and assistant to Albert R Broccoli."

I turned the card over like I expected to see "Fooled you" printed on the other side.

Shirley leaned closer to me and I handed her the card.

"Who is this Broccoli guy?" she asked.

"He produces the James Bond films," I said.

"Like *Goldfinger*," Shirley said. "I just dig that Honor Blackman as Pussy Galore."

Grainger managed one of his lop-sided grins. "I cast Honor in that role after seeing her as Mrs Gale in *The Avengers* on TV."

I held up my hand. "Hold up a minute. We don't know who you really are."

"I just handed you my business card."

"Anyone can pay a fiver for a bunch of business cards from the local printer. I could get some saying I'm the Duke of Edinburgh."

Grainger nodded like I'd just explained the meaning of life.

"I understand," he said. "Especially after the inept way I've introduced myself. But it's real. I am who the card says I am."

"Then what do you want with us?" Shirley demanded.

Grainger turned to Shirley. "I want to offer you a part in the next James Bond film."

"Gee, me a film star. What'll my Ma say about that?"

I lifted my glass off the bar and had a good pull at my gin and tonic. This was moving too fast.

I said to Grainger: "Let's assume you are who you say you are. Do you have authority to go around offering parts in a big movie? And even if you do, why Shirley, when you've never met her before?"

Shirley flashed me an angry look. "Why not, buster?" she said.

"I don't suppose Marilyn Monroe got cast in *Gentlemen Prefer Blondes* because Howard Hawks saw her walking down the road."

Grainger raised his hands, palms out, in a calming gesture.

"Good questions. They deserve an answer. Let's move to that table at the back before I answer them. Besides, that scruffy guy behind the bar is earwigging our conversation."

Jeff stopped wiping a grey tea towel around a grimy glass and said: "Don't mind me. I got offered a film part once. But I turned it down because of the billing."

"They wouldn't give you a starring role?" I asked.

"No, they wanted to charge me a hundred quid to be in it."

None of us had anything to say to that. So we picked up our drinks and moved to the table.

Grainger had a swig at his lager and said: "First, this is on the level. I can recommend actors for a screen test, but the final decision on casting is the director's"

"You could've spoken to me yesterday at the Café Royal," Shirley said.

"I wasn't sure you'd be right for the part then. I didn't want to raise your hopes and dash them. Besides, it doesn't look good for me if I recommend actors who don't make it onto the screen. That's why I wanted to see more of you – how you move and whether you looked like you had the confidence to carry off a screen role. I didn't realise you'd spotted me following you."

Shirley sipped her Campari. "As a follower, you've got all the subtlety of a troop of 'roos."

Grainger grimaced. "Looks like I fouled up."

I said: "What made you pick out Shirley?"

"Well, this part requires a girl with two qualities. She must be beautiful and she must be Australian."

Shirley laughed. "And your eyeballs pinged out on springs as soon as you saw me."

Grainger's cheeks reddened. "Actually, I heard your Aussie accent when you were talking to someone. That's what got my attention. The other bit fell into place when I'd taken a look at you."

"Why do you need an Australian girl?" I asked.

"It's in the plot. We're making *On Her Majesty's Secret Service* as the next movie."

I nodded. I'd read Ian Fleming's book a couple of years earlier.

I said: "That's the one where the villain, Ernst Stavro Blofeld, has recruited twelve girls to act as angels of death?"

Grainger nodded. "The girls come from all over the world. There's an English one – we've already signed Joanna Lumley for that part – a Hungarian, American, German, Chinese, and so on."

"And Australian," Shirley added.

"Yes. In the story, they're all suffering from allergies – one of them can't stand chickens. Blofeld pretends to be curing them when, all the while, he's really developing a killer virus. He plans to use it to blackmail the world to pay him a ransom and forgive his previous crimes. Blofeld is holed up in this clinic at the top of a mountain in Switzerland. James Bond arrives in disguise and has to stop Blofeld. Of course, before that he seduces some of the girls."

"Jeez!" Shirley said. "I have to go to bed with Sean Connery. He's old enough to be my father."

"He's only thirty-seven. But, in fact, he's backing out of the Bond movies. We've hired a new actor, George Lazenby. He's an Australian, too. And only twenty-seven."

"Sounds cool," Shirley said. "If I'm filmed in bed with him, what do I have to wear?"

"A dab of perfume behind the ears normally suffices," Grainger said with a grin.

Shirley laughed.

I said: "*Ahem*. You've not got the part yet."

"I'll be a shoo-in," Shirl said.

"I think you'll be great," Grainger said.

"You should think it over carefully," I said. "Your modelling career is taking off. And you don't normally have to hop into bed with itinerant Australians."

Shirl flashed me an angry look. "So what? When they cry lights, camera, action, are you jealous you're not getting any of the action?"

I frowned. Picked up my gin and tonic and had a good pull at it.

I said: "It's the lights and camera I'd be worried about."

Grainger said: "All this is done discreetly. In the old Hollywood days, they insisted the man and the woman each had one foot on the floor in a bedroom scene."

"Kinky," Shirl said.

"Besides, I haven't seen a full shooting script yet. I don't even know whether the Australian Girl has a steamy session with James Bond."

"You need to think carefully about this," I said to Shirley. "You don't want to regret a hasty decision."

"What's to regret? If I get the part, I've got a film career. If I don't, I'm still a model." She turned to Grainger. "Where's the contract, buster?"

Grainger grinned. I didn't like the way he did it. If sharks grinned, they'd do it that way before they ate you.

He said: "Let's get the preliminaries out of the way first."

I said: "I hope the preliminaries don't involve Shirley keeping one foot on the floor."

Shirl bristled at that. I could feel her body tense beside me.

Grainger's eyes misted with worry. He shook his head. "Nothing like that. We'll do a screen test – just to make sure Shirley is right for the role."

"In a few weeks' time, I suppose," I said.

"Tomorrow," Grainger said.

He rummaged in his pockets and pulled out a sheet of paper. Handed it to Shirley. "There's the address of the screen test studio in Soho. Can you be there by eleven tomorrow morning?"

Shirl took the paper. Glanced defiantly at me. "Sure, I can."

"Great," Grainger said. "Broccoli will be there."

"Cripes," Shirl said. "I'm being auditioned for a film role by a vegetable."

"Don't make jokes about green vegetables in front of Mr Broccoli," Grainger advised. "Or even behind his back."

"What should I wear?" Shirley asked.

"Come as you are. We'll arrange any costume changes we need at the studio."

Grainger picked up his lager and drained the glass.

He stood up and offered his hand to Shirley. "It's been great meeting you. I'm sure we're going to enjoy working together."

"Can't wait," Shirley said.

Grainger waved a hand at me and headed for the door. He disappeared and Shirley turned to me.

"What's got your goat, buster?"

"What do you mean?"

"You were trying to give him the knock-back all through our talk."

"I was just trying to test whether he was for real."

"Course he was for real. I could see that as soon as he faced up to us."

"You'd called him a creep earlier."

"That's before I knew he was a film hot-shot. You don't want me to be in a film because it'll cast a cloud over your paddock."

"That's got nothing to do with it. I just didn't want you to end up disappointed."

Shirl necked her Campari soda in one shot. "Oh, I won't be disappointed. But you might be. You don't think of what I might want. You just charge ahead like a bull…"

"…in a china shop?"

"No. Like that bull in the labyrinth. The one that used to eat people."

"You're thinking of the Minotaur. He was half bull and half man."

"Yeah! In your case I wonder which half was which."

"Anyway, the Minotaur was killed by Theseus who found his way out of the labyrinth with the aid of his girlfriend Ariadne's ball of thread."

"If you ever find yourself in trouble, don't bank on me helping you find your way home, buster."

This was getting out of control. I'd never seen Shirley as angry as this before. I drained my gin and tonic.

I said: "I think we need another drink."

"Not for me. I've got a screen test in the morning. But you stay and have as many as you like."

"I thought I'd come back to your flat. I could help you with a little practise for the screen test. Especially if it involves Lazenby and you wearing only perfume behind the ears."

"Forget it, buster."

"We could always each keep one foot on the floor."

"In your case, tonight you can keep both of them there."

NINE

As it happened, I slept that night with both feet in the bed.

My only disappointment was that there weren't two feet beside mine.

When I woke, my feet were still in the bed. And they were cold. The blankets had slipped during the night.

It added to my general sense of ennui.

Perhaps I'd been a crime reporter for too long.

For a few minutes I lay in the bed rubbing my feet together.

I thought about the row I'd had with Shirley. I hadn't liked Grainger. He was one of those cocky types who think the world owes them a living. I hadn't liked the way he'd ogled Shirley, although she didn't seem to mind. Still, perhaps one man's ogle was one woman's appreciative glance. And, maybe, if Grainger was who he said, his job was to ogle likely talent for Cubby Broccoli's films.

But I wasn't happy about Shirley taking the screen test. It all sounded a bit too pat to me. I was proud of the fact that Shirley had made a big success as a photographic model. But she'd never been an actress. So why was Grainger in such a big rush to get her to the Soho studio?

I could think of two reasons and I didn't like either of them. The first was that Grainger had already lined up an actress for the screen test, but he needed a couple of others to satisfy Broccoli that he was getting a choice. If that were the case, Shirley would take the test, be given the thumbs down and tossed out. A humiliating experience.

But not as humiliating as the second. The casting couch had been notorious in Hollywood since the nineteen-thirties. I'd never heard it used in Britain. But now Shirley was unexpectedly caught up in the movie world, perhaps that was the fate she faced. And she wouldn't get the choice about keeping one foot on the floor.

I climbed out of bed seething with anger. But as I took a long hot shower, I realised there was nothing I could do. Shirley had taken against me simply for sounding a note of caution. But if anything bad happened, she'd find I was still on her side.

In the meantime, I had to pursue the Winterbottom murder story. I had to find the evidence that would prove to the dunderhead Tomkins that the Widow wasn't the killer.

I stepped out of the shower and towelled off vigorously.

I was a crime reporter. I would always be a crime reporter I told myself.

And I would crack this story.

* * *

Forty minutes later, I pushed through the swing doors into the newsroom.

The place was gearing up for the first deadline of the day. I nodded hello to Phil Bailey, said "hi" to Sally Martin. They smiled back but then looked away.

What was the problem?

Had I grown horns out of the top of my head?

I sat down at my desk feeling slightly miffed. I reached for last night's final *Chronicle* which Cedric had draped over my Remington.

But before I could pick it up, my telephone rang. I lifted the receiver.

Frank Figgis said: "Get in here, *pronto*."

I said: "*Assolutamente, il mio editor di notizie.*"

I stood up and headed to Figgis' office *rapido*.

I knocked on his door and went in before he could say "Enter".

He was sitting at his desk. He'd just stubbed out a Woodbine. He was blowing the smoke down his nose.

I said: "If you could blow it out of your ears, you could turn that into a stage act."

Figgis said: "I'm glad you're taking an interest in the theatre."

I sat down on the guest chair. "If there's a murder at the Hippodrome, I'll be the first through the doors."

"You may be there anyway," Figgis said. "You must've seen last night's *Evening Argus*." He pushed his copy across the desk.

It was the same edition I'd bought the previous evening on Brighton station.

I picked it up like it was a diseased bandage peeled from a plague victim's open wound. I unfolded the paper and pointed at Jim Houghton's front-page story.

I said: "This is the most outrageous piece of reporting since Horatio Bottomley accused Kier Hardie of being in league with the Kaiser during the First World War. Houghton is trying to suggest my only interest in getting Mrs Gribble off a murder charge is so that I can retain my rooms."

Figgis nodded. "I agree. It's outrageous. But it's in print – and it's out on the streets. One hundred thousand copies give or take a quire."

I leaned back in the chair. My heart thumped in my chest. I was breathing heavily.

"I'll sue Houghton for libel," I said.

"No you won't," Figgis said. "I've already had the night lawyer take a look at the piece. He puts the chances of you winning a libel case at no more than fifty-fifty. Besides, the matter has been taken out of my hands."

"By whom?"

"Who do you think?"

"His Holiness."

"He called me up to his office first thing this morning. He wanted me to fire you on the spot, but I refused."

I sighed. "Thank you."

"You may not when you hear what the deal is."

"There's a deal?"

"The best I could get him to accept under the circumstances. He believes that if readers think we're harbouring a reporter who's in a murder conspiracy, it will cost us circulation. And advertisers."

"But we could hit back in our own columns. Give me half an hour and I'll write an article that'll make Houghton's piece look like so much wastepaper."

Figgis shrugged. "I'd do that but I've received my orders. All part of the deal."

"What is it?"

"I take you off crime reporting."

"You can't do that. I'm the best crime reporter in town. In the county. Perhaps even the country."

"Why be so modest? What's so good about the rest of the world?"

"But crime reporting is my life."

Figgis leaned forward. He nodded sadly. "I hate that it's come to this. But that's the way it is."

"So I'm back on general reporting. That may not be so bad. Sometimes, it includes crime."

"You're not back on general reporting," Figgis said.

"Not court reporting?"

"It's worse than that. You're being assigned to entertainment."

"What? You want me to dress up as a clown and make the kiddies laugh?"

"Don't be ridiculous. You're going to be the entertainment reporter."

"But that's Sidney Pinker's beat."

"We're short-staffed at the moment because of the holiday season. This is the only way I can keep both subjects covered. A straight swap between you and Sidney."

"But Sidney won't want to mix with all those rough criminal types."

"I've already spoken to him. Says he can't wait."

I knew Figgis was lying. Sidney would hate the hurly-burly life of a crime reporter. He'd spent years lounging in the front row of the stalls at the Theatre Royal on premiere nights.

I slumped in the chair. I couldn't believe what I was hearing. For four years, I'd been the *Chronicle's* crime correspondent. I'd landed scoops that had hit our own front page and been taken up by papers all over the country. And now I was being pushed out.

I said: "Do I have time to think about whether I want to make the move?"

Figgis shook his head.

"It's this or your cards. No job."

"Is there any way back?"

"I don't know. Perhaps when this whole Winterbottom business is cleared up, Pope will change his mind. But don't bank on it. In the meantime, you steer clear of crime reporting."

"But Sidney... He's had no experience of crime. At least not the kind he'll be reporting on."

"He's in the tearoom. You're to brief him on the stories you're covering so he can take them on. He'll return the compliment."

"So that's it?"

"Not quite," said Figgis. "Tomorrow morning, I want you back in the newsroom with a story for the entertainment page."

"Comedy or tragedy?" I said.

"I don't care – as long as it's not a farce."

* * *

I stomped back into the newsroom in half a mind to storm Gerald Pope's office and tell him I'd quit.

But what good would that do?

I'd be out of a job without a reference. And with scant chance of picking up another post on a daily – let alone as a crime reporter.

The newsroom went quiet as I crossed to my desk. Suddenly, everyone had something to do that involved them rummaging in a drawer. Or rearranging the papers on their spike. Or sharpening their pencils.

Everyone knew what had happened – you can't keep secrets on a newspaper.

Besides, Sidney Pinker wasn't in the tearoom, after all. He

was beside my desk. He hopped from foot to foot like the ground underneath was burning the soles of his powder-blue loafers.

He was wearing a well-cut pink jacket and light brown chinos. He had a blue cravat knotted around his neck. His hands flapped from side to side.

I walked up to him and said: "At ease, Sidney. I know you hate this as much as I do."

Sidney let out a sigh which sounded like the Royal Scot steaming into Kings Cross.

"I'm pleased you see it like that, dear boy," he said. "You must know I had nothing to do with this."

"We're both the victims of a stitch-up."

"Fates. We're like the star-crossed lovers, don't you think?"

Sidney rested a consoling hand on my shoulder.

"No, I wouldn't go that far," I said.

Sidney removed his hand. "Oh, please yourself. But, really, I don't know what to do."

I glanced at the newsroom clock. "In twenty minutes, there'll be a press conference at Brighton police station. It'll be to report progress on the Winterbottom murder case. As the conference will be given by a detective chief superintendent called Alec Tomkins, there won't be any. He'll have nothing useful to say, but you can ask him an awkward question."

Sidney's cheeks coloured. "I really don't think I could."

"Yes, you can. Find your inner strength."

"*Oooh*, that's what my friend Brett said to me only the other evening."

"Ask Tomkins whether he's made an arrest. He won't have done, but he'll say one is imminent. But don't bother to write it down, because it won't be."

"But what do I do when I get back here? Mr Figgis will want some copy."

"Don't let that worry you, Sidney. I'll write something and use your catchline on the top folio so Figgis and the subs think it's come from you."

"But people will see me hanging around the newsroom with nothing to do."

"As a crime reporter, you shouldn't be here. You need to be out meeting contacts. Pick up some leads."

"I don't have any contacts, dear boy. At least not in crime. The people you deal with seem, well… rather rough."

I sat down in my captain's chair to make it clear to Sidney that the desk didn't come with his new role.

He pulled a face which made him look a bit miffed. But he perched on the edge of my desk.

I said: "I want you to tell me what you're working on. I'll need to turn in some showbiz stories to keep Figgis off my back."

Sidney clapped his hands together. "That's what makes it so damnable."

"What's damnable?"

"The fact that I'll miss out on covering the biggest showbiz story in Brighton for years. You've heard about the beach party."

"Who hasn't?" I said.

"Well, I've lined up a big interview tomorrow with the guy who's behind it. Perry Turner, who runs *Seabreeze* Radio. It's tomorrow morning. Mr Turner is sending a launch to pick me up from Palace Pier and take me out to the ship. I was going to wear my bell-bottom jeans and the sailor's jacket I bought in a little boutique I know in the North Laines."

"Spare me the fashion notes, Sidney. Who do I meet at the pier?"

"Perry's colleague and fellow DJ, Zena Lightheart."

I grabbed a sheet of copy paper and made a note.

"Do you have any background on the beach party?" I asked.

"Perry was going to tell me during the interview. He's suggested that he's attracted a big name to headline the show."

"Any hints?"

"No, but Perry planned to give me an exclusive tomorrow. At the moment, he's staying on the ship to avoid any trouble."

That had my attention. In my experience, where there's trouble, there's news.

I leaned closer to Sidney. "Trouble? What trouble? Tell me more."

"Well, you know Radio *Seabreeze* broadcasts the latest in music – it can be quite daring. Have you seen that Lulu's skirts? I've seen bigger pelmets. It's attracted some attention, I can tell you. And not the kind of attention Perry wants."

"And what kind of attention is that?"

"Have you ever heard of the National Purity Army?"

"I've seen a couple of pieces in the nationals," I said.

As far as I'd heard, the so-called army were largely a bunch of prissy madams or saloon bar bigots who had a fit of the vapours if they heard a naughty word uttered in public. They'd all become riled up a year earlier when the theatre critic Kenneth Tynan had become the first person in Britain to say the word "fuck" on live television. The prissy madams and saloon bar bigots should never have heard it. Tynan had used the word in a late-night satire programme on the BBC.

There'd been the predictable outrage with 133 Conservative and Labour members of parliament signing House of Commons' motions condemning Tynan and the BBC. One Tory MP even suggested Tynan should be strung up. But it all died down after a few weeks. Except for the prissy madams and saloon bar bigots who ganged together to set up the so-called

National Purity Army. Their mission: to persecute anyone whose minds weren't as narrow as theirs.

From what I'd heard, nobody really knew who'd started the Army or who ran it. But the group had a "Pure in Heart" logo which they'd had printed on stickers. The stickers would appear overnight on posters advertising *avant-garde* films or the covers of library books with four-letter words. As far as I knew, no one had ever suggested the Army members were violent types. But extreme prejudice sometimes comes out in exaggerated forms.

I said: "Why is Perry Turner worried about the Army? After all, they're on land and he's out at sea. And they haven't got a navy. At least, not yet."

"It seems they've become a lot more active in the Brighton area lately. And the beach party will be on land. There'll be a big stage erected near to Palace Pier. And there's going to be a large hospitality area. Plenty of scope for the Army crowd to make trouble."

This sounded promising. An entertainment story with the chance of a crime twist. Perhaps my time on the entertainment desk wasn't going to be wasted after all.

I said: "Who's the commander behind this trouble?"

Sidney's gaze flicked round the newsroom, like he was just planning to divulge the code number to the Bank of England's vault.

"The name Perry Turner gave me was Jeremiah Puttock."

"Puttock," I said.

I rolled the name around my tongue. "Doesn't sound very pure to me. With a slip of the tongue he could make an arse of himself."

TEN

Two hours later, I was standing outside Baz's Book Bazaar, a dirty bookshop in Queen's Road, not far from Brighton station.

Baz specialised in erotic reading material. In the window, there were dog-eared copies of novels with titles like *He Heard The Snap Of Her Knickers' Elastic*, *She Did It Anyway*, and *Three Times A Night (And Four On Saturday)*. Inside, there were cheaply printed magazines called *Naughty Girls* and *Big Ones*. I knew all this because Baz also stocked the *Evening Chronicle*. He wanted to give the place a veneer of respectability.

Normally, Baz would do a brisk trade for furtive types who'd hang around outside and then nip in when they thought no one was looking. But not today. There were half-a-dozen protestors in the street holding placards with slogans like NO SMUT HERE, DOWN WITH DIRTY BOOKS, and CLEAN UP BRIGHTON.

After I'd waved a reluctant Sidney off to his first press conference at the cop shop, I'd tracked down Jeremiah Puttock. (I'd looked up his address in the telephone directory, if you must know. Crampton, master researcher.)

I was about to set off for his house when Susan Wheatcroft steamed back into the office from a meeting at the Chamber of Commerce. She announced to the newsroom: "Hey, guys, there's a bunch of weirdos marching in circles outside Baz's Book Bazaar. They call themselves the National Purity Army or some such. They won't get a salute from yours truly."

Susan's timely appearance had saved me a wasted trip to Puttock's house. And, so, I was reviewing his army.

There were three women wearing floral print dresses and scarves knotted under their chins. There were a couple of men. One, an old geezer, leaned heavily on a walking stick. The other, a spotty youth, wore a tweed jacket fastened at all four buttons and flannel trousers which ended just above his ankles.

They didn't look like the kind of army that would win many battles.

Jeremiah Puttock stood on the kerb and issued a sharp order: "Keep marching round in circles, troops. Then the officers of the law can't move us on."

"'Coz we're already moving, eh?" said the spotty youth.

"Bright lad, that one," Puttock proudly announced to the rest of the troops.

Puttock was a short pudgy man who looked like he lived on suet puddings. He had a round fleshy face and wide lips. Stringy grey hair fell over his forehead and hung in scrawny tufts around his ears. He had a bulbous nose with a cleft in its point. He was wearing a plain grey suit which was frayed around the trouser turn-ups.

He held up a sign chalked on a blackboard. It had originally read BORN AGAIN! It seemed some passer-by had rubbed away the lower curve of the B so that it read PORN AGAIN! None of his fellow army had noticed. I didn't like to be the one to point it out.

Which was just as well. When I introduced myself as a gentleman of the press, he waved the sign in the air and shouted. "Halleluiah! Our word is to be heard."

I said: "This protest may be worth a paragraph on an inside page."

Puttock said: "Surely, the sins of this store of Satan's salacious secrets should feature proudly on your front page. And why not a ringing editorial praising our campaign on an inside page?"

"What is your campaign?"

Puttock drew himself up to his full height (five foot six) and declaimed: "It is to stop this man Baz selling the most corrupting of publications. One which depraves our young and leads the unwary on the thorny path to Hell."

I said: "Cut the preaching and answer the question."

Puttock shot me a wounded look and said: "This shop is the only one in Brighton which sells a certain magazine. And we want it banned from our town."

"Which magazine?"

"*Health & Efficiency.*"

I laughed.

The magazine had been around since the turn of the century. It had originally specialised in articles about improbable diets and herbal remedies. But in the years since the Second World War, it had become the magazine of choice for serious nudists. (And, probably, frivolous ones as well.)

Puttock frowned. "This is no matter for levity."

"The magazine is more than sixty years old. Why protest now?"

"Because of the latest issue. The most disgusting yet. Eight pages of photographs of nude tennis matches. Including mixed doubles. I've always had my suspicions about a sport that includes 'love' in its scores. What have you to say to that?"

"New balls?"

Puttock flashed me a dirty look. I needed to tone down the levity.

I pointed at the marching protestors. "Is this the whole army or just the advanced guard?"

"One day our massed ranks will march proudly in their thousands," Puttock said.

So this was the full complement, after all.

"And are you the commander of the army?"

Puttock pushed back his shoulders and said: "You may address me as Colonel Puttock."

"Is there a general?"

Puttock's grey eyes shifted nervously from side to side.

"We have a leader," he mumbled.

"Who is it?"

"This is not the time to reveal their identity. We are a movement – and do you know what a movement does?"

"It moves?"

"It grows. The small but highly-trained platoon you see today will grow into a great battalion. And when that happens our leader will march proudly at the head of our column."

"Can't wait," I said. "Meanwhile, perhaps you could tell me why you're opposed to the beach party Radio *Seabreeze* has organised?"

"Because it will be a festival of filth," he said.

He turned to his troops: "What will the beach party be?" he bellowed.

"A festival of filth," they chanted.

"Actually, I thought I'd go anyway," the spotty youth said.

Puttock glared at him. "Vernon, see me later for a lecture on the true meaning of purity."

He turned to me. "Some of our younger recruits still have much to learn."

I said: "Vernon may have a point. I don't see that there will be any filth at the beach party."

Puttock pursed his lips. "There will be dancers of the female persuasion."

"You mean girls. What's wrong with that?"

"It's those girls that appear on television."

"The Beat Girls? What's wrong with them?"

"They move parts. Parts that shouldn't be moved. At least not that way."

"You mean they sometimes wiggle their puttocks, I mean, buttocks?"

"Disgusting. The name of the Beat Girls should be expunged from history."

I said: "I've heard it will be. They're changing their name to Pan's People."

Puttock threw up his hands in horror. "Even worse. Pan, the Greek god of debauchery."

"And dance," I added.

Puttock's troops had gathered in a group to earwig our argument.

A middle-aged matron with a beaky nose sidled up to Puttock. Her placard read: NO COVER-UP FOR NUDES. Perhaps not exactly the message she'd intended.

She grinned sheepishly at Puttock. "All right if we pop off now, Jerry? We're going to have a Wimpy. Care to join us?" She winked. "You can dip your chips in my ketchup."

Puttock cleared his throat noisily. "That won't be possible today, Maureen. I'm speaking to a member of the press."

Maureen winked at me. "I've never seen a member of the press."

Looked as though several of the troops needed that lecture on the true meaning of purity.

Puttock coughed again. "Good afternoon, Maureen."

Maureen shoved her placard into Puttock's hand, scowled at him, and marched off. Puttock propped Maureen's discarded placard against the wall.

The troops drifted off in a raggle-taggle group towards the Wimpy.

I asked: "You're not a fan of hamburgers?"

"I prefer to dine alone," Puttock said stiffly.

"Never married?"

"If you must know, my wife left me two years ago. Ran off with a travelling salesman in pickles and condiments." Puttock let out a long sigh. "Eleanor didn't understand me. Evenings now, I settle down in my back parlour with a simple supper and a good book."

He'd looked me in the eye as he'd said it. As if to stress his sincerity. And his purity.

But I hadn't believed a word of it.

* * *

I left Puttock tidying up his group's discarded placards while he contemplated a lonely night at home.

Or not.

Twenty minutes later, I parked the MGB just around the corner from Puttock's house. There was something about him I couldn't understand. When you've been around as many crooks, conmen, and ne'er-do-wells as I have, you can smell the trouble. And Puttock reeked of it.

I sensed a crime exclusive. Figgis had warned me to steer clear of crime. But as the beach party was involved, I could tell him it was an entertainment story.

Puttock lived in a tree-lined crescent out towards Wood-ingdean. It was a street of modest detached houses and cottages. The kind of place where people like to pretend they keep themselves to themselves. In reality, it would be a street of curtain-twitchers where nobody could move a muscle without someone else knowing.

I planned to call on some of Puttock's neighbours to find out what they knew about him. At first, I was worried that Puttock would spot me if he returned to his place. But most of the houses were separated by high hedges and had elaborate porches around their front doors.

The ability to cold call on someone you've never met and ask them intimate questions is a skill you learn fast if you want to get on as a reporter. There are two main ways to do it. If you plan to ask them about something you know they'll want to talk about, you knock on the door and dive straight in.

If you want to ask about a topic they might not want to talk about – like what they think of a neighbour, for example - you ask them about something else and steer the questions round.

When I use the second tactic, I pretend I'm conducting a survey on a subject they'll feel passionate about. I decided to make my survey about what people would like to watch on the telly. At a suitable point in the conversation, I'd ask them what others in the street think, like that man – er, Mr Puttock, is it? – who lives at number twelve.

A brilliant ploy.

Couldn't fail.

But by the time I'd knocked on nine doors, I wondered whether I was wasting my time.

Number sixteen, two doors along from Puttock's place, was a cottage built out of ochre bricks. It had a steep roof and two dormer windows. The front door was tucked into a neat porch fronted by oak beams.

The door was opened by a middle-aged woman. She wore a cream blouse and beige slacks. She had straw-coloured hair permed into tight curls and hazel eyes that peered at me suspiciously.

She said: "Whatever you're selling, I've already got one."

I said: "That's just as well, as I don't have one with me today."

"What one?"

"The one you've already got."

"Why are we having this conversation?" she asked.

"Because I'd like to ask you some questions."

"You've called at other houses in the street," she said.

"You've been watching me."

"An old habit, I'm afraid. In the war years, I was a spotter."

"One of those who watched out for enemy aircraft approaching."

"Never missed one. Especially the doodlebugs towards the end of the war. Sharp-eyed Sylvia they used to call me."

Sylvia crossed her arms in an impatient gesture.

She said: "Well, I haven't got all day. What do you want?"

I decided to plunge straight in.

"I want to ask about one of your neighbours."

"Old Puttock at number twelve."

"How do you know?"

"Because I watched you call at eight and ten. Then you missed him and went straight on to fourteen."

I grinned. "Still sharp-eyed, then."

Sylvia gave a little nod of pleasure.

I said: "I've heard that Puttock is involved in a war, too."

Sylvia raised a quizzical eyebrow. "War?"

"On filth. Not the kind you find at the bottom of your dustbin. The kind that's said to feature in late-night television shows or X-rated films at the cinema. The kind that you can find in the racy books in Baz's Book Bazaar."

Sylvia gave a mirthless laugh. "I could tell you something about Jeremiah Puttock."

"I wish you would."

"The postman around here is hopeless. We're always getting other people's mail by mistake. About six months ago, a big brown envelope came through the door. Well, I wasn't expecting anything. Picked it up and it was addressed to Puttock. The envelope was so big it had torn as it came through the letterbox. There was a magazine inside."

"Not the *Church Times*, I bet."

"You'd bet correctly. It was a magazine called *Girls That Do*. I must admit my curiosity was piqued and I accidentally ripped the envelope tear a bit more. It seemed to be a contact magazine. A kind of directory of women from a certain profession."

"Not bus conductors, I assume."

"You assume correctly. Well, I put the magazine through the letterbox when he was out one morning, so he'd think it'd been delivered by the postman. But over the next few weeks, a young woman used to turn up at his house around half-past seven every Tuesday. Maudie over at fifteen mentioned it all casual to him one day. Like she was interested in whether she was his daughter or something. He just snubbed her, said the woman was a cleaning lady, and he wished neighbours would mind their own business."

"Have you seen the woman?" I asked.

"A few times. I'll tell you, no cleaning lady of mine would step into the house wearing stilettos like those. I'd end up with holes in the hall carpet. At first, I wondered whether she was anything to do with the man who turned up every Friday evening. Regular as a dose of Epsom salts."

"What man was this?" I asked.

Sylvia shook her head. "No idea. Had a fancy car, though. One of those Jaguars. Flash job in racing green."

That had my attention.

Winterbottom had owned a racing green Jag.

I said: "Did it have a detachable hood – one in a tan colour?"

Sylvia shot me a suspicious look. "Know it, do you?"

I shook my head. "Just an idea. A lot of them are like that. What was the man like?"

"Couldn't really see. He used to go into the house. Stayed less than five minutes and came out. Heard raised voices once between him and Puttock, but couldn't make anything out."

"Nothing else?"

"Sometimes the man was carrying what looked like a narrow piece of paper. Could've been an envelope I suppose. Perhaps he was collecting a letter."

Sylvia gave me a sharp look.

She said: "Anyway, I'm telling you all this, but I don't know who you are."

"Private detective. Client is his ex-wife Eleanor. All to do with money. Isn't it always?"

Sylvia nodded. "I can't stand here all day. My Henry will be home for his tea in half an hour. I haven't even boned the herrings yet."

She shut the door and I strode away from her house. I didn't care whether she looked out of a window and saw me.

I was confident I knew now what that personal matter was between him and Winterbottom. Ted Wilson had told me he had a suspicion that Winterbottom had added blackmail to his investment services. And it looked as though Puttock's hypocritical lifestyle had made him a prime target.

But did that mean Puttock was now a murder suspect?

I climbed into my MGB wondering what to do next. There was no way I could present this to Figgis as entertainment.

ELEVEN

I perched on the edge of the guest chair in Frank Figgis' office.

I said: "Just think of the headline. Dirty book campaigner has a bit on the side."

Figgis exercised his smoker's cough and settled back into his chair.

He said: "There are three things wrong with that. Point one. The headline is ambivalent. You could be talking about a book campaigner who hasn't washed for a few days."

"The subs will think of a way to reword that."

"That won't be enough because of point two. We have no means of knowing whether the young woman arriving at Puttock's house was a tart."

"What else could she have been?"

"Someone who's popped in for a *Bible* class, from the sound of Puttock."

"Wearing six-inch stilettoes?"

"Remind me where in the *Bible* there's an injunction that thou shalt not wear high-heeled shoes. In any event, point two pales in comparison with point three."

"Which is?"

"I've told you, you're off crime stories. Entertainment – that's your beat now."

I leaned forward over the desk. Caught a whiff of Figgis' stale Woodbines. Leant back sharply.

"This is an exception," I said. "Besides, I was following up Puttock as an entertainment lead."

"He's no comic or crooner."

"He's a man who's launched a campaign against the beach party that Perry Turner is organising. Says it will be a festival of filth. There must be a story in it."

Figgis reached for his Woodbines. Opened the packet, found it was empty. Scrunched it. Tossed it in his bin.

"But you weren't following the Turner angle," he said. "Your argument is that Winterbottom had found out about his lady friend and was blackmailing him. That gave Puttock a motive for murdering Winterbottom. If that isn't a crime story, I'll stop editing newspapers and get a job wrapping fish and chips in them."

I said: "I thought I might just visit Puttock and put one question to him. Are you seeing a fancy woman? Was Winterbottom blackmailing you? Did you kill him?"

"That's three questions."

Figgis thumped his hand on his desk so hard the chipped mug holding his pencils fell over. The pencils rolled across his desk and clattered onto the floor.

"Now look what you've made me do."

I bent down to pick up the pencils.

"Leave them," Figgis snapped. "And leave me. But leave me with this warning. You go within a mile of Puttock and you're finished here. Is that clear?"

I looked Figgis firmly in the eye. "As clear as a picture."

"What do you mean, 'As a clear as a picture'?"

"I was thinking of the American use of the word 'picture'. They use it sometimes instead of 'film'. Like the ones you see at the cinema. Except they sometimes call them picture houses."

Figgis gave me a flinty look. "Which picture house? I mean cinema?"

"I had in mind one in Kemp Town."

"What film?"

"I was thinking of that cinematographic masterpiece *Naughty Night Nurse Does Her Rounds*."

Figgis twisted his neck. Looked out of his window. Stroked his chin. Had one of his gravelly coughs. Switched his attention back to me.

"You wouldn't dare."

"Not intentionally, of course. But it's so easy for something to slip out. You'll understand, late at night in the pub after you've had a couple."

Figgis relaxed a little and leant back in his chair. He knew he had to do a deal.

"You know I can't countermand Pope's orders."

I nodded. "Understood."

"This has to be unofficial."

"The way I like it."

"Pinker mustn't suspect you're encroaching on his new territory."

"He won't know what I'm doing."

"And, as far as His Holiness is concerned, you're still entertainment reporter."

"If I had a party horn, I'd blow it."

I stood up and headed for the door. Turned and faced Figgis.

He had that leprechaun grin on his face which meant he thought he'd won the bout.

He picked up a fat envelope from his in-tray. "We must make sure you turn in plenty of entertainment copy."

He handed me the envelope. "Here's your next assignment. Good luck."

I went out feeling I'd just plucked defeat from the jaws of victory.

* * *

Back at my desk in the newsroom, I thought over what Figgis had said.

I suspect he thought I wouldn't go through with my threat to blab about his visit to the Continentale. Besides, we were a cynical lot in the newsroom. We'd have a laugh, shrug our shoulders, and think no more about it.

But it would matter to Figgis. Behind the wizened face, the scruffy clothes, and the smoker's cough, there was a man with a finely chiselled *amour propre*. And why shouldn't he have it? In my book, he was one of the best news editors in Britain.

He also knew that Pinker would make a hash of the crime reporter's beat. Figgis couldn't allow the *Chronicle* to fall behind the competition in crime stories. Crime sold papers. And if circulation fell, he'd have His Holiness on his back. Figgis needed me to ferret around the Winterbottom killing in the background.

But it wouldn't be easy. I'd have to make sure His Holiness didn't find out. And I'd have to double up with the entertainment job. That was a real downer. Not least because the talk of cinema and films had reminded me that it was the day of Shirley's screen test. She'd stomped out on me last night.

I'd broken a golden rule – never let the sun go down on an argument. I should have apologised to Shirl. Made it clear I supported her chance for stardom. But, deep down, I was worried about Grainger's true intentions. Do film talent scouts really pluck the stars of tomorrow from people they've seen on the street? It didn't see very likely. But, perhaps, it did happen.

I would just have to push all these thoughts to the back of my mind. Shirley would be back in the evening on the London train. I'd meet her at the station. We'd kiss and make up. I'd enjoy that bit. Then I'd take her for a delicious dinner. Perhaps English's Oyster Bar. They say oysters are an aphrodisiac. But I'm not sure that's true. The last time I had half a dozen only four of them worked.

I picked up the envelope Figgis had handed me. I shook out the contents. A motley collection of papers and photographs cascaded onto my desk. A jasmine scented musk rose up from the stuff. Like it wanted to say: follow your nose, big boy, and I'll show you a good time.

I picked up one of the photographs. It was a professional one in colour. But the print had done the rounds of theatrical agents. It was creased down one side and a corner had folded over.

But all this was mere detail. The girl in the picture would grab attention no matter how many creases and dog-eared corners this photo had. She was one of those girls where you're not sure where to look first. Being a gent, I started with her face. It was a perfect oval, like the women have in those pre-Raphaelite paintings that hang in Brighton art gallery. She had softly pronounced cheeks which, dammit, actually were rosy. Her wide lips were parted in a smile which revealed a row of teeth as perfect as a dowager's pearls. Her blue eyes danced with mischief and her button nose turned up in a kind of arrogant after-thought from her upper lip. Her blonde hair fell in thick tresses to her shoulders.

Further south, she was just as striking. She had an hour glass figure that packed in the full sixty minutes without a second to spare. She was wearing a red leotard, seamed tights, and dancing shoes. Nothing else. But, then, when a girl's job is to kick her legs up high enough to catch a giant under the chin, she doesn't need frills and furbelows getting in the way.

The girl's name was printed at the foot of the photo: Crystal Starr.

I looked at the picture just long enough to be sure I could recognise her again on a dark night and then put the picture back on the desk. I rummaged through the other material. There was a *curriculum vitae*. Crystal, it turned out, came from West Bromwich in the Midlands. She was nineteen and her real name was Bertha Spinks. She'd trained at the Muriel Doggett Dancing Academy in Walsall. She'd had her first stage role at the age of fifteen in a pantomime at the Masonic Hall, Rowley Regis. Last year, she'd been a member of the chorus in the summer show *Splash!* at the Landmark Theatre, Ilfracombe.

So it looked like she'd hit the big time at Brighton's Palace Pier Theatre.

I rummaged among the other stuff from the envelope. There were a few press cuttings I didn't bother to read and a note. It read: "Please come to the stage door at half past six o'clock and ask for Crystal xxx."

Well, that was something. You didn't often get kisses in crime reporting.

The stage door was round the back of the theatre facing out to sea.

I opened the door and stepped into a long corridor with whitewashed walls. The place smelt like an old boot cupboard at the end of a wet winter. Deep in the building someone was knocking out a rag number on a honky-tonk piano. I remembered that Winifred Atwell, the popular Trinidadian piano player, was the show's top-of-the-bill.

Off to the right, a booth was built into an alcove. An old bloke with lanky grey hair, bags under his eyes, and a walrus moustache scowled at me through the booth's window.

He said: "You don't look like your typical stage-door Johnny."

I said: "That's because I'm a stage-door Colin."

"Anyway, you're early. Most of the Johnnies don't turn up 'til after the show. And you'll need to have a bunch of blooms and a bottle of champers if you want to glimpse a chorus girl's trim ankle."

"Trim ankles went out with the Edwardian age, grandad. In the Swinging Sixties, we're into creamy thighs."

"Dirty bugger."

"Vulgarity is disappointment's handmaiden," I said. "But enough of this persiflage. I'm here by appointment. At Miss Crystal Starr's invitation."

The old bloke pulled a face like: what can you expect from a girl like that?

He said: "Are you, indeed? Her dressing room's down the corridor, first right and third door on your left. You can't miss it. And if you do, you'll end up falling off the side of the pier."

I didn't miss it.

It was dressing room number 17. Except that one of the screws had come out of the seven so that it swung from side to side when I knocked.

A trill voice with a nasal Midlands accent called out: "Come in, my knight in shining armour."

I opened the door and stepped inside.

I said: "I left my cuirass out in the rain and the rivets have rusted."

Crystal was sitting on a stool at a dressing table with a large mirror and a lot of lights.

She swivelled on the stool. She looked me up and down like I was a rack of lamb in a butcher's window and she couldn't decide whether to go for the whole joint or just have a couple of chops.

She said: "That's a facer. You ain't who I thought you were."

I said: "I'm sorry. I'll try to be someone else next time."

"Yeah! But don't bother. I quite like you."

"Who did you think I was?"

"Suleiman the Sword Swallower - 'cept his real name is Marlon. He comes from Reigate and talks quite posh like they do down there. He also eats razor blades and closes the first half. The management like it that way - 'coz the audience don't see the ambulance come to pick him up when a razor blade goes down the wrong way on account of they're guzzling booze in the bar."

I pulled a card out of my pocket and handed it to Crystal. "Colin Crampton, *Evening Chronicle*. Sidney Pinker arranged to interview you for a feature in the paper. But Sidney's engaged elsewhere."

"Engaged," Crystal wailed. "He didn't tell me he were getting married."

"Sidney's not the marrying kind. He's engaged in other work."

Crystal's pert little mouth turned down at the corners.

"Are you married?"

"No."

Crystal's eyes sparkled with life and she smiled. She stood up and crossed the room. Picked up another stool and put it down next to hers.

"Why don't you perch your bum on that and tell me all about yourself?" she said.

"I've got a better idea." I pointed at her stool. "Why don't you park yourself there and tell me all about you. I'll write it down in Pitman's in my notebook."

She sat down and put her hand on my knee. She winked at me.

"Are you gonna make little old me famous?"

"You'll be the toast of Brighton. Not to mention Hove. And, by the way, it's not compulsory to fondle the interviewer's knee while you're answering his questions."

Crystal pulled a mock pout. "It's just that I like something to do with my hands." She gave me a fat wink. But she took her hand off my knee.

I took out my notebook and pencil. I licked the point on the pencil. It tasted better than usual.

I said in a business-like tone: "How was it you became a dancer?"

"It's all on account of my mom."

"She always wanted you to become a dancer?"

"No, she wanted me out of her hair when my Uncle Denis came round. 'Coz he weren't really my uncle. My mom used to tell me he came round for a dance – so I should go out and learn how to do the waltz and stuff. But he didn't come to dance. Not unless you count the horizontal hokey-cokey."

"You mean...?"

"Yeah! Twice a week, Mondays and Thursdays. Except when there were a bank holiday."

"Why not then?"

"Because my dad were home on bank holidays."

"Happy home, then?"

Crystal raised a well-plucked eyebrow. "Not so you'd notice. Anyway, it couldn't last. Denis came round for his dirty dancing Friday one week, instead of Thursday. Forgot it was Good Friday."

"A bank holiday."

"My Dad caught him in a cheeky Charleston. Threw me out."

"Why you?"

"The old soak said it were my fault. I should have told him. How was I to know? I was learning to dance."

"Where did you go?"

"I raided the box he hid at the back of his shed. The box where he stashed his beer money and caught the first train to London. Got off the train at Euston station in London and this spiv came up to me and said, 'You look like a dancer. Wanna job?' So, as I had nothing else planned, I said, 'Might do.'"

"And ended up dancing in a strip club," I said.

Crystal's eyes opened. "How did you know?" She grinned. Gave me a playful punch on the arm. "Hey, you're not one of those dirty mac types who used to sit in the front row? You've seen my act."

"Certainly not. But I am one of those reporters who knows that crime gangs target single girls arriving in London."

"Yeah! Well, you're right there. Anyway, I only stayed at the Strip-a-Go-Go for a couple of weeks. I did the round of theatrical agents in the day and stripped in the evenings. It were the pantomime season. One day I met an agent who said he'd just been let down. One of the dancers he'd booked into *Babes in the Wood* as Second Toadstool turned out to be eight months pregnant. He took one look at my belly and gave me the part."

"A star was born," I said.

"Yeah! It don't always feel like that."

Someone rapped twice on the door. A treble voice cried: "Overture and beginners, five minutes, Miss Starr."

"Young Cyril," Crystal said. "He's forty-three but I don't think his voice has broken yet."

She turned back to the dressing table. Reached for a powder puff. Dabbed it round her face.

"Got to go," she said. "Dress rehearsal tonight. But, say, perhaps we could meet later. I guess a guy like you must know where we could dance the night away."

I closed my notebook. Shoved it back in my pocket.

"It's a tempting offer, but I'm afraid my typewriter calls. Got to write up your interview."

Crystal pulled a disappointed face. "Another time, then. Never know your luck. I might teach you the horizontal hokey-cokey."

I went out and closed the door. It wasn't the kind of offer you got after a fraught exchange with Alec Tomkins.

But at least I wouldn't need to see Crystal again.

* * *

Back at my desk in the newsroom, I pulled my old Remington towards me.

My hands poised over the keys while I thought about what to make of the interview with Crystal.

For her age, she was a tough little cookie. But, then, I guess her life had made her that way. And she was in a demanding profession where there was always somebody waiting to step into your shoes.

I decided for my first outing as an entertainment reporter, I would give Crystal a piece that she'd want to cut out, stick in a scrapbook, and proudly show to her grandchildren.

I began: "Crystal Starr is a dancer with light feet and an effervescent personality..."

I suppose the interview with Crystal should have cheered

me up a bit. But there was no getting away from the truth. I was depressed.

It had all started with Gribble's arrest – and the realisation that I could lose my rooms. I was no closer to getting the Widow off Tomkins' trumped-up charge. Then there was the bust-up with Shirley over her screen test. And, finally, Figgis moving me onto the entertainment beat.

To cap it all, I now had to watch Sidney Pinker's back as he made a hash of covering the Winterbottom killing. And do it without Pinker or anyone else realising.

I'd taken on some challenges over the years, but one at a time. I just couldn't work out how I was going to put everything right.

What made it all worse was that I couldn't contact Shirley. There was no answer from her apartment's phone. And she'd not called me. I wondered whether she'd stayed in London after the screen test. Would Grainger be behind that? It wouldn't be difficult to tempt a star-struck girl with the offer of dinner at the Savoy and an overnight stay in a plush suite. Was that how the casting couch worked?

I didn't know. And I knew I would only work myself into a state by thinking anymore about it.

Back at my lodgings, I thought I'd have an early night. Perhaps everything would look better in the morning light.

But by the time I'd showered and climbed into my jim-jams – a red and blue tartan pattern, if you must know - my mind was buzzing like a chain-saw. I tried reading – Ernest Hemingway's *A Moveable Feast* – but I couldn't keep focused on the words. Finally, I tossed the book aside and turned on the radio. Out of curiosity, I tuned in to Radio *Seabreeze*.

Kenny Ball and his Jazzmen were playing their way through *Midnight in Moscow*. I liked the number, but it was nearly midnight in Brighton and I needed to get to sleep.

I reached for the off button, but the record ended and a husky late-night voice said: "That was Mr Kenny Ball with a time check in Russia. And now stay tuned for a recorded message from our sponsor."

A man's voice came on. Smooth and unctuous. The kind conmen use when they're targeting a mark. The voice said: "When you've worked hard, you deserve the best that life can offer you. Why not make your money work hard, too, so that you can pay for that new bijou villa by the sea or a long lazy holiday on the Riviera? I can help you double your money in just one year without any risk. You can have everything you ever wanted. And more. This is honest Claude Winterbottom, the double-your-money or your money back financial adviser. Get in touch today."

There followed an announcement about a telephone number, but by then I was reaching for the off button.

So, Winterbottom had advertised his dubious services on Radio *Seabreeze*. I couldn't understand why the ad was still running when Winterbottom was dead. But perhaps he'd booked a series and the station didn't know he'd been killed.

Suddenly, tomorrow's visit to the pirate ship didn't look like such a chore after all.

I turned over in bed and went straight to sleep.

TWELVE

So there I was at the end of Palace Pier at eight o'clock the following morning.

I leant on the rail and looked out to sea. It was a balmy morning with the sun already well risen over the Seven Sisters cliffs out to the east. Small waves slapped rhythmically around the pier's supports. Seagulls divebombed eddies in the water hunting for fish.

And far out to sea someone had switched on an electric sewing machine.

I listened intently as the burr turned to a buzz and a black dot appeared in the distance.

The dot turned into a speedboat which left a trail of white foam in its wake. Its twin outboards roared as the boat flashed a semi-circle to line up with the pier's landing stage.

The engines died and the boat bobbed on the swell. It was a handsome craft, sleek and fast, which sat low in the water. I wouldn't mind owning it myself.

A lithe girl with long blonde hair, braided with coloured beads, climbed out of the seat behind the wheel. She was wearing a knee-length kaftan over blue jeans. She jumped nimbly over the prow onto the landing stage.

She walked up to me in a slinky way which definitely took my mind off the boat.

She had green eyes, like a cat's, pale cheeks, and button lips that would beat a zip-fastener any day.

She said: "Hi, you must be the dude I'm picking up."

I grinned: "Sure, you can pick me up any time."

"Gee! That line was original – two centuries ago. I'm Zenobia."

"Queen of Palmyra in ancient Arabia."

Her eyebrows arched. "Hey, smart *hombre*, don't get too cocky. The queen got canned by some Roman emperor guy."

"Aurelian. He imprisoned Zenobia when she tried to take over his empire in Syria and Egypt."

"Yeah! Just shows what happens when you get above yourself. I thought I'd hit you with the full handle, you being a gentleman of the press and everything. But you can call me Zena."

"Well, Zena, perhaps we should hoist the skull and crossbones and join the pirates."

Zena ignored that and led me along the landing stage to the boat.

We climbed aboard. She fired up the outboards and sat behind the wheel. I slid into the seat beside her.

She turned to me and asked: "You ain't got a problem with boats? You gonna need a bucket?"

"Crossed the English Channel once in a force ten gale. Didn't throw up once. Mind you, someone tried to kill me."

Zena arched her eyebrows again. "Yeah! Happens to me all the time."

We pulled away from the landing stage and Zena swung

the wheel so we turned in a half circle. Then she leaned on the throttle and the boat lifted from the water like it wanted to fly.

I shouted above the roar. "How long have you been on the *Seabreeze*?"

Zena relaxed in her seat as the boat bounced over the swell. "Joined the crew a few months back. Perry – Turner that is, the head honcho – said he needed a DJ who spoke fluent Yank. Needed a voice that sounded cool to the hip cats who tune in. And a cool head to keep the team afloat."

"Not literally, I hope."

"No. But that rust-bucket ain't no destroyer. We sure keep those bilge pumps running at night."

"How did you meet Perry?"

"Oh, you know. A guy meets a gal. Makes a proposition."

"And the gal comes running?"

Zena gave me a sharp look. "When there's a guy involved, I mosey on by at my own pace."

Spray from the prow splattered the windscreen. Zena laughed. Twisted the wheel back and forth so the boat shimmied through the water and more spray hit the glass.

I said: "How long does this journey usually take?"

"Not more than twenty minutes unless there's a sea mist. Look."

She pointed ahead.

Sitting low in the water was the *Seabreeze*, a hulk of a ship that looked like it had never wanted to float.

A couple of minutes later we came alongside a Jacob's ladder that hung down from the stern. Zena climbed out of her seat, stood on the prow, and looped a rope around the ladder.

She climbed on to the first rung of the ladder and looked down on me. "Follow me up, but hold on tight if you don't want a wet ass."

I grinned, grabbed the ladder, and followed her own perfectly dry ass up to the deck rail.

I was helped over the rail by two muscle-bound guys. One had an anchor tattoo on his forearm and a ring through his left ear. He had a thatch of thick black hair that fell to his collar and a straggly beard.

The other had a head as bald as a billiard ball. He had broad shoulders and a paunch for a belly. He had a pierced heart with the name Carmen tattooed on his neck and another heart with Serena on his left arm. I guess that must have taken a bit of explaining at one time. But perhaps not. Weren't sailors supposed to have a girl in every port?

Zena turned to the hairy one and said: "Meet Kenny Todd, our boatswain."

Todd extended a hairy hand and said: "They call me Blaster."

The bald one shouldered his way forward. "I'm Knocker."

"Known to his ma as Noddy Wells," Zena added. "He's our chief deckhand."

Knocker growled a laugh. "And only deckhand."

"The Ancient Mariner's retired, then?" I said.

Blaster and Knocker exchanged puzzled looks.

"Yeah! We don't like anyone, we make them walk the plank," Knocker said.

"I'd forgotten the plank. Every good pirate should have one," I said.

Knocker bristled like he wanted to say something but couldn't find the words.

Zena stepped between us. "I think we should go below."

"Below what?" I said.

Her eyebrows arched again. But I knew what she meant.

We left Blaster and Knocker scowling at us and passed

through a door into a cabin with a couple of upright wooden chairs and a table.

Zena pointed at one of the chairs. "Make yourself comfortable."

She turned her back on me, opened a door, and disappeared into another part of the ship.

I sat on one of the chairs and tried to make myself comfortable, as instructed.

The door opened and a man walked in.

He was one of those thirty-year-old blokes you just know is going to turn into a ball of blubber before he's forty. He had a round face with heavy jowls. He had piggy eyes with lids like shutters that hung heavily over them. He was wearing jeans held up by a thick leather belt. He'd recently let it out a notch. I could see the worn hole where he used to secure it. Hadn't made a lot of difference. His belly still hung over the belt like it wanted to leave home.

He grinned at me in that sloppy way folk do when they want you to think they've stumbled across you by accident but have really come to have a good look.

He said: "I'm Charles Dunn. People call me Chunky." He forced a laugh. "Never been able to tell why."

I joined him in the ersatz merriment to ease his tension.

"Anyway, I jockey some of the sessions on the air."

He relaxed a bit and the belly flopped lower. Perhaps if he took up yoga, it would hit the floor.

He said: "Perry is just finishing his set. Asked me if you'd like to take a look over the boat. Only if you want to."

I said: "Lead the way, *matelot*."

Dunn flashed another sloppy grin.

We stepped out of the room into a long passageway in the centre of the ship. It had some sort of corrugated rubber stuff on the floor and was lit by bulkhead lights behind metal grilles.

Doors painted different colours led off either side of the passage. The place smelt of old oil.

Dunn pointed and mumbled as we passed them.

Red door. "Library, where we keep the discs. Filed under artistes, in case you were wondering."

Green door. "Green room, natch! It's where we prepare our sets."

Yellow door "Ship's office. Just a load of paperwork. We all hate it."

We turned a dog-leg in the passage. There was a last door. A black one.

Dunn walked by. Said nothing.

I said: "What's behind the black door?"

"Nothing."

"It can't be nothing. It has to be something."

"Yeah! What I meant to say, it's nothing worth talking about."

"The kind of subject I find most interesting."

"Not this one. It's a bore."

"A bore door."

Dunn flashed a guilty grin.

"Yeah! Let's leave it at that. A bore door."

Dunn hustled me out of the passage on to the open deck in the centre of the ship. He pointed at a structure towards the stern. It was like a metal framed cube with lots of windows. Serious looking aerials sprouted from the roof and pointed towards the land.

Behind one of the windows I could see a man wearing headphones. He was hunched over a microphone and talking fast.

"Our studio one," Dunn said. "That's Perry inside finishing off his set."

I asked: "Is there a studio two?"

Dunn looked away. Thought about something. "We only have one show running at a time, so we only need one studio."

"Logical to call it studio one, I guess."

I let a little silence hang in the air. Dunn said nothing. Looked down and studied his shoes. Plimsolls with sweat marks around the toes.

So I said: "I guess a ship like this has to be self-sufficient."

Dunn pointed to a companionway towards the stern. "Down there leads to the galley, ward room, and heads – you'd know them better as the lavs. It's also where we have our cabins."

"Can I take a look-see?"

Dunn glanced at his watch. "No time. In three minutes, Perry finishes his set and I take over. Besides, you don't want to see down there. It's not exactly up to Aristotle Onassis' standards. Let's take a look at the studio."

Dunn hustled along the deck towards the studio. I tagged along behind, still wondering what was behind the black door.

Dunn beckoned me over to one of the studio's windows.

Inside, there was a tall slim man with fair hair brushed back from his forehead. He sat behind a console with a microphone that looked as though it had been wrapped in a dead mole. He had those well-etched lines on his face which make a man look more distinguished as he grows older. (At least, that's what I'm hoping.) He had a square chin straight out of a nineteen-fifties adventure comic only slightly offset by a pointy nose.

He looked up and saw Dunn and me with our noses pressed against the glass like a couple of kids sizing up toys in a Christmas shop window. He held up a disc, leaned into the microphone and his mouth moved. He placed the disc on a turntable and lowered the pick-up. He leant back and flicked a switch at the side of his console.

The Kinks' *Sunny Afternoon* blasted over the speakers. Dunn started to jig like he'd pulled the best-looking bird at the disco. Perry waved his arms in time with the beat. I tapped my foot and got out my notebook. It would do no harm for Perry and his number two to enjoy themselves.

I wanted the number one in a good mood when I asked him some tough questions.

* * *

Perry Turner held a thin cheroot between his index and middle finger.

He pointed it at me like it was an air-to-surface guided missile.

I said: "I thought pirates usually smoked a clay pipe."

Turner grinned. "That's only in Blackbeard films. But, hey, we're not real pirates. We're cool guys and gals who think the freedom of the airwaves is as important as the freedom of the sea."

"So you're not so much a disc jockey, more a freedom fighter?"

"Hey, I like that. You can write that in your article."

We were in Turner's cabin at the prow of the ship, just behind the wheelhouse. It was furnished with an old oak desk piled with manila files. There was a tower of wire baskets overflowing with the things. There was one of those office chairs on wheels behind the desk. A small sofa, and a couple of tub chairs upholstered in velvet, were grouped in front of the desk.

There was a bank of filing cabinets along one wall.

But what grabbed my attention was a life-sized cardboard cut-out of Cliff Richard propped in the corner. I'll say this. It looked a lot livelier than the original. I strolled over and took a closer look. Knocked into it – accidentally on purpose, you understand - and it slipped sideways.

Surprise! Behind it, were two crates of champagne. I noted the marque – Pol Roger – and crossed back to the chairs.

Turner flopped onto the sofa. I lowered myself into one of the tub chairs.

I pointed at the cut-out. "Has the real Cliff been on board?"

"We've invited him, but he's not yet been able to find the time."

"So the crates of champagne aren't for him?"

"No. But you can mention in your article that Cliff is thinking about coming on board."

"I'll need something meatier than that to make a decent piece."

"What about our beach party?"

"The whole town already knows about that. The place is plastered with posters."

"Yeah, that's the way we like it." Turner grinned again.

I said: "Where do you get the money to mount a big show like the beach party?"

Turner fumbled with a pile of papers on his desk as though he expected to find the answer in them. "Sponsors," he said.

"Sponsors usually insist on their name all over the publicity. You know... the Brighton beach party is proudly sponsored by Muggins' Laxative Chocolate. Your posters don't have anything like that."

"Yeah! See your point. But it's just our sponsors like to play it close to their chest."

I thought about that for a moment. Was I missing something? Sponsors were paying money to keep their name out of it. That was a novelty.

"So what's in it for them?" I asked.

"I'm not supposed to say."

"Then why have you accepted an interview with the *Chronicle*? 'Mr Perry Turner had nothing to say,' doesn't make much of a story."

Turner rose from the sofa. Paced over towards the window. Stood gazing at the sea while his hands twitched nervously together behind his back.

He turned and faced me with the cheesiest grin this side of Cheddar on his face.

"We wanted to keep it a surprise for the sponsors. You see we'd guaranteed that their money would buy them the opportunity to meet the biggest names in rock."

"The Beatles?"

"No."

"Who then?"

Turner stretched out his arms in an "ain't this fabulous" gesture. "The Rolling Stones."

My eyes widened like I was on one of those wake-up drugs. "You mean with Mick Jagger, Brian Jones, Keith Richards and Bill Wyman?"

"Don't forget Charlie Watts on drums. Are there any other Rolling Stones?"

"Only ones that gather no moss."

"We've been keeping it a secret. They'll play the closing set at the party, which ends at midnight – when we let off a ton of fireworks. In fact, the champagne in the crates is all for them."

I said: "Those sponsors must have stumped up some big cheques to pay for this."

"Fattest you'll ever have seen," Turner said. He relaxed. Seemed to be enjoying himself. Too bad. I had another question.

"Did the sponsors include Claude Winterbottom?" I asked.

Turner's body tensed. He started entwining his fingers nervously again.

"Who?" he asked.

"Claude Winterbottom. Investment consultant. Because if he was a sponsor, you'd better have cashed his cheque. He died three days ago."

"Don't think I've ever heard the name."

"That's strange. He advertised on your radio station. Honest Claude or something like that. I heard one of his ads last night. Just as I was dropping off to sleep. It certainly woke me up, as he'd been murdered."

Turner crossed the cabin back to his desk and sat down.

"I remember now. He visited us a few weeks ago – navigated here in his own motor cruiser. Wanted to see if any of us were interested in investing in one of his schemes. No chance. All our money is tied up. But we gave him a tour of the ship and he paid for a short run of ads. Even recorded it in our studio, while I was ashore. The series must've had time still to run. But I'll make sure any future ads are pulled from the schedule."

"That's the least of Winterbottom's problems now. So when do these sponsors get to meet the Stones?"

"Immediately they've finished their set. We're setting up a VIP hospitality suite in a marquee. It'll be in a closed area of the beach behind the stage."

"Riff-raff and journalists excluded?" I asked.

"We won't be inviting the press," Turner said in a strained voice.

He looked like a man who wished he was somewhere else. Like the front-line of a pitched battle.

But he managed to force one of his cheesy grins. "Say, we can't neglect the press. Let me play a request for you on my next show. Which song would you like to hear?"

That caught me off-guard.

"Er... I've just thought of one. How about *Midnight in*

Moscow – Kenny Ball and his Jazzmen. Came out a few years ago, but you'll have a copy."

Turner frowned and looked at the ceiling. "Not sure we have," he said. "In fact, now I come to think of it, I'm certain we haven't. I'll find something from the current charts and play it for you. And, now, if you'll excuse me..."

Turner stood up and moved towards the door. I closed my notebook and followed him. Evidently, the interview was over.

We stepped out onto the deck.

"Zena will take you back to the Palace Pier. I hope we'll see you on board again."

He stepped back through the bulkhead door to his cabin and slammed it shut.

I was left wondering why Turner should lie over something as trivial as a record. I knew for a fact he had a copy of *Midnight in Moscow* on board.

I'd heard him play it last night.

THIRTEEN

I thought more about *Midnight in Moscow* as Zena powered me across the waves to the Palace Pier.

I was beginning to wonder whether I really had heard it played on the radio. I was sleepy and perhaps I'd mistaken something else for it. Or perhaps I'd been asleep and it had been a dream.

No.

None of that was right. The disc had played right before Winterbottom's slippery advert.

I looked at Zena. Her blonde hair streamed in the wind. She had a tight hand on the tiller. Her eyes scanned the sea ahead.

I said: "What is it that Perry has against *Midnight in Moscow?*"

Zena looked at me like I'd just asked her to jump overboard.

"What?"

I repeated. "Why doesn't Perry like *Midnight in Moscow?*"

"The Kenny Ball number? It's news to me that he doesn't."

"He told me the station doesn't have the disc."

Zena frowned. "I don't get it. It's ancient history in the charts, but it still grooves. I spun the disc in my show a few weeks ago. Don't recall Perry grousing about it."

"Perhaps he's had a run-in with Kenny Ball in the past. Bad blood over something he said about Kenny in a show?"

"No way. Perry's new to the disc jockey business. He's a jock who's barely won his spurs. Doubt he's even met Ball."

"He seems to know The Rolling Stones."

"Yeah! Admit that caught my attention. Perry's so square. Less Rolling Stone. More Stonehenge. I didn't even realise he'd clocked they were on the scene."

"So how's he managed to book a top act?"

Zena shrugged. "Beats me. Must've had a contact somewhere. Agent, maybe."

"I suppose that explanation's as likely as any," I said.

I hadn't even convinced myself.

I said goodbye to Zena when she dropped me off at Palace Pier.

My second outing as an entertainment reporter had produced a scoop of sorts.

Nobody knew the Stones were planning an unscheduled gig in Brighton in two days' time. (Gig – I was even picking up the lingo.) It was a story that would be worth a par or two in the national tabloids. I could make myself some freelance lineage. The *Daily Mirror* would pay me five shillings a line and take twelve lines. Three pounds. Enough to buy Shirley a slap-up dinner to celebrate her film stardom. Besides, after a trip on the ocean waves, I felt I owed myself a bonus. I stopped off at Marcello's on the way back to the *Chronicle* and phoned the story through to the *Mirror's* newsdesk.

Back in the *Chronicle* newsroom, I gave the story the full front-page treatment. For the time being I didn't speculate on how Turner had lured the famous group to headline his beach party. My reporter's instinct told me there was more to tell about that. I wanted to be the first when the full story broke.

I'd just rolled the eighth and final folio out of my Remington, when my phone rang.

I lifted the receiver and a voice that reminded me of muck spreading on a newly ploughed field said: "I'm thirsty."

I'd rarely known a day when Ted Wilson wasn't.

I said: "If I were to assist you in quenching your thirst, would I return from the encounter enriched in knowledge?"

"If you mean would you get a tasty tip-off, the answer's yes. Ten minutes."

The line went dead.

* * *

I stepped into Prinny's Pleasure nine minutes later and walked up to the bar.

Jeff was dusting the fluff off the lid of a jar of pickled eggs. It had been on the end of the bar ever since I'd been patronising the place. I'd never seen a punter buy one.

Jeff twitched a thumb at the corner table at the back of the bar.

"He's already there. And he's stood you a gin and tonic, just as you like it."

"One ice cube, two slices of lemon."

I walked up to the corner table and took the seat next to Ted.

I nodded towards Ted's large scotch and said: "You seem in fine spirits – in more ways than one."

Ted took a good pull at his drink. "Might be."

I took a sip of my own drink. "You've got something Tomkins doesn't know about."

Ted frowned. "How do you know that?"

"First, you've invited me round here. You never do that. Second, you've bought me a drink. And, third, you've got a look on your face like you've just bagged the biggest potato at a beggars' feast."

"Yeah! And the leg off the chicken."

"Spit it out then."

"The potato or the chicken?"

"The information. Will it be something that gets Mrs Gribble off Tomkins' absurd murder charge?"

Ted scratched his beard. "Can't promise that, but it upends the case he's made against her."

I had a good pull at my drink, while Ted took out a small notebook.

He said: "We've spent three days going through the paperwork in Winterbottom's flat. You should have seen it – eight filing cabinets packed with papers. Boxes of papers in his bedroom, out in the utility room, even on his balcony. It was clear the guy was a grade one scamster, so weird that he decided to keep all the paperwork. If the fraud squad had got hold of that stuff while he was still breathing, they'd have had him inside for twenty years. None of your open prison nonsense, either. But that's another story."

"So stick to this one."

Ted gave his beard a little tug. Decided he didn't like that and smoothed it down.

He said: "We found scores of letters from Winterbottom's mug punters who'd lost their money. Plenty of nasty ones, too, but most of them general abuse. Sticks and stones stuff for a man like Winterbottom."

"But there was one letter that wasn't just sticks and stones stuff?" I asked.

"Three, to be precise."

"Recent?"

"No dates on them. But one had been left in the envelope. It was post-marked just three weeks ago. And making some hard threats that would turn your stomach. Well, not perhaps yours, but it would have your Shirley reaching for the smelling salts."

"More likely a can of Fosters. But let's leave Shirley out of it for now. I take it, in the tradition of threatening letters, it wasn't signed."

Ted smirked. "That's where you're wrong. It was signed Astraea."

That had my attention. "Just Astraea?"

"Yeah! Not even Mr Astraea or Mrs Astraea. We don't even know whether we're dealing with a man or a woman."

"It's a woman."

"How can you be sure, know-all?"

"Because Astraea was the Greek goddess of purity. She was a celestial virgin and, the legends say, lived with mortals during what the Greeks called their Golden Age. But when the world became too wicked for her, she ascended to heaven and became the constellation Virgo. Get it? Virgo, virgin. Anyway, the legend says that one day she'll return to Earth and drive away all the wickedness."

Ted gawped at me. "How do you know all this stuff?"

"Reading," I said. "You should try it."

"Well, she wasn't driving away any wickedness in her letters. There wasn't anything pure about them, either. Especially about the bits of Winterbottom she was going to cut off before she croaked him. Or what she was going to do with them. *Ugh!* I'll never let a morsel of toad-in-the-hole pass my lips again."

"He'd taken her money?"

"A small fortune as far as we can make out from the letters."

I hoisted my glass and drained the drink. Called for Jeff to bring us both refills. I was thinking hard.

Jeremiah Puttock was a member of the National Purity Army. Could he be linked to purity goddess Astraea? When I'd met him and his fellow purists outside Baz's dirty book shop, they'd seemed sincere in their views but not especially militant. Not the kind who'd write about how to cook a meal of body parts baked in batter.

So was this Astraea linked to the National Purity Army or was she just pure on her lonesome? Perhaps Puttock could tell me more. After all, he'd refused to name the army's leader. Could that be Astraea?

Herbie Stubbs had told me a preacher type had visited Winterbottom. I wondered whether that could be Puttock. If Astraea was head of the National Purity Army, she could have ordered Puttock to get the money back from Winterbottom. But the slimy investment scamster would have looked for ways to get Puttock off his back. What better than to turn the tables and find a way to blackmail him?

"Why haven't you taken this to Tomkins?" I asked Ted.

"Because he'll just bury it. He's already decided your landlady is the fall-guy for the Winterbottom killing."

"She's the fall-girl," I corrected.

We fell silent while Jeff served us our new drinks.

I said: "This is an interesting tip-off, but I can't see where it's leading. There are already suspects Tomkins ought to question – Crouchpenny and Puttock for a start. As a story, the Astraea letters would make a Gothic tale, but they don't lead anywhere. Because we don't know who Astraea is."

"That's where I thought you could help. You've already mentioned the purity goddess angle. We didn't know about that."

I said: "I could poke around in the morgue and see if it

throws up anything. But I'll have to do that quietly. Officially, Pope has banned me from writing crime stories. I'm supposed to be the paper's entertainment writer."

Ted smirked. "Couldn't have picked a better man."

He drained his second scotch in a single gulp and hurried out of the pub.

I lingered over my gin and tonic. I wanted a quiet moment to think through what Ted had just told me.

I already knew that Puttock's mail-order love-life made him a blackmail target for Winterbottom. I suspected that had made Winterbottom a murder target for Puttock. But if there was a shadowy Astraea figure in the background – one that had lost money to Winterbottom - that blurred the picture. Especially if Puttock had known Astraea through his purity campaign. If both had a reason to bump off Winterbottom, could they even have worked together on the project? After all, with their twisted minds, perhaps they thought it wouldn't be wrong to make sure Winterbottom ended up purely dead.

There was only one way to find out whether any of these theories held up. I had to interview Puttock again.

* * *

I'd rung the bell on Puttock's front door three times before I suspected he'd scarpered.

But I haven't been a crime reporter all these years without letting a little thing like an unanswered door put me off. Of course, I was forgetting. I was now an entertainment reporter. Still, I knew that folks with something to hide, didn't answer the door when the press came calling. They crept under the table or stowed away in a convenient wardrobe.

So I walked up a passage at the side of the house and tried the backdoor. I rattled the handle like I was Burglar Bill.

Locked. Rattling would usually get a hidden culprit to break cover. Nothing.

There was a frosted glass window in the door. I tried peering through, but it made the room behind look like a heavy mist had settled in.

I could've tried the other windows, but there didn't seem much point. Puttock clearly wasn't at home. But when was he coming back?

Maybe Sharp-eyed Sylvia at number sixteen could throw some light on the matter.

She had her front door open before I was halfway up her garden path. There was a big grin on her face.

"Didn't think it would be long before you were back, now that this has happened," she said.

"Now what's happened?"

"Old Puttock's flown the nest."

"I know. I've just called on him."

"I saw you. And you went round the back when you shouldn't have."

I smiled. "I won't tell if you won't. When did he leave?"

"Just after lunch. I was just grilling a Welsh rarebit when I heard a taxi draw up."

"How did you know it was a taxi?"

"They always sound their horn with a couple of *beep-beeps* to alert their fare. Well, I pulled the rarebit out from under the grill – because there's nothing worse than burnt rarebit – and had a quick peek. Puttock crept down his garden path like he'd just snuck out of the Bank of England with the day's takings. Had a suitcase with him big enough for them, as well. Heavy, too. The cabbie had a couple of tries to heft it into the cab."

"I don't suppose you know where he was going?"

"Who do you think I am? Madame Arcati? I'm no clairvoyant."

"Did you note the number plate on the taxi?"

"I'm not Fabian of the Yard, neither. But I'll tell you this. From the size of the luggage, Puttock was going a long way away – and he didn't plan to come back any time soon."

* * *

"If I were going to be a goddess, I wouldn't want the purity job," Mabel Berridge said.

"Me neither," Elsie Deacon said. "With all that purity around, you'd feel you had to rinse your smalls out every day rather than save them for the big wash on Mondays. Now if I were in line for a goddess, I'd settle for Aphrodite."

"Isn't she the goddess of love and beauty?" Freda Wallace asked.

Elsie brushed her grey hair away from the mole on her cheek. "That's right."

"Don't you think you're a teensy-weensy bit under-qualified for that role?" Freda said.

"And what do you mean by that?" Elsie demanded.

"Now, now ladies," Henrietta Houndstooth said. "That's enough Greek goddesses for now. Any more trouble and I'll take on the role of Circe."

"Who's she when she's at home?" Mabel demanded.

"She's the goddess of magic with the power to turn her enemies into beasts. And, as for where she lives, I believe it's Mount Olympus, with the rest of the gods."

"Not the flats down Edward Street, like Elsie," Freda said.

Henrietta threw up her hands and wiggled her fingers like she was casting a spell. "I said that's enough goddess talk."

I was in the morgue at the *Evening Chronicle*. It was about half an hour after I'd left Sharp-eyed Sylvia. I'd decided the only way I'd be able to track down Astraea was to see whether we had any information in the files.

But it wasn't going to be easy.

It never was when Mabel, Elsie and Freda started to squabble. They were known around the paper as the Clipping Cousins. The clipping part was accurate. They snipped the articles from each day's paper and filed them under the names of the people and sometimes places mentioned. The "Cousins" was just the way we journalists talked about them in the newsroom.

Henrietta Houndstooth was the morgue's manager. She kept the peace. More to the point, she had an encyclopaedic knowledge of what was in the files. And even more about what wasn't.

I'd asked her whether we had anything about Astraea in the files. She'd screwed up her eyes as though she was trying to remember some distant fact.

She shook her head. "We don't get much call for Greek goddesses around here."

I explained that Astraea was a *nom de guerre* for a mysterious figure connected to Jeremiah Puttock, currently a Winterbottom murder suspect.

I said: "I've got a theory."

Henrietta grinned: "I thought you might have."

"I think she's someone who's been in the news before but doesn't now want personal attention for her National Purity Army campaign."

"Why not?" Mabel asked.

"Perhaps because she doesn't want the personal flak you get when you hold extreme views. Or, perhaps, she wants to keep out of the spotlight because her organisation has sinister plans."

"Like taking over Britain?" Elsie asked. "I'd like to see her take over my Bill. Someone's got to get him out of that armchair of an evening."

I said: "Maybe if we search the files of extreme organisations, we'll pick up some clues, perhaps a fleeting reference to Astraea."

"Like the National Socialist Movement and that foul Colin Jordan," Henrietta said.

"Or the ridiculous League of Empire Loyalists," Elsie said.

"Or that loathsome Racial Preservation Society that's just been set up," Freda said.

"Those and others, including those American-backed private churches where the message of Jesus got lost on the way to the bank," I added.

Henrietta frowned. "It will take hours to look at all the files we have on extremist dingbats."

"Just too busy," Mabel said.

"Haven't a minute to spare," Elsie said.

"Rushed off our feet," Freda added.

This was a problem. Without the Cousins' help there was no way I could trawl the files.

I leaned on the edge of Henrietta's desk. "Pity," I said. "I noticed Forfar's had one of those extra-large Victoria sponges in their window. Lashings of cream in the middle. The strawberry jam was spread so thick, it was running down the sides."

Mabel winked at Freda. Elsie nodded at Henrietta.

"Well, maybe we could spare a few moments," Henrietta said.

I returned with the Victoria sponge half an hour later.

The table in the centre of the room was strewn with manila files.

The Cousins were bent over the files. Mabel was grinding her teeth. Elsie scratched the mole on her cheek. Freda let out a stream of irritated grunts.

The work wasn't going well.

They didn't even look up when I plonked the sponge in the middle of the table.

Over at her desk, Henrietta said: "This is hopeless. These files are just full of loons and misfits. Astraea could be any of them."

"Remember, she's a woman," I said.

"How do we know that? There are men in this town crazy enough to masquerade as a woman. Some who enjoy it."

Henrietta had a point. I hadn't considered it.

I said: "Why don't you all take a break? It was worth a try, but we're not going to track down Astraea this way."

The Cousins pushed the files into the centre of the table. Mabel picked up the sponge. Elsie fetched a knife to slice it. Freda brought plates from their little pantry. Teamwork!

Henrietta leant back in the chair. "It was always going to be a long shot," she said. "We were never going to see the name Astraea written in black and white."

I stiffened like an electric current had just passed through my body. I felt like I'd just been touched up with a cattle prod.

"What did you say?" I said.

Henrietta looked up with worried eyes. She'd caught the urgency in my voice.

She said: "The name Astraea won't be printed in black and white."

Black and white.

The words had triggered a distant memory in my mind.

"You know the daily feature we run towards the back of the paper – Twenty-five Years Ago?"

162

"Don't I just? I have to research the item each day," Henrietta said.

It was always a single paragraph snippet from the paper twenty-five years ago. The kind of space-filler papers use in their back pages.

I said: "A few months ago, the item was about a woman named Black who'd married a man named White. I remember the woman said she looked forward to her new name because it made her feel more pure. I thought it was an odd thing to say."

Henrietta was already up and moving towards the shelves where the bound back issues of the paper were stacked.

She heaved down a volume from 1941. Turned the brittle pages.

"Here it is," she said.

I peered over her shoulder. The article described how Sir Roger White, a baronet, had married a Miss Millicent Black at St Peter's church, Brighton. There was a picture of the happy couple. White was grinning manically at the camera. Millicent was frowning at him.

I said: "Do we have any cuttings filed on Sir Roger and Lady White."

Henrietta disappeared into the shelving stacks where the cuttings were stored in hundreds of filing cabinets. She was back in less than two minutes with a thin file.

There were just two cuttings inside. The first was dated 12 October 1941, six months after the marriage. It reported how Sir Roger had died in the Royal Sussex County Hospital from what it called a "French disease".

"What does that mean?" Henrietta asked.

"It means syphilis," I said.

The second cutting was dated 11 March 1942. It reported how Sir Roger had left his fortune – two hundred and three thousand pounds – to his wife, Lady Millicent. She'd told a *Chronicle* reporter: "This is dirty money, but one day I will make it clean."

I said: "I don't think she planned to give it a rinse at the laundry."

"Do you think she's Astraea?" Henrietta asked.

"If she's not, I'm Momus," I said.

"Who?" Mabel asked with a mouthful of cream sponge.

"Momus, the Greek god of writers and poets."

"You're no poet, and you know it," Freda said.

FOURTEEN

I left the morgue feeling pleased with myself.

But it's never wise to display hubris in the face of Greek goddesses – even would-be goddesses eating Victoria sponge. Nemesis is never far behind.

I thought it wouldn't take me long to track down Lady Millicent White's address. The telephone directory is always the first book of reference. She wasn't listed.

The press cuttings had mentioned that Sir Roger and Lady White had lived in Ovingdean, a suburb of Brighton with big houses. But, happily, not many of them. That meant it shouldn't take me too long to search the electoral register to see if Lady Millicent was registered to vote. That is, if she still lived in Ovingdean. I thought it likely. Wealthy people who live in nice houses in smart parts of town rarely have an incentive to move.

I'd just heaved the Ovingdean register off the bookshelf on the far side of the newsroom, when Cedric stepped through the door.

He hurried over to me waving an ominous looking piece of paper.

"I've been looking for you, Mr Crampton. Mr Figgis asked me to give you this."

"What is it? My dismissal notice?"

Cedric smiled, but not enough to make me think he'd entirely dismissed the idea as possible.

"No, just a story in your new job as entertainment reporter. You get all the luck, Mr Crampton."

He gave me the papers.

"With a job like that, you could walk into Sherry's and pull any bird in the place," he said. He wandered off.

I took a quick look at the paper. Figgis wanted me to interview an amateur actor. The bloke had taken the part of Henry Ormonroyd, the drunken photographer, in a revival of J B Priestley's play *When We Are Married*.

Well, good luck to him.

I had a quick word with Sally Martin. (I'd done a couple of favours for her recently.) She agreed to take it on.

Which left me at my desk hurriedly poring over the Ovingdean electoral register.

And, as I suspected, Lady Millicent still lived in the area. I quit the newsroom certain I wouldn't meet any genuine Greek goddesses. But not about much else.

Lady Millicent's house turned out to be a large two-storey place built in a mock Tudor style.

There were lots of blackened bricks, oak beams and casement windows with diamond-shaped glass. It was a double-fronted property which I could see an estate agent describing as "spacious". And, for once, he wouldn't be wrong. The place

was surrounded by a brick wall, about three feet high. The wall
was topped by the kind of railings with sharp pointy tops that
would make sure any intruder got a rip in his trousers.

Beyond the wall, there was a lawn. A youngish bloke was
pushing a mower up and down.

I sat in the car wondering what to do.

It might not be good tactics to march up to the front door,
ring the bell, and demand to speak to Astraea. For a start, the
bloke pushing the mower could be a problem if there were
trouble. And I didn't know who else might be in the house.
There was even the chance that Lady White was not at home.
After all, even Greek goddesses had to nip down to the grocers
for a pint of milk from time to time.

I decided to sit it out for a bit and see whether anyone
arrived or left.

After ten minutes the mowing stopped and the gardener
disappeared. He was back two minutes later and started clipping a privet hedge which ran along the side border of the
house.

I watched him clip away and tried to keep myself interested. But I was beginning to think I was wasting my time. I'd
either have to take a risk and knock on the door. Or beat it and
think up another plan.

I was still debating that when a young woman stepped
around the edge of the house. It wasn't Lady White. She was
too young for that. If Astraea had been in her twenties when
she'd married in 1941, she'd be mid-fifties now. This woman
was no more than thirty-five, perhaps even younger.

She had dark brown hair, clipped short in a severe cut that
could have had her mistaken for a man from the back. She had
a round face with high cheek-bones and pinched eyes. She had
a stocky figure and walked with a determined tread. She was
dressed in a grey blouse and tan slacks.

She called across the garden: "Luke, make sure you sweep up those clippings before you go."

Luke waved to her: "No worries, Magda."

"Make sure there aren't."

"Off anywhere nice?"

"No."

"Oh, just wondered."

"You're not paid to wonder."

Luke looked ruefully at his shears and turned back to the hedge.

Magda headed for the gate and stepped into the road. She began to walk away from me.

Magda? A foreign name. Middle European, possibly?

I climbed out of the car and headed after her.

Magda may have carried some excess weight, but she knew how to move it.

I puffed along twenty yards back.

Magda headed out of Ovingdean to the Falmer road and turned left towards Woodingdean.

She got herself in the groove and powered up the hill.

As I hustled along, I tried to think why a young middle-European woman would be living with Lady White. *Au pair*, seemed the obvious answer. No doubt someone with a title in front of her moniker would feel she deserved a bit of help around the house.

But, then, Magda seemed to have a certain amount of authority. She'd left Luke in no doubt who was boss. Would an *au pair* have the confidence to do that? I had no answers. And, besides, I was hot. My shirt had stuck to my back. And my socks had started to itch.

At the crossroads in Woodingdean, Magda turned left and marched along Warren Road. I wondered how far she was heading. The road led to Brighton racecourse. But the gee-gees weren't running today. Besides, Magda didn't look like a betting woman.

A couple of hundred yards along the road, Magda stopped. She reached into her handbag and took out something. I couldn't see what it was. Then she went up some steps and into a building.

I hurried up and looked at the building, surprised and puzzled. It was Woodingdean library.

For a moment, I stood around in the street wondering whether I should follow Magda in. After all, she didn't know who I was. I can play the part of eager bookworm as well as any library-goer.

But that could create difficulties later on. If I called on Lady White and Magda saw me, she might remember me from the library. That could be awkward.

I was musing on this when I glanced down the road. Coming up the street from the racecourse end was Knocker, the bald-headed deckhand from the *Seabreeze*.

What on earth was a salty sailor like Knocker doing on dry land?

I didn't want him to see me, so I nipped smartly round the corner into a small lane which ran down the side of the library.

I peered around the corner. Knocker was less than fifty yards from the library. He paced along with his head down.

And then Magda shot out of the library, glanced towards him, and turned to make her return journey.

I slunk further down the lane to make sure she didn't see me as she hurried by.

When she'd gone, I scooted up to the top of the lane and peered round the corner. Two minutes later, Knocker came out of the library carrying a book. Even twenty yards away, I recognised the book by its distinctive cover.

It was *Chitty Chitty Bang Bang* by Ian Fleming.

Knocker turned back the way he came and trotted down the road. Looked like he was eager to read a story about a car that flies.

I leant against an old flint wall that skirted the boundary of the lane and wondered what to do next.

My mind felt it was throbbing like I'd just been posed a tough move in three-dimensional chess. If I was right and Lady White was Astraea, that would make her a mortal enemy of Perry Turner and his *Seabreeze* Radio beach party.

No purity there. A festival of filth, Jeremiah Puttock had called it.

Yet here was Noddy Wells – Knocker to his mates and, for all I knew, his enemies as well – using the same public library within minutes of Astraea's *au pair*. Could that be coincidence? It didn't seem likely.

For a start, Magda had spent three minutes inside the library, barely enough time to browse even one shelf. She'd shot out like the place was on fire – and she hadn't borrowed a book. At least, not one I could see.

As for Knocker, he looked like the kind of guy whose lips moved as he followed the words.

I could think of only one link between Lady White as Astraea and Knocker and the *Seabreeze* crew. Winterbottom. He'd taken Lady White's hard-earned cash and could have spent at least some of it advertising his crooked services on Turner's radio station.

And now Winterbottom was dead.

I crept out of the alley and looked carefully both ways to make sure none of the other players in this drama were lurking nearby. The street was clear of pedestrians. A red and white Brighton Hove & District bus roared down Warren Road. A couple of cars tooted at one another as they swerved to avoid a crunch. An old boy on a push bike pedalled by.

I walked down the road and stepped into the library.

A young woman was sitting at the issues and returns desk. She had mousey hair held back on each side of her forehead by a comb. Her hair was tied in a bun at the back. Her lips were pressed together in concentration as she thumbed through some library cards. She had a pair of tortoise-shell glasses perched on the end of her pert little nose. She was the lady librarian from central casting. I hoped she was the kind who, in the last reel, throws off the glasses, pulls out the combs, lets her hair fall free in luxurious tresses, and looks into the camera with a winsome smile.

I walked up to the desk. A name plate read: Yvonne Garland, Assistant Librarian.

I said: "Excuse me, I'm looking for a copy of *Chitty Chitty Bang Bang*. Do you have one in the library?"

Yvonne looked up from her library cards, took off the tortoise-shells but didn't shake her hair out of the bun. (Well, not everything happens like it's in a film.)

She said: "Strangely, that book has just been borrowed. Were you looking for children's books in general or works by Ian Fleming?"

I said: "I just noticed my old friend Magda come out of the library, but she was away before I could speak to her."

"That will be the lady who comes in every few days to consult the dictionaries."

"Yes, Magda was always one for words. Where are the dictionaries? Something I'd like to look up myself."

Yvonne pointed to a bookshelf on the far side of the room.

I crossed the room and studied the books. The library was well equipped with dictionaries. There was the two-volume version of the *Shorter Oxford English Dictionary* – shorter because it wasn't the full twenty-one volume work. There was a copy of *Chambers* and a *Roget's Thesaurus*.

The shelf below held some English and foreign language books. There was an English-German dictionary and others for French, Spanish, Dutch, Polish, Hungarian and Russian. I stood and wondered which book Magda had consulted. The books were all neatly shelved. But the English-Hungarian dictionary hadn't been pushed back on the shelf as far as the others.

I picked it up. It was new and looked like it had been hardly used. I wondered why it was stocked in a library in Woodingdean. But perhaps someone had requested it. Perhaps even Magda, if she were Hungarian. I held the book in my hand and opened it at random. It fell open at a page that had obviously been more used than the others. One of the English-Hungarian pages towards the back of the book.

There was helpful indexing at the top of each page.

The page I was looking at read: review-revolution.

* * *

I left the library wondering what the hell to make of that.

An otherwise little-used English-Hungarian dictionary falls open at what seemed to be a much-used page. Review-revolution. A choice or an accident? I had no idea.

If I was right and Magda was a Hungarian *au pair*, it wouldn't be surprising if she occasionally wanted to consult an English-Hungarian dictionary. But if you needed a book regularly, why not buy one?

And, anyway, that didn't explain the appearance of Knocker. He hadn't been there to consult a dictionary. He'd borrowed a book, but was that the main reason for his visit?

I wandered back towards the main road while I thought about these things. At the crossroads in the centre of Woodingdean, there was a small parade of shops. A newsagent, a fish and chip shop, a general store, and a funeral director.

As I approached the crossroads, Magda hurried out of the general store. She had a large carrier bag under her arm. I could just see a packet of cornflakes and a bag of sugar poking out of the top. She bustled down the road. With a load like that, it was clear she was heading for home.

I decided not to follow. Instead, I waited for her to round a bend in the road and hurried across to the shop.

It was a cramped little place with dark brown shelves that seemed to crowd in from the walls. The air smelt of smoked bacon and damp cardboard.

A glass counter to the right held cold hams, sliced meats, and wedges of Stilton and Cheddar cheese. A severe looking woman with a pinched face and brown hair braided in plaits stood behind the counter. She was wearing a blue-striped apron over something grey underneath.

Over by the far wall, a table held baskets of fruit and vegetables. An old man with hunched shoulders was running his hands over a bright yellow honeydew melon.

The woman said crossly: "Stop fondling that melon, Mr Harris."

"I was just seeing whether it was ripe, Mrs Saunders."

"You never buy melon."

"Not surprising, at your prices."

I walked over to the counter and said: "My wife and I moved into a house in Crescent Drive a couple of weeks ago. We're looking for somewhere that does weekly grocery deliveries."

Mrs Saunders' mouth cracked into what I think was a smile. Or it could have been a snarl.

"That we do, Mr, er..."

"Trumpington-Smythe."

"As you can see, we stock only the finest provisions – and at very reasonable prices. Stop poking that tomato, Mr Harris."

"It'll be a large order. Fresh fruit and veg. Cheese and ham. Few rashers of bacon. Eggs, bread, milk. I can pop in with a full list in a couple of days."

"We shall be honoured to have your patronage and I assure you of our best attention at all times. And don't you dare do what I think you're planning with that aubergine, Mr Harris."

She tried another grin. "He can't stop admiring how fresh our vegetables are."

I said: "That's good to know. And, by the way, did I see Magda come out of the shop just before I popped in?"

Mrs Saunders' bushy eyebrows jumped a bit at that. "You've met Miss Groff already?"

I nodded. "A couple of days after we moved in. We ran into her in the library. She was consulting the English-Hungarian dictionary."

"Really. That surprises me. Miss Groff has been here for, let me see, nearly nine years. She came in 1956."

That had my attention. I vividly remembered newsreels of the Hungarian revolt. Pictures showed refugees – 200,000 of them in the end – fleeing across fields from advancing Russian troops. What had started as a student protest in October was crushed by the Red Army in November.

I asked: "Has Miss Groff lived here ever since?"

"She's shopped with us for many years. Her English is excellent."

"Is that so? We only met her briefly, but intended to invite her to one of my wife's musical soirées. I always thought she'd be a wonder on the clarinet. Such a pity that she plays the flute. Still, the biscuit consumption is huge. So great business for you."

"I believe Miss Groff plays the pianoforte. Perhaps she could accompany your wife. In an unguarded moment, Miss

Groff admitted to me she'd studied the instrument at the Tchaikovsky Academic Music College in Moscow."

So, Magda Groff had studied with Russians, but fled from their troops when they invaded her country. She played the piano, but preferred to work as an *au pair*. Miss Groff was a puzzle of contradictions.

"Will there be anything else, Mr Trumpington-Smythe?"

"Not for the present, Mrs Saunders."

I headed for the door.

"I wouldn't let the old dragon see what you're doing with that banana," I whispered to Harris on the way out.

* * *

I stepped into the street and paused under the shop's awning.

I wanted to take a good look around. I was pretty sure that Magda and Knocker had headed off to where they were going. But this afternoon was turning out to be full of surprises.

I made a point of studying a pyramid of canned baked beans in the shop's window while actually looking at the reflection.

Across the road, a young bloke in a well-cut suit and trilby hat had been leaning on a lamp-post. And not, I suspected, like George Formby, in case a certain little lady passed by. For a start he didn't have a ukulele. But he did have a copy of *The Daily Telegraph* which he'd pretended to read. He'd folded it as I came out of the shop.

Big mistake.

His clumsy action had drawn attention to himself.

I didn't know who he was. But I've been followed before – and he had follower written all over him.

I sighed. If it wasn't one thing, it was another.

FIFTEEN

I studied the baked bean pyramid in the shop's window for a little longer

I needed to plan how to handle Matey, my follower.

I had three options. One, I could let Matey follow me back to the office. He'd discover I worked at the *Evening Chronicle*. But, I expected, he already knew that.

Two, I could shake Matey off. His newspaper folding fumble suggested he was new to the game and I didn't think it would be difficult. In which case, he'd have to crawl back to his boss and admit he'd failed. The boss would find someone sneakier to follow me. I might find it harder to spot the replacement tail.

Or, three, I could turn the tables. Let Matey follow me. But when he thought his task was done, follow him as he headed back to base. Perhaps I would discover who'd set the tail on me.

It had to be something to do with the Winterbottom murder but I couldn't figure out what.

If I were to stand any chance of turning the tables on

Matey, I had to work out where he'd originally picked me up. He wouldn't have known that I planned to stake out Lady White's place. So it must have been before then.

I'd discovered that Astraea could be Lady White back at the *Chronicle*. So that's where Matey must have picked up my trail. Careless of me. I'd been followed from the *Chronicle's* offices in the past – usually by rival journalists who wanted to discover who my contacts were because they had too few of their own. Matey would have followed my MGB in a car of his own and parked nearby – but out of sight – while I watched Lady White's house.

There was a phone box twenty yards down the street. I sneaked a peek at my pursuer as I strolled down to it. He was studying the bus timetable like he wanted to commit it to memory.

I stepped into the phone box and called the *Chronicle*. The switchboard put me through to Phil Bailey in the newsroom.

I said: "Phil, how would you like to borrow my MGB for the evening?"

Phil laughed. "What is this? Some kind of scam? The car is your pride and joy. What do you want from me?"

"The loan of your beaten-up old Wolseley."

"I accept there's a dent in the offside wing and the upholstery has faded a bit, but the motor's still a goer."

"My apologies to you and the car. I would like to borrow your passion wagon for one evening for purposes I will reveal to you afterwards."

"It's not illegal, is it?" Phil sounded wary.

"No. It's for a story."

"And I definitely get your MGB for the whole evening?"

"Until midnight. We meet outside my lodgings at the witching hour and return each other's cars."

"And there's no catch? Like it has no petrol? Or it's been impounded by the cops?"

"Would I make a generous offer like this with a catch?"

"Well... okay. You're on."

I grinned. "I'll leave my MGB at the front of the *Chronicle's* offices. Leave your motor in Figgis' reserved parking spot round the back. I should be back to the newsroom in about an hour."

I pushed out of the phone box feeling like I was just about to win a prize.

* * *

It was easy to lead Matey back down the hill to Ovingdean, where I'd parked my MGB.

It was still where I'd left it, just fifty yards from Lady White's mock Tudor mansion. I sat in the car and took another close look at the house. There was no sign of Luke, the gardener, or Magda Groff. I fiddled about with stuff in the glove compartment for a bit. I wanted to give Matey time to get back to his own car, so he'd be able to follow me.

He marched by on the other side of the road and never once sneaked a glance at me.

He disappeared round a corner. So, his own car was parked in a side road.

I fired up the MGB's ignition and took off. But slowly to give Matey plenty of time to fall in behind.

On the drive back to the *Chronicle*, I worked out what I would do next. After I'd parked outside the office, Matey would pull into the road nearby. He'd see me walk into the building and assume I was there for some time. I hoped he'd hang around to see if I left again. That was a flaw in my plan. If Matey decided his work was done when I'd returned to base, he would take off smartly. I'd have no time to follow him in Phil's Wolseley.

But I didn't think he'd leave immediately. He'd want to see whether I planned to stay in the office or leave quickly. So, he'd hang around for a few minutes at least. Probably for long enough to see Phil dash out with my car key and race off. Matey wouldn't quite know what to make of that. But he wouldn't follow Phil. He'd wait to see if I emerged on foot.

While he was thinking about that, I'd have fired up the Wolseley and would have taken up position ready to follow him when he left.

* * *

Which is why an hour and a half later I was sitting in the Wolseley wishing for Matey to move.

It was past eight o'clock, nearly two hours after I'd arrived back at the *Chronicle*, before he finally started his car and drove off.

His first stop was a fish and chip shop. He went inside and spent forty minutes treating himself to a cod and chips supper.

I sat in the Wolseley and listened to my own grumbling stomach.

Matey emerged from the chippie looking like a man who's just feasted on a banquet. He climbed into the car and moved off.

He drove out of town towards Lewes. At Falmer, he turned into a lane and dropped his speed. He slowed the car and manoeuvred on to a narrow driveway which led to a large detached house that stood well back from the road.

I drove slowly by to make sure I could clock Matey's car on the driveway. It was there with two other cars, one a red Jaguar E-type – a phallic symbol on four wheels. The other was a

Rover P4, a stylish car for the gent who thought he deserved a Bentley but didn't have the necessary readies.

But it was the house, not the car, that had my attention. I drove further down the lane and parked in a lay-by.

The house was a smart Lutyens villa built at the turn of the century. Probably for one of Lewes' prosperous merchants. Or perhaps for a professional type like the barristers who had chambers in the town.

I knew it was as elegant inside as out. I had been inside once but I never wanted to go inside again.

* * *

Three years earlier, the whole country was gripped by the trial of Septimus Darke, the gangster who'd held Brighton in the grip of his terror for years.

Day after day, I sat at the reporters' table in Lewes Assizes and listened to the evidence against Darke. The cops knew that Darke was behind at least four murders, beating up rivals, illegal gun running, drugs, and prostitution. And that was only the opening salvo on the charge sheet.

But as the case opened, I was shocked at how few witnesses were appearing for the prosecution. It wasn't hard to work out why. Darke was standing in the dock, but the tentacles of his criminal organisation stretched deep into Brighton. Some witnesses had been bought off. Others had been frightened off. At least one had disappeared.

After three days of prosecution evidence, it was beginning to look as though the case against Darke could collapse. And then, on the fourth day, the prosecution called a surprise witness, a Mrs G. The judge agreed she could give her evidence behind a screen so she could not be seen by Darke.

It transpired that Mrs G claimed to have been the secret

lover of Jed Hodgkin, Darke's feared enforcer, who'd died after a gun battle outside the Masonic Provincial Grand Lodge of Sussex in Queens Road, Brighton.

For months, there had been pillow talk. "*Oooh*, Jed, it just excites me when you tell me things like that. It makes me want to..."

"'Ere then. I betya didn't know that...*oooh*, is that you getting excited, darlin'?"

Mrs G had been shrewd enough to keep a diary of everything she was told. There was massive press speculation over who Mrs G was. The Fleet Street press pack were on her trail. But I thought I could outwit them and make a name for myself.

In the secure parking area near to the court, I'd spotted an Austin Cambridge – grey with a red stripe. A driver was dozing in the front seat. There was one of those little strips stuck in the back window that garages often affix after they've serviced a car. It came from a garage in Falmer, not far from Lewes.

I reckoned the car was waiting to drive Mrs G back to whichever safe house she was being held in during the trial. There was no way I would be able to follow the car. There'd be a back-up car a hundred or so yards behind it ready to pick off any pursuer. But, perhaps, I could trace the Austin from the Falmer garage.

I rigged one of the sparking plugs on my MGB so it wasn't firing correctly. Then I drove – with some embarrassing backfires – to the garage and asked if they could fix the problem. They could.

"I thought you'd be able to help," I told the mechanic – Dickie - as I slipped him a generous two-pound tip. "The guy down the road from me – the one with the grey Austin Cambridge with the red stripe – recommended you."

"Ah, that would be Neville from Village Way. Nice guy.

Don't know what he does. Thanks for the couple of quid. I'll make sure I don't spend it wisely."

I never found out whether Dickie spent his two quid unwisely or not. In fact, I wished I'd kept the money. For Dickie was clearly on a retainer from the people who ran the house in Village Way. Later that night, two burly types in cheap suits visited me at my place in Regency Square. They invited me to take a ride with them. It was clear from their expression that a refusal would offend.

They took me to the house in Village Way where I was met by two suave men in expensive Savile Row suits.

The first introduced himself. "My name's Conan."

I turned to the second. "That must make you Doyle."

"How did you guess?" he said.

They gave me a plate of smoked salmon sandwiches and a glass of champagne. They made it clear it would be my last meal unless I listened very carefully to what they had to say.

They told me that Mrs G was a very special person. She did not wish to have unwanted attention from anyone, especially members of the press. And that intrusions would be met with "severe repercussions". I munched the sandwiches and drank the champagne, and started to enjoy myself.

Because I'd already worked out who Mrs G really was. I knew she had never been Hodgkin's mistress. I laid it all out for them. I'd sat in court and heard Mrs G swear blind that Hodgkin had told her he'd provided the guns for the Eastbourne bank job. In fact, I'd had that information from a contact close to Hodgkin, who later told me he'd been wrong. It was someone else who'd provided the automatic rifle which gunned down a bank teller.

But Mrs G had stood in the witness box and without a blush to her cheeks had repeated the story including the incorrect details in my newspaper report. By the end of her first morning's evidence, I knew that Mrs G was a plant. Probably a member of the security services briefed to play the part of the secret mistress of Darke's enforcer. She'd been told to provide the evidence Darke's henchman had frightened other witnesses out of giving.

I summed up. "The upshot, Mr Conan and Mr Doyle, is that the security service is attempting to pervert the course of justice, albeit in a good cause. One word from me to the judge and you'll find yourselves standing in the dock."

The two looked at one another like they'd just forgotten their real names. They headed to another room. I heard phone calls being made. I heard loud voices. And then I heard some silence while they decided quietly what to do.

They returned to the room. The result was like that scene in *Alice in Wonderland* when all the characters run a race around the lake to get dry. The Dodo bird declares: "Everybody has won, and all must have prizes." Conan and Doyle's prize was that I would keep quiet while they continued with their deception to jail Darke. My prize was another glass of champagne and a lift home by the guys with the cheap suits.

But it was a dirty deal – and I never wanted to mix with their kind again.

* * *

I drove half a mile down the road and pulled into a lay-by.

I thought long and hard about what I knew. Matey, I now assumed, must be a member of the security service. Probably MI5. Probably not licensed to kill, like James Bond. At least, I hoped not.

I knew that the latest he'd picked me up was when I'd visited Lady White's house. His car had been parked just around the corner from mine. But could he have followed me there from the *Chronicle*? I hadn't spotted a following car, but I couldn't be sure.

There was another thought in my mind. Could he have been watching Lady White's house? After all, if she was the mysterious Astraea – and the boss behind the National Purity Army - she could be of interest to MI5. The army sounded like the kind of shadowy organisation that could have a darker underside.

I was certain of only one thing. I wasn't going to solve the mystery by sitting in a lay-by.

I started the old Wolseley and headed back to the *Chronicle*. I couldn't wait to get my own MGB back.

* * *

It was after midnight by the time I inserted my key in the front door lock of my lodgings and crept into the hall.

I took a moment to savour the silence – and then remembered why. The Widow was still banged up in the cells at Brighton cop shop charged with murder.

I stared for a moment at Holman Hunt's *Light of the World* on the wall. But he just looked like an old bloke who'd got up in the middle of the night and couldn't find the loo.

I had a quick look at the hall table in case anyone had taken a message from Shirley. Nothing. I couldn't understand it. How long did screen tests take? This was the second night I hadn't heard from her.

I was just about to head up the stairs when the door at the end of the passage opened. Clarence Birtwhistle, who occupied what the Widow called the garden room, limped up the hall.

He shot me an embarrassed grin. "Glad I caught you before I nodded off. You've had a visitor."

"Shirley?"

"No. A lady. Well, not exactly a lady. More of a girl. Although that doesn't quite do her justice."

"Who is it?"

"She didn't actually give her name. But she did say you were old friends. So I thought it would be all right if she came in to wait."

"In my rooms?"

"Certainly not in mine. She'd put my budgie off his millet."

I left Clarence gawping and pounded up the stairs.

Crystal Starr was wearing my dressing gown and sitting in my easy chair. She was reading the interview I'd written about her in the *Chronicle*.

She looked up as I walked and said: "What does effervescent mean?"

I said: "Why do you want to know that?"

"Because it says here, 'Crystal Starr has an effervescent personality.'"

"It means bubbly... in your case, vivacious and enthusiastic."

Crystal grinned. "I like that. And you wrote it all about little me."

I said: "Why are you here?"

"Because I wanted to thank you for writing this nice article about me."

"Why does that involve wearing my dressing gown?"

"Well, you wouldn't want to see me all naked - not just yet. It wouldn't be right. I'm not that kind of girl. First, we should get to know each other for a time."

She glanced at a little gold watch on her wrist. "We could give it, say, five minutes?"

"I think you should get out of that chair, go into the bathroom, and put your clothes back on."

Crystal crossed her legs and winked. "That article was

great. They've given me a solo dance spot in the show as a result. Couldn't have done it without you. Don't you want to claim your reward?"

"I'll get my reward at the end of the month."

"Not sure the show will run that long, lover boy."

"I mean my reward is my salary cheque which arrives on the last day on the month."

Crystal shook her head and pouted. "Pity. I thought I'd quite enjoy it this time."

I grabbed the upright chair, turned it round and sat on it backwards. Kept the back of the chair between Crystal and me.

"You mean you make love with reporters who've written about you."

"Only if they write nice things like you. But it's mostly the agents and so-called impresarios who want to get inside my knickers. It's all part of the game."

"Not for me."

"Yeah! I can tell you're different. That's why I'd do it anyway."

This was getting difficult. I never thought I'd welcome a time when the Widow was prowling the landings and knocking on the door of any room where a bedspring creaked.

I said: "Where are your lodgings?"

Crystal shot me a sly grin. "We can't do it at my place. Cheap theatrical digs. The fat slob who runs the place will want some, too."

"I was offering to drop you off when I go out. After you've changed out of my dressing gown, that is."

Crystal's eyes opened with surprise. "You're going out? You only just got in."

"Something's just come up."

"That's what I was hoping, lover boy."

"Well, tonight we're not sleeping together. Get changed."

Crystal pouted again, stuck out her tongue at me, and climbed out of the easy chair. She sloped off to the bathroom.

I frowned. I'd hoped to hit the hay, but inventing an appointment seemed the only way to get rid of Crystal.

Crystal came out of the bathroom dressed in a flimsy blouse and a mini-skirt. She stomped across the room and handed me the dressing gown.

I said: "One day, you'll find the man of your dreams."

"I already have."

"You'll have to introduce me some time."

* * *

I dropped Crystal off outside a cheap boarding house in Madeira Place.

She leaned over and gave me a lingering kiss on the cheek.

"Crazy you gotta work at this time of night," she said.

"A reporter never sleeps," I said.

Crystal winked. "That's what I'd hoped. Another time, maybe."

"Can't wait," I said. Out of politeness, you understand.

Crystal slid out of the MGB. She skipped up the steps of the boarding house, turned as she opened the door, and waved before she went in.

I sat in the car for a minute. I felt tired but strangely keyed-up.

I wished Shirley was with me. I couldn't understand why she wasn't back in Brighton. Even more, why she hadn't got in touch.

I fired the engine, put the car in gear, and pulled out into the traffic.

I planned to drive back to Regency Square but when I

reached the junction of Madeira Place with Marine Parade, I turned left. Away from Regency Square. Towards Ovingdean.

There had been something nagging away at the back of my mind since I'd seen Magda Groff and Knocker at the Woodingdean library. I wondered whether Matey who'd pursued me had really been told to follow one of them.

I parked just around the bend from Lady White's house between two street lamps – in the darkest part of the road. I climbed out of the car and looked around.

The street was deserted. On the other side of the road I saw a pair of green eyes as a cat slunk by. A light breeze rustled the canopy of trees that shaded the footpath.

There were no cars parked on the road – and I took the trouble to look up a couple of side streets. There were no lights on at Lady White's house. No car on the drive either. Perhaps there was no one at home.

I opened the gate and crept into the garden. I hid in the shelter of the hedge Luke had clipped. He'd done a good job.

I made my way up the side of the house wondering why I was doing this. There was no logical explanation. I was firing on instinct.

I worked my way around to the back of the house. Half way along the back wall I could see a pair of French windows. A breeze rustled the hedge and one of the French windows blew back on its hinges.

I edged forward. I looked into the room – a sitting room – but couldn't see anything. I crept inside and bumped into a thin bloke with a big head.

No, it was a standard lamp with one of those fancy shades.

I switched the lamp on. It had a low-watt bulb, but shed enough light for me to see around the room.

One of the cushions from a sofa was on the floor. A magazine rack had been knocked over. A drift of *Country Life* had slid across a Persian carpet. A tumbler of whisky and soda stood undrunk on an occasional table by the sofa.

I moved across the room.

From somewhere, a bluebottle rose and buzzed angrily around. I swatted it away and moved behind the sofa.

A woman was slumped on the floor, her limbs fanned out at crazy angles. Her hair was matted with dark red blood. Lady White was a quarter of a century older than the picture I'd seen of her in a *Chronicle* cutting. But she'd not lost her disapproving look over the years.

The killer had wiped the blood from his weapon on an antimacassar that he'd tossed beside the body.

I felt my body shake with shock. I leant on the back of the sofa for support. My insides felt like they'd been tied with elastic. My mouth had become dry.

I moved around the sofa and reached for the whisky and soda. I downed it in one.

Lady White wouldn't be needing it now.

SIXTEEN

I dragged my gaze away from Lady White's body.

That wasn't difficult to do. Her head had been hit so hard the thick cranium had cracked like an egg. Grey matter had oozed from the split. Blood had pooled on the floor. Two fingernails on her right hand were broken. Lady White had evidently fought her attacker.

But my immediate concern was whether that attacker was still in the house. After all, the French windows were still open.

A sturdy oak door on the far side of the room had been left ajar. I crept over and eased it gently open with my elbow. You won't find me leaving my dabs for the cops to find. (Yes, I had had the presence of mind to wipe my dabs off that whisky glass.)

I stood silent, held my breath, and listened for a sound. The creak of a floorboard. The scrape of a drawer pulled open. The soft pad of a leather shoe sole on a tiled floor.

Somewhere upstairs a tap dripped.

Otherwise, silence.

Unless the attacker was lying doggo, I was as convinced as I could be that they'd scarpered.

I walked swiftly across the room to the French windows. I knelt down and examined the catch. It was in a good condition and hadn't been forced. There was no sign of splintered wood or the kind of deep scratch marks you see with most forced entries. And I've seen plenty.

(Made one or two as well in the cause of the greater good.)

There were three possible explanations for the lack of marks. One was that the French window had been left open. Quite possible. It was a pleasant June evening. Or, two, the window could have been shut but unlocked. No doubt it was locked before bedtime, but Lady White was still dressed so hadn't retired for the night. And, three, the French windows could have been locked and the caller had knocked and been let in. That seemed unlikely as a caller would surely have knocked at the front door.

As I pondered that conundrum another puzzle hit me. Where was Magda Groff? There was no sign of her. Could she have gone out for the evening? Or could she also be lying dead in another room?

I crossed the room again and went through the oak door. I wrapped a handkerchief around my hand so I could open and close doors without leaving fingerprints behind. It was an elegant house designed for gracious living. I looked into a dining room with a ten-seater table and handsome sideboard. There was a modern kitchen, a study, a utility room, and a couple of others, one which seemed to be for sewing and the other for reading.

No sign of Magda.

Upstairs, Lady White had her own large bedroom with a four-poster bed and a bathroom in tasteful pink (if you like that sort of thing). There were three guest bedrooms and another bathroom. A corridor led to the back of the house where there was a final bedroom. It was away from the rest and had a cheap door – no fancy bevelled woodwork - which is always a give-away when you're searching for the servants' rooms in these grand houses.

I opened the door and went in.

Magda – alive or dead – I was pleased to see was not at home.

The room was square and characterless, like the architect had forgotten about it until the last minute and wasn't sure what to make of it. It had wallpaper which featured bunches of grapes hanging on a vine. There was a small window on one side which looked out over the garden at the back of the house.

The room had an iron bedstead with a lumpy mattress covered by a grey Terylene counterpane. There was a bedside table which held a couple of books in a foreign language – probably Hungarian.

On the far side of the room, a television set rested on a chest of drawers. That had my attention. Even I didn't own a telly. This was a flash job, too. A Philips with a twenty-three-inch screen. I walked over and took a closer look. Something was strange. The back panel had been taken off. It was on the floor down by the side of the chest of drawers.

I peered around the back and looked at the wiring and valves inside the TV. I'm no engineer, but it looked to me as though some parts had been removed. Behind the television, a thin cardboard box had slipped between the chest of drawers and the wall. I used my handkerchief-covered hand to pull it out. The box was empty but had once held a television ultrasonic remote-control device. I remembered someone had told me they existed, but hardly anyone had one. But Magda Groff evidently did. Although there was no sign of it. I searched through all the drawers in the chest. Empty.

I peered into the dismantled TV and tried to work out what it all meant. Had Lady White provided the TV for her employee? Or had Magda bought it for herself? If so, she must have been earning a decent salary to afford it. But why should she take it to bits? The obvious answer was that it had gone wrong and a TV engineer had called. Or had the person who'd killed Lady White taken the set apart? If so, why?

I had no answers.

There was a transistor radio to the right of the TV. For no particular reason, I turned it on. The Beach Boys were coming to the end of *Sloop John B.*

The record ended and a familiar voice crooned: "And that was the Beach Boys – and don't forget our great Brighton beach party tomorrow. Now to see us through the small hours, Ol' Blue Eyes is back – Mr Frank Sinatra with *Strangers in the Night.*"

Chunky Dunn was hosting the graveyard shift.

I switched off the transistor.

So Magda Groff listened to Radio *Seabreeze.* No reason why she shouldn't. But was that her only connection with the station? Could it really have been just a coincidence that she'd visited Woodingdean library minutes before Knocker?

I parked that thought at the back of my mind.

One of those cheap utility wardrobes was rammed into the corner of the room. I opened the door. Inside a couple of wire hangers held a faded pair of jeans and a blouse with a rip in one sleeve. A single sandal lay on the floor of the wardrobe. I picked it up and turned it over. A black blob had stuck to the sole. I sniffed. It was tar, the kind it's possible to pick up on Brighton beach if you step in the wrong place.

I slumped down and sat on the edge of the bed. There were only two thoughts in my mind.

Either Magda had left Lady White's house before she was killed.

Or she'd killed her employer and made a run for it.

Neither hypothesis made any sense. Magda had shown no sign of leaving earlier this afternoon when I'd watched her visit the library and the grocers.

Had Magda and Lady White fallen out in a row which went too far? It was possible, but it didn't seem likely. Not by the way Magda had cleared the room of her possessions.

And where was she now?

But I would have plenty of time to ponder that.

I knew what I had to do next. I went downstairs, found the telephone, and called the cops.

* * *

Detective Chief Superintendent Alec Tomkins looked at me like I'd just slaughtered a convent of nuns.

His lips twisted into his trademark snarl. "I could arrest you for breaking and entering," he said.

I said: "For a start, you know that I didn't break anything. And I only entered when I'd suspected a crime had been committed. I thought there might be a need for urgent medical help."

We were in interview room one at Brighton Police Station. It was an hour after I'd called the cops. Ted Wilson had been the first to arrive. Tomkins had turned up ten minutes later obviously wearing his pyjamas under his usual greasy grey suit. He'd left Wilson to investigate the crime scene and ordered me back to the cop shop.

"You have a nasty habit of turning up at places just after a murder has taken place," he said.

"You have a bad habit of not turning up before to stop it happening."

Tomkins cleared his throat and rustled the papers in front of him.

I said: "It's clear the Winterbottom and White murders have the same *modus operandi*. You should release Mrs Gribble immediately."

Tomkins said: "I'm not so sure. We don't know whether she has an accomplice. Perhaps she works as a team. Her accomplice has committed the second murder. Doesn't let Gribble off the hook."

"That's a ridiculous theory, even for you. For a start, the Widow doesn't go in for accomplices. She prefers victims. And, secondly, she'd never kill someone if there was the alternative of making his life a misery. In this case, her life. But she never knew White."

"But she knew Winterbottom."

"She never killed him. If you're going to keep her in jail, you'll need to convince a court that she's committed the White murder from behind bars."

Tomkins leaned back in his chair and stroked his chin. He leaned forward with a smirk.

"You're only standing up for Gribble because your fellow hacks have given you a hard time. They think you want her out of jail so you can keep your cosy billet at her place."

"My fellow hacks will be eating their words – and they won't find it a tasty diet."

"I won't fall for that bluff. They won't want to lose face."

"They'll have to one way or another. Because either you release Mrs Gribble now or I'll advise her to go to court in the morning. Her lawyer will argue that new evidence proves she has no case to answer. Are you prepared to stand up in court and say you do have that evidence?"

Tomkins cleared his throat noisily again.

I said: "There'll be much less press attention if you let Gribble out now. The papers will write about you as the one who put an injustice right. You might even get a favourable mention in the *Chronicle*."

Tomkins knew he was beaten. He stood up and headed for the door.

"Make sure you spell my name right. I'll tell the turnkey to release Gribble now. She'll be in the reception area in ten minutes. Just get her out of here."

He stomped out of the room and slammed the door after him.

* * *

Frank Figgis took a match out of his box of Swan Vestas.

He pinched the end of the match and used it to pick out the breakfast bacon which had stuck between his teeth.

I said: "Do you have to do that?"

"Bacon and eggs for breakfast is a British tradition."

"Picking your teeth with an old match isn't."

"You may be right. In French restaurants they provide them on the table."

"Matches?"

"Toothpicks."

"That's more useful."

"Not if you want to light a fag afterwards."

He foraged a piece of bacon rind from between a couple of molars, turned the match round and struck it on the box.

It gave off a little sulphur flare as he lit his Woodbine.

I said: "We're not in a restaurant, French or British."

"Too right. We're in my office. So what have you got to say for yourself?"

I slapped several folios of copy on his desk.

"When you read that, you'll want my crime reporter byline back on the front page faster than you can say toothpick."

Figgis growled something I couldn't make out and picked up the folios.

The smoke started to rise faster from his fag when he became excited. By the time he'd reached the last folio he was giving a good impression of the Flying Scot trying for the London to Edinburgh record.

He put the folios down and stubbed out his dog-end.

He said: "If this stands up, it'll put us right ahead of the rest of the press pack. They'll look like a bunch of lazy losers who can't get off their fat arses."

I said: "Tomkins will be confirming every word of Mrs Gribble's release at this morning's police press conference. No doubt through gritted teeth. He'll have to admit a search for a new suspect. Probably Magda Groff. I want to be at that conference."

Figgis stood up. Walked over to the window and looked out at the Pavilion Gardens. He didn't want to face me. That meant bad news.

He said: "You can't be at the press conference. Sidney Pinker is still acting crime reporter – His Holiness' orders."

I pointed at the folios on his desk. "Surely this changes everything."

"It will do – at least, I hope it will - when Pope sees it. But until then I'm under orders – pain of the grand order of the boot – to keep you away from murders. I've risked a lot letting you do it on the sly."

"Pope will know I'm back in harness with a clean conscience when he reads that story on the front page." I waved an angry hand at the folios on Figgis' desk.

Figgis spoke to the window pane. Wouldn't turn to look at me. "You won't have a byline. It'll have to be Pinker's"

"Sidney could never write something like this."

"I know that. You know that. I expect even Pinker knows it. But Pope doesn't."

I could feel the flush round my neck. It always came when I was angry. There wasn't anything I could do to control it.

"Well, can't you go upstairs and see Pope now?"

"He's taking a day off. He calls it meeting important contacts. In fact, he's at the golf club schmoozing a bunch of bores we'd never want to write about."

"Which golf course? I'll go and show him what a hole in one really means."

"No, you won't. Because if you do, you'll ruin everything."

"I thought Pope had already done that."

"Only until tomorrow. I promise I'll see him first thing tomorrow and you'll be back on crime. There's much more to the Winterbottom and White murders than meets the eye – and only you can winkle out the full story for us."

I relaxed back in my seat a little. "And, for today, I can continue working on the story as long as I keep quiet about it?"

Figgis returned to his desk and sat down. He nodded.

"Then I'll be on my way."

I stood up and headed for the door.

"There is one other thing," Figgis said.

I turned at the door.

"And what's that?"

Figgis held up an envelope. "Take this. You are still entertainment reporter. Consider this your last assignment."

I leaned over Figgis' desk and snatched the envelope from his hand.

"I hope this isn't what I think it is," I said.

* * *

Of course, it was.

I opened the envelope and took out two tickets for the opening night of *Seaside Follies*, the show at the Palace Pier theatre. It started at half past seven that evening.

There was a note from Figgis in the envelope: "500-word review on my desk by eight-thirty tomorrow morning. And none of your quirky sense of humour."

I screwed up the note and tossed it in my bin.

Damn Figgis!

Damn Pinker!

If I was sitting in the front row of the theatre, there'd be little chance of avoiding Crystal Starr.

Cedric was drifting around the newsroom collecting up first edition copy for the subs. He spotted me and loped on over.

"You're girlfriend Sheila..."

"Shirley."

"...sorry, Shirley, rang while you were in with Figgis."

"Why didn't you call me?"

"She was in a rush. Something about a make-up test. But she asked me to give you a message. She's back in Brighton this evening. Suggested you come round to her flat at half-seven."

Cedric gave me one of his toothy grins and drifted off towards the subs' room.

And damn Shirley!

But, perhaps, not.

If Shirley was back in Brighton, I'd have the perfect defence for fending off unwanted advances from Crystal.

I took a sheet of notepaper and envelope out of my desk drawer. I scribbled a note to Shirley. I asked her to meet me at the theatre. I put one of the tickets in the envelope in case she couldn't get there before the show started."

Cedric reappeared on the other side of the newsroom. I waved him over and handed him the envelope.

"Could you deliver this note?"

Cedric squinted at the address on the envelope. "Hot contact is it?"

"I hope so," I said.

* * *

Figgis had warned me to keep quiet about any crime reporting I did.

So I slipped out of the office and walked round to Marcello's.

I borrowed Marcello's phone and called Ted Wilson.

I said: "It's too early for the amber liquid, but if you shoot round to Marcello's there's a full English breakfast waiting for you with extra fried bread."

Ted said: "I want three sausages as well."

"Done."

I replaced the receiver.

Marcello said: "Don't you have phones in your office?"

"What are you moaning about? You're getting a giant order." I gave it.

Marcello's eyebrows jumped north. "Nobody eats three sausages and two fried breads."

But the plate of steaming food was on the table when Ted walked in.

Ted sat down, stroked his beard a couple of times, and picked up the knife and fork.

I gave him a few minutes to demolish one of the sausages and half of the fried bread.

Then I asked: "Well?"

"Well, what?"

"What's the latest on the White killing?"

"Tomkins put out an all-points bulletin on that Groff woman this morning. He won't catch her. She'll have been on the Newhaven ferry that sailed last night."

I nodded. He was probably right.

I said: "Anything else?"

Ted cut into his tomato. "Not much."

"What do you mean, 'not much'? Even Tomkins would organise some door-to-door enquiries in White's street. Check whether neighbours saw anything."

Ted munched some bacon. "Nope."

"What the hell is going on, Ted?"

"Can't say." He scooped up a forkful of mushrooms.

I grinned. "The case has been taken out of Tomkins' hands."

"That's your view." Ted had egg yolk dribbling down his beard.

"Who's taken the job? Is it the London cops? The Metropolitan police?"

Ted scraped up the last of the baked beans and shoved them in his mouth. He burped so loudly two secretary types at the front of the café giggled.

The lights came on in my mind.

I said: "It's the security services. MI5." Suddenly, I began to make sense of it all. Of why I'd been followed by Matey. He was one of them.

Ted grinned: "I could do with a coffee after that blow-out," he said.

SEVENTEEN

I left Ted to slurp his coffee alone.

I needed time to think. I headed off along Madeira Drive towards Black Rock. The beach was busy as the bucket-and-spade brigade flocked onto the shingle. A couple of coaches drew up and eager holidaymakers scrambled out and darted off towards the Volk's railway. Out at sea, the horizon was blurred by a sea fret. Somewhere beyond the mist Radio *Seabreeze* was spinning a disc for Doreen from Portslade or Wayne from Worthing.

Ted hadn't surprised me when he'd confirmed that MI5 had taken over the White case. Not after my experiences with Matey. I'd tried to look as though I wasn't much interested. Otherwise, Ted would have stung me for a currant bun as well as the coffee.

But he'd grabbed my attention, all right.

MI5 were the kind who lurked in corners or behind bushes. They were supposed to keep an eye on spies who sold secrets to our enemies. But too often they'd turned out to have been looking the wrong way. They'd missed the arch-traitors Guy

Burgess and Donald Maclean, two of the notorious Cambridge Spy Ring of undercover communists at the university.

A kid with an I-spy badge could have spotted them. Burgess was a drunkard who once dropped a secret document when he lurched out of a pub. Maclean's friends said he was a chatterbox who'd astonish listeners by blurting out secrets. But they'd both absconded to Moscow before MI5 had got out of bed.

MI5 had missed Kim Philby, another Russian spy, too. He'd skipped from his job as a journalist in Beirut and later turned up in Moscow.

I'd heard rumours that there were more than three Brits in the Spy Ring. But, so far, no one had fingered anyone else. Besides, I couldn't see that spying would have any connection with Lady White's killing or Winterbottom's murder.

I trudged on past the miniature golf course and the children's playground trying to make sense of it all. Even if White had been on MI5's radar, I couldn't see why Winterbottom should have been in their sights. He was just a common-or-garden fraudster. Winterbottom had fleeced a fair proportion of Brighton's population before someone interrupted his breathing. A simple police case. Although evidently not for Tomkins.

I couldn't make sense of any of it. And it wasn't going to be easy to try. Not while I had to do my crime reporting in the shadows. Not while I was still officially the entertainment reporter.

And that meant being in the audience at the Palace Pier theatre for the opening night of *Seaside Follies*.

* * *

That evening, as instructed by Frank Figgis, I was in an end seat in the front row.

But Shirley wasn't next to me in hers.

I'd kept an eye on messages coming into the newsroom during the day. Nothing from Shirley. On my way to the theatre, I'd called at her flat. Nobody at home.

So you can imagine I wasn't in a jolly mood as the house lights went down and the orchestra struck up the overture. I swivelled my head and looked back up the aisle. Perhaps Shirley had returned to Brighton on a later train. Perhaps she would read my note, see the ticket, and hurry around – at least for the second half of the show.

When you want something so badly, you cling to false hopes. Perhaps that's what I was doing. But I badly wanted Shirley in the seat beside me.

The curtain rose on six chorus girls in a high-kicking can-can routine. Crystal was second from left. What's that advice producers give to chorus girls before they go on? Tits and teeth. Well, Crystal certainly fitted the bill on both counts. She wasn't a bad dancer, either. I'd give her that. Nor were the others. It wasn't exactly the *Folies Bergère* but it was a lively opening to the show.

I wish I could say the same about the rest. The girls were followed by the kind of comedian who relies on witless patter and an endlessly repeated catchphrase – "blimey, what a facer" – rather than genuine humour. I found myself looking for Shirley several times during his act. There were jugglers who spun plates. There was a singer who sang *I Dreamt I Dwelt in Marble Halls*. There was a magician who produced eggs from behind his ears. And there was a ventriloquist with a talking dog.

I glanced at my watch. The show had been running for fifty minutes. The interval must be coming up. The compère, a young comedian who appeared in a TV game show, bounced onto the stage.

He grabbed the microphone. "And now folks, there's a special treat in the show tonight. We're havin' a bit of class. No, doesn't mean there'll be a teacher. It's not that kind of class. I mean something you'd normally turn off if it were on TV. Like the *Epilogue* or a bloke in a dinner suit playing something by Rips-his-corsets-off. Or should that be Rimsky-Korsakov. Yeah! It's big break time. And I don't mean for wind, that fat bloke at the back. *Phew!* We've got the lovely Crystal Starr you first saw in the girls' chorus at the beginning. She was second from the left. Lovely. Both of them. She'll be doing a dance she's choreographed herself – and that can't be bad because I can't hardly say choreo-gruff... Dancing the *Prelude to the Afternoon of a Faun* by Du Bussy... No, the conductor is signalling to me that it's not two words. At least I think that's what his hand-signal means. It's Debussy. French bloke. But I know you won't hold that against him. Take it away, *maestro*."

The music started cool and calm. The lights went down so that one spotlight cast a dappled light at the centre of the stage. As though it were a glade in the middle of a dense forest. The stage stayed empty for the first few bars as the flute and clarinet created the atmosphere.

Then Crystal appeared.

I heard the quiet gasp as she stepped gracefully into the spotlight. She was dressed in a skin-hugging yellow-tan costume. Some points were lighter and some darker so that she appeared almost as a ghost.

She moved her limbs like they each had a life of their own. It was a slow dance in line with the sensual music. Not what the audience were expecting. But as the dance continued, the rustle of toffee papers and the coughs of smokers grew silent. A kind of intensity settled over the auditorium. As though nobody wanted to miss a single note of the music or a movement of Crystal's body.

For almost ten minutes we stared in rapt attention. And then the music – soft chords – faded slowly as Crystal sank to the floor. For a few seconds, a silence hung over the audience. It was almost as though the vibrations of the last chords were suspended in the air.

And then the cheering and applause exploded. The audience rose to their feet. Me, too. Who would have thought Crystal had something so perfect in her? Especially anyone watching her dance the can-can at the start of the show.

I glanced around again to the aisle. No Shirley. I wished she could have seen this.

The applause subsided and the auditorium resounded with little thumps as everyone folded down their seats. When everyone had settled, Crystal rose from the floor and walked to the front of the stage.

A microphone appeared from the footlights and rose up to meet her.

Crystal stepped up to it and gave a becoming bow.

Behind me, I heard the doors at the back of the auditorium burst open and swing shut.

I glanced around. Shirley was standing at the end of the aisle. I waved my programme so she could see me. Even though the house lights were dimmed, I saw a radiant smile appear on her face.

She started her way down the aisle.

On stage, Crystal gripped the microphone. "This was my first ever solo dance on a public stage," she said. A ripple of applause ran through the audience. "I want to dedicate it to my boyfriend who is in the audience tonight."

Heads swivelled to see who the lucky guy was.

Crystal pointed. "He's sitting in the front row. And there he is, my wonderful boyfriend, Colin Crampton."

A spotlight from Hell, swung through the auditorium and settled on me.

I glanced back. Shirley was half way down the aisle. She'd stopped. She had the tense look of a tiger who's about to attack.

Around me I could sense people applauding. Someone patted me on the back.

My head was spinning, but Crystal was speaking. "Only last night, Colin told me he couldn't wait to see me again."

An awful image bruised my mind like a blood-stained frame from a slasher flick.

I'd told Crystal: "*A reporter never sleeps.*"

She'd winked and said: "*That's what I'd hoped. Another time, maybe.*"

And I'd foolishly replied: "*Can't wait.*" Out of politeness.

But Crystal had taken it as the start of a beautiful friendship.

From the stage, Crystal waved at me.

More cheers broke out.

I turned round to face Shirley. The spotlight dazzled me. I moved out into the aisle and shaded my eyes.

Shirley's fists were planted firmly on her hips. Her lips were compressed and her eyes were on fire. I half expected gouts of flame to shoot down her nose.

She screamed: "You... you... you... Bluebeard."

She turned and pushed through the fire exit onto the pier.

The audience gasped. Some of them laughed. They thought it was part of a surprise act.

I ran up the aisle.

Behind me, I heard Crystal gulp back a sob and then shout: "But I still haven't told you I love you."

The hubbub of an audience who didn't know what to make of it all buzzed behind me as I raced towards the exit.

On stage Crystal shrieked: "*Yeeeeeooooooow!*"

I charged through the exit doors on to the pier.

A salty breeze hit me in the face. Clouded my eyes for an instant. I stopped and rubbed them. Looked about.

Shirley was striding down the pier towards the sea end.

I started after her and shouted: "Shirley, I can explain."

She glanced over her shoulder: "Keep away from me, you gutter rat."

I picked up my pace, but Shirley was twenty yards ahead and striding like she needed to outrun a volcanic eruption.

She vanished around the edge of the theatre. Into the open area at the end of the pier where they keep the fairground rides.

I hurried after her.

The fairground was closed. Deserted. Shirley strode past the bumper cars. Past the helter-skelter. Past the waltzer.

I shouted after her: "Where are you going?"

She turned round, faced me and yelled: "To throw myself in the sea. After I've drowned you."

I tried a new tack. "Did you get the part?"

"What part? Oh, the Bond film. Yeah! They cast me as the Australian Girl. It was gonna be so perfect. Especially when I read in your letter that you were thrilled that I was gonna be in a film. And all the time you were a double-dealing, two-timing snake."

"I didn't know what Crystal was going to say," I shouted.

"Yeah! I bet you didn't."

Shirley turned and stalked towards the railings at the end of the pier

I went to follow her but was distracted by a movement from behind the ghost train.

Someone was coming up the steps that led down to the landing stage.

No, it was two people.

They stepped round the edge of ghost train.

Blaster and Knocker from the *Seabreeze*.

Blaster was carrying a heavy holdall. A big brown leather job which strained at its handles. Knocker had a baseball bat. And he wasn't planning a home run.

The pair gawped at me with open mouths.

Blaster said: "What're you doing here? There ain't supposed to be no one here now."

Knocker said: "Yeah! We didn't invite no guests."

Shirley heard the question and swivelled round.

Blaster saw her and grinned. "I get it. You're after some private nookie. Moonlight on the sea, bit of romantic chat, and before you know it, her knickers are round her ankles."

"Shut your filthy mouth, you ape," Shirley screamed.

"Yeah! Shut your cakehole," Knocker said. "We're here to do a job."

"And what job might that be?" I asked.

Blaster said: "None of your business."

"It's a drugs hand-over," I said. "That's the secret of the *Seabreeze*."

"You know too much," Blaster said. "That's dangerous."

"Let's croak him and float him out to sea," Knocker said. "Night like tonight, he'll have sunk before morning comes."

Blaster grinned. "If we give him the old heave-ho, we could deliver the goods and have the girl afterwards. Bit of a bonus."

Shirley marched closer. "Don't you try your luck with me." She thumbed dismissively towards me. "You can do what you like with him."

I said: "Don't I get a say in my fate?"

"Shut your trap," Knocker said.

Shirley sidled up to Blaster. "You want me to be your floosy?" she said.

Blaster's tongue lolled out of the side of his mouth.

"What do you want out of it?" he asked.

"This," she said.

In one swift movement, Shirley kicked him on the ankle, then kneed him in the groin.

He dropped the bag, howled in agony, and grabbed his nether regions.

Shirley seized the bag and made a run for it.

Knocker took off after her. I raised a leg and tripped him up. He hit the deck like a ton of wet seaweed. But his hand still gripped the baseball bat.

Shirley was heading for the helter-skelter. I couldn't make out why. There was no escape up there.

She reached the bottom step and clambered up. Round and round as she climbed higher.

Knocker scrambled to his feet. Blaster was down on his knees with his face twisted in pain.

Shirley reached the top of the helter-skelter. She came out on the platform like the queen of the world.

Knocker stepped back to look up.

Shirley yelled: "Watch this, you scumbags."

She whirled the holdall round and round her head. When it was travelling fast enough, she let go. The holdall sailed through a perfect arc. It hit the sea ten yards from the pier.

Knocker and I heard the splash and raced to the rails.

The bag bobbed uneasily for a moment in the swell. And then a wave bigger than the rest overwhelmed it. Slowly, it filled with water and slipped beneath the briny.

"You'll pay for this," Knocker said.

He raised the baseball bat. I ducked but I was too late. A flash of multi-coloured lights exploded in my head.

And then everything went black.

* * *

Somebody was holding my left hand.

My fingers had been balled into a fist. But this person had uncurled them.

I opened my eyes. My vision blurred like a smudged water-colour. A group of people stood around me. They muttered to one another and shook their heads.

I moved my neck. My bones creaked like a rusty hinge.

Crystal had knelt down beside me. She saw my eyes open. "You're alive. Glory be! I thought you were going to die. And you've only been my boyfriend for one day."

"Not even that."

"That's not what you said in the car last night. You said you couldn't wait to see me again. Well, here I am, lover boy. All glammed up and ready to go."

My head pounded like a busted piston.

A beefy bloke with a toothbrush moustache leaned over and said: "You dirty git. I bet you gave her one and now you're trying to talk your way out of it."

I said: "Why don't you mind your own business?"

"Well, if that's your attitude I'll leave you to it."

I heaved myself up so I could rest my body against the back wall of the theatre.

A woman with brown hair held back by tortoiseshell combs said: "I think they're going to make up. That's nice. It reminds me of last week's story in *Woman's Realm*."

The woman next to her said: "If we don't hurry back, we'll miss the second half. It opens with that young singing and dancing bloke who wears them tight trousers. When he dances, it looks like he brought his budgie with him."

A murmur ran around the crowd. Evidently, I wasn't dead. So there was nothing to see.

I said to Crystal: "You've got it all wrong about us."

She snivelled, searched for a hankie, but couldn't find one. I gave her mine.

She blew her nose. "I'm gonna keep this hankie and embroider your initials on it. It will be a lifelong reminder of the love that could not be."

My mind had started to clear. Vision had come into focus. And I realised something was wrong.

"Where's Shirley?" I asked.

"You mean that other girl. She was at the top of the helter-skelter when I ran round the corner."

"What happened to her?"

"I could see immediately she wasn't the kind of girl for you. I mean, what kind of girl goes up a helter-skelter when there are two men after her?"

"Did the men go up the helter-skelter?"

"I'm not sure. As soon as I saw you, I rushed over and cradled your head in my arms."

"Very thoughtful. But what happened to Shirley?"

"I kissed you tenderly on the forehead. I wanted to before you died. But you didn't and then I heard Shirley screaming. I nearly told her to be quiet as you were sleeping."

I felt my stomach churn and bile rise in my throat.

"But where did she go?" I croaked.

"The last I saw of her, the two men had grabbed one arm each and were dragging her down the steps to the landing stage. I could hear her yelling all the way down. Then the outboard motors kicked in and I didn't hear her anymore."

I pushed against the wall of the theatre and levered myself to my feet.

"Where are the police?" I asked.

"We don't need police, lover boy. Besides the manager doesn't like the rozzers at the theatre. It puts the punters off."

I said: "Aren't you in the second half of the show?"

Crystal's hand flew to her mouth. "Oh, my golly. I have to dance as Pierrette in the opening number. I must fly. Don't go away, precious one. I'll be back as soon as I've tripped the light fantastic."

Crystal raced away and hustled through the stage door.

I rubbed my head. A lump only about the size of a basketball had risen behind my left ear. A dull ache had started behind my eyes. And I felt like I could curl into a ball and sleep for a month.

I wasn't in great shape for what I had to do next.

* * *

Alec Tomkins' lips parted in a feral grin I knew always meant bad news.

He said: "Mrs Tomkins doesn't like me being called out at night. Especially when we've gone to bed. I have to climb over her to get out, on account of my side is up against a wall."

"Puts you between a rock and a hard place," I said.

Tomkins sniffed because he couldn't think what to say to that. Instead, he said: "However, tonight I shall make an exception to my distaste at late-night calls."

"What, you mean you'll act like a police officer faced with a serious crime?"

"Less of your cheek."

We were in interview room one at Brighton Police station. The clock on the wall was only twenty minutes shy of midnight. Tomkins had a steaming mug of coffee in front of him. I had a glass of water and two aspirin. I took the tablets and swallowed some of the water. Felt a bit sick.

I said: "You've heard what happened on Palace Pier tonight?"

"Yes, you were the star of the show."

"Shirley and I stumbled on a drug handover. It's obviously being run from the *Seabreeze*. Two plug-uglies from the ship were on the job. They never got to hand the drugs to their buyer because Shirley snatched them and threw them out to sea."

"I'd call that destroying the evidence."

"I'd call it preventing a crime. And protecting young people from the evils of hard drugs. Besides, the plug-uglies grabbed Shirley. I think they've got her as a prisoner on the *Seabreeze*."

"That's as maybe. I don't see what you expect me to do about this. That *Seabreeze* is moored outside the three-mile limit from our shores. The ship's outside the territorial limit. She's in international waters. My job is policing Brighton, not the Spanish Main."

"It's not the Spanish Main and no law-abiding citizen will object if you board the ship and seize the drug-runners. You'll be the hero of the town. Mrs Tomkins might even agree to take the side by the wall."

Tomkins reached into his inside pocket. Brought out a small leather folder. Flipped it open and showed me his warrant card.

"See that card," he said. "Outside the boundaries of Brighton, it doesn't carry that much weight."

"It must do when kidnapping is the crime."

"We don't even know that Miss Goldsmith was kidnapped. From what I understand, you were unconscious when she disappeared."

"Crystal told me Shirley was grabbed by the two drug runners."

"That's not what she told me. Crystal Starr said Miss Goldsmith was walking out on you. Sensible girl, if you ask me. She's probably run home to her mother."

"Her mother lives in Adelaide. And Shirley's not the running home type. Her life may be in danger on the *Seabreeze*. If you can't take action, get in touch with someone who can."

Tomkins slurped at his coffee.

"Not easy. Lot of telephone calls. People – important people – don't like being dragged from their beds in the middle of the night. Might see what I can do in the morning."

"The morning could be too late."

"Anyway, nothing we can do now. We don't have a boat to reach the *Seabreeze*. We're not the Royal Navy, you know."

I slumped back in my chair. I felt a cold fury building inside me. I wanted to leap up and plant a punch on Tomkins' oversized nose.

This was all my fault. I should never have argued with Shirley about her film job in Prinny's Pleasure. If I hadn't, none of this would have happened.

And now she was a prisoner out at sea.

Tomkins looked at his watch. Buttoned his jacket. Stood up and crossed the room.

"Nothing more to do at the moment. If I go home now, I can get a few hours kip before the morning."

I followed Tomkins out of the room.

He glanced at me. "Can't do anything without a boat."

On that point, he was right. And I didn't have a boat either.

EIGHTEEN

I stepped into the street outside the cop shop cold with fury.

Yes, cold. Forget that talk about people getting hot under the collar. Real anger – I call it fury – doesn't generate heat. Because fury lurks in a dark and cold part of our soul. It's a place which is forever icy because it's surrounded by fear.

And as I stood in the street and stared, like I was transfixed by the cop shop's blue light, I felt real fear. Not just that I would lose Shirley for ever.

My fear was that Shirley would lose her life.

Like Winterbottom.

Like Lady White.

Two dead already because they'd got in the way. In the way of what I didn't yet know. But it must be something big. Because, as Winterbottom and White proved, anyone was dispensable.

Well, Shirley wasn't dispensable. Not to me. Not to her mum in Adelaide.

And not, apparently, to Cubby Broccoli who wanted her in

his next James Bond film. I was determined she would be there.

But she was a prisoner on the *Seabreeze*. Tomkins had no plans to do anything about that for hours. Perhaps for ever. And even if he did, it could be too late. The *Seabreeze* could have hauled up its anchor and sailed into the night.

I needed a boat. I didn't have a boat.

But I knew someone who had. And who wouldn't be needing it tonight. Or ever again.

Claude Winterbottom.

He'd kept his motor cruiser moored in Shoreham harbour. Herbie Stubbs, the porter at Embassy Court, had told me. Stubbs even said he'd seen a picture of the craft in Winterbottom's flat.

And Perry Turner had told me Winterbottom had sailed the craft out to the *Seabreeze*. So why shouldn't I?

I could immediately think of three reasons why not. One, my knowledge of seamanship was limited to a session on the pedalloes at Brighton beach when I was a kid. Two, the harbour was four miles long and I had no idea where Winterbottom would have moored his boat. Three, a motor cruiser needed a key to start it. That key was almost certainly somewhere in Winterbottom's apartment – vacant, locked and bolted.

Obviously, this was a plan that couldn't fail. Because it couldn't start.

I crossed the road to the telephone box opposite the police station and pushed inside.

I took out my notebook and turned to the pages at the back where I kept phone numbers. I shoved four pence in the slot and dialled a number.

The phone was answered: "This is a recorded message. Susan Wheatcroft is in bed making mad passionate love to

Cary Grant. Sean Connery and Gregory Peck are already waiting in the sitting room for their turn. So unless you're delivering another bottle of gin, please call back in the morning."

I pressed the call box's button A, waited for the pennies to drop, then said: "You know me, Susan, the shameless queue jumper."

Susan slurred: "Colin? Hey, Cary, stop that. There's a real man on the line."

I said: "You haven't really got him there?"

"A girl can dream. But with you on the line I don't have to. Say, why don't we talk dirty until your money runs out? Then you can come round. But remember to bring more gin."

"Susan, I need your help. It's about Shirley."

"She can come, too. I don't mind sharing."

"Susan," I said firmly. "Shirley's life is in danger."

There was a moment's silence at the end of the line. Then Susan didn't sound tipsy anymore. "You're serious, aren't you?"

"Deadly. But you can help."

"Anything. What is it?"

* * *

Ten minutes later, I was in the telephone box outside Embassy Court on the seafront.

Before scrambling into the box, I'd sauntered past the front entrance and looked into the stylish art deco foyer. The night porter was sitting behind the desk. Not stylish at all. Unless you count picking your nose as an art form.

I'd laid a plan with Susan. She'd divert the night porter away from his desk long enough for me to sneak into his lodge and snatch the spare key to Winterbottom's flat. Then I'd hoof it up to the flat, search it for the key to his motor cruiser, and make my getaway. If Susan played a blinder, I might even have time to return Winterbottom's key to the porter's lodge before he came back.

I lifted the receiver and dialled Susan.

This time, she came on the line all business-like.

I said: "I'm in place. Give me two minutes then make the call."

I replaced the receiver and left the phone box.

There was a post box just to the right of Embassy Court's entrance. One of those sturdy ones the Victorians installed. All cast iron and red paint.

It was big enough for me to hide behind and watch the show.

A couple of minutes passed. The porter reached down to a drawer in his desk and pulled out a paper bag. He reached into the bag and brought out a doorstep of a sandwich.

The phone rang. He looked at the phone. Looked at his sandwich. Thought about taking a bite before answering the phone. Shook his head in exasperation and put his sandwich down. Lifted the receiver.

I could imagine what Susan was saying. "Oh dear, I didn't know who to ring. And then I thought of that brave man who works nights in Embassy Court. I'm Estelle Throstle. You must have seen me. I live in the flats immediately opposite you. I'm looking out of my window and there's a young girl in the street and this rough looking tramp has stopped her. He keeps pointing at her handbag. I think he wants to steal her purse. If only a brave man like you could intervene, I'm sure the tramp would leave her alone. Oh dear, I think she's crying."

The porter's body had stiffened. He said something. Probably, "Call the police".

Susan would have that covered. "Oh, I dialled 999 once.

But they told me it was only for emergencies. And this won't be an emergency until the tramp has taken the girl's purse. You could stop it now. Please say you will."

The porter stood up. Looked uncertainly towards the door. Shrugged his shoulders. Said something into the receiver.

I could imagine Susan saying: "Oh, the girl has run round the corner into Norfolk Street. Please hurry. You can stop something very terrible."

The porter said something else and replaced the receiver. Like a soldier going into battle he strode towards the doors and went outside.

I waited for him to clear the building, then scooted through the door. The lodge was behind the desk. I'd never been in there, but these porters' lodges were all the same. They had a board with a row of numbered hooks. The spare key for each apartment hung on a hook ready for the time when the duff occupier had locked themselves out.

I raced into the room and there it was – the board with the keys. Which was Winterbottom's apartment? Number 27. I ran my gaze along the line of keys.

An empty space.

The hook was there, but the key wasn't.

I took a deep breath. Felt my heart skip a beat or two.

This wasn't how it was supposed to work out. The girl and tramp ploy wouldn't keep the porter out of the way for more than five minutes. Ten at the most. Any less, and it wasn't going to give me enough time to search for a missing key.

What if the police had confiscated all the keys?

No! That didn't make sense. Winterbottom was a victim not a criminal. At least, not this time. Besides, the porters would need a key in case of fire.

If there was a key, why wasn't it on the hook, like the

others? Answer: because the owner was dead. He'd never need it again. So perhaps it had been put in a safe place.

Under lock and key.

It had to be somewhere nearby. It would be in the porter's desk.

I raced out of the lodge into the foyer.

The porter sat at a desk which had a pedestal with three drawers on the right-hand side

I yanked open the top drawer. Old crisp packets and stale sandwich crumbs.

Middle drawer. Street maps of Brighton and a telephone directory.

Bottom drawer. A cardboard box. Took it out and pulled off the lid. It was full of keys. Some had tags, some didn't. I rummaged among them. Room 27 with its tag was near the top. I grabbed it. Closed the box's lid, shoved it in the drawer, slammed the drawer, and raced for the stairs.

I poked my head cautiously around the stairwell which led on to the second-floor landing.

Empty.

I crept on to the landing and moved swiftly to number 27. Put my ear to the door and listened. A precaution, and not a silly one. More than one person has watched with dismay as their plans fell apart because they weren't careful enough.

I slipped the key into the lock, opened the door and stepped into the apartment. I closed the door silently behind me.

There was just enough light from the windows of the sitting room for me to see dimly around the room. I crossed to the windows and drew the curtains, then turned on the lights.

I stood there looking round the place like I was an estate agent wondering whether I should describe it as "cosy" (translation: pokey) or "full of character" (translation: riddled with woodworm).

The question was: where would Winterbottom have kept the key to his boat? I wandered around the place in a vague way, like I'd paid half a crown to look round the stately home of a minor duke. I had some time to search, but not an unlimited time. Even if the porter returned, I could slip down the back stairs. But I was worried about the lights. The curtains weren't thick enough to blank them out entirely. If someone outside realised the lights were on in Winterbottom's apartment, they would surely raise the alarm.

I moved from the sitting room along the corridor to what looked like an office. There was a desk and chair and a handsome cabinet. It had that deep patina which comes from age and a lot of money. It also had a lot of fancy drawers with wooden knobs, worn with age. Winterbottom had arranged a selection of framed photographs of his motor cruiser on the top of the cabinet.

I tried some of the drawers. I found the keys, together with a manual for the boat, in the third from the top. I flipped through the manual and checked the key and ignition information. I studied the picture of the key in the manual with the key I held in my hand. They looked the same, but then I'm no locksmith.

I closed the drawer, switched off the light, and hurried out of the room.

Downstairs, the porter hadn't returned so I slipped the door key into the box in the bottom drawer of the porter's desk.

I was in the phone box opposite Embassy Court, thanking Susan and asking for a further favour, when the porter reappeared.

Goodness knows what he'd discovered because he strode by like a conquering hero.

* * *

Twenty minutes later, I pulled the MGB into the kerb next to a telephone box in Shoreham.

I called Susan. The final favour I'd asked – for tonight at least - was to call the duty harbourmaster. The work of ports is governed by the tides, and you'll always find someone near a telephone. I'd asked Susan to find out where Winterbottom's motor cruiser was moored in the harbour.

Susan said: "Finally tracked down the deputy assistant harbourmaster. Or it may have been the assistant deputy. Anyway, he was quite a salty sailor type. Offered to come round and furl my sails any time."

I grinned, but I didn't have time for this. "Susan, did he tell you where Winterbottom's cruiser was moored?"

"Place called Surry Boatyard. Gee, what a girl has to promise to get a guy to part with his secrets."

"I owe you a big one," I said.

Susan laughed. "Now that sounds like my kind of promise."

I replaced the receiver. Once that kind of conversation starts, it invariably leads to trouble.

Surry Boatyard was less than half a mile from where I'd parked. I drew the MGB alongside an old warehouse.

The wharf was quiet – and unlit. But a gibbous moon cast a wan light over the scene.

In this part of the harbour floating pontoons snaked out into the water. The boats – small yachts and motor cruisers – were moored alongside the pontoons.

I sat in the MGB for a moment and watched the pontoons rise and fall as the water moved under them. I thought about the foolish row I'd had with Shirley. The time when she'd stormed out of Prinny's Pleasure. I'd been an idiot then to try and stand in the way of her ambition.

Perhaps I was being foolish now thinking that I could rescue her from a pirate radio ship run by drug dealers. But there were no other options. And, I thought, I did have a couple of things going for me. Turner and his crew would never think a lone sailor would try to snatch Shirley from them. And, at night time, I might just catch them off-guard.

I climbed out of the MGB and headed to the spot where Susan had told me Winterbottom's motor cruiser was moored.

I found it tied up at the end of one of the pontoons. I recognised it immediately from the photos in Winterbottom's apartment. It turned out to be a more modest craft than I'd expected. It would be open to the skies, but it had a tight tarpaulin arrangement that fitted over the open part of the boat.

I climbed onto the prow – I might as well get into character if I were becoming a seaman – and began to loosen the tarp from the hooks that kept it secure. By the time, I'd taken the tarp off and stowed it in a locker at the aft, the boat's interior looked a bit like that of a saloon car. There were two seats at the front, one with a steering wheel and two at the back.

The boat bobbed up and down rather becomingly on the swell of the water. Not enough to have me doing the old heave-ho over the side, but enough to remind me this wasn't a saloon car. And I wasn't on *terra firma*.

I took a quick look around the boat. Behind the wheel – larger by a factor of two than the one in my MGB – there was a dashboard. I could make out some dials, one for fuel and another probably for engine revs. A third could have been for speed – but I was a bit hazy about all that knots per hour stuff. And I'd been right. I needed the key. I reached into my pocket, inserted the key, and turned it. An array of lights appeared on the dashboard. Not enough to illuminate Piccadilly Circus. Plenty to reassure me I'd be able to navigate on the open seas. There was a compass behind a glass panel next to the captain's seat. I checked that it pointed to the north. It did. I took that as an omen that I was good to set sail.

Stout ropes held the boat to the pontoon fore and aft. I cast them off like I was Captain Smollett setting the *Hispaniola* on course for *Treasure Island*. Then I fired the engine. The roar echoed around the harbour. A squadron of snoozing seagulls took off, and squawked angrily in the air.

I eased the boat forward. The engine purred as the craft rocked gently from side to side. The moon cast a finger of light across the water and I followed it until I reached the harbour entrance. Then I turned away from the moonbeam, set a south-east course and headed into the open seas.

* * *

An hour later, I looked around me and wondered where the *Seabreeze* was.

I must still be in the English Channel. I couldn't have strayed into the North Sea... yet. The one conclusion was that there was a lot of sea and finding a ship in it was not easy.

What seemed to make it more difficult was the fact I was low down in the motor cruiser so I couldn't see far. I'd tried standing up, but that only put me about six feet above the water. And it made the boat rock dangerously.

I'd dredged up some old memory from maths lessons at school. You can work out how far the horizon is away by measuring how far you are above the water, calculating the square root of the figure, and then multiplying it by 1.17. A bit of quick mental arithmetic put the square root of six at about

2.5 and that multiplied by 1.17 gave me a figure of roughly three. So unless I could get within three miles of the *Seabreeze*, I wouldn't be able to see it. In practice, I probably needed to be nearer as it was night.

And the moon had just retreated behind a cloud.

If, in the morning, I ended up being rescued by the lifeboat, this wouldn't look good.

I decided my problem had been setting a south-east course. I didn't know whether that was accurate enough to intercept the *Seabreeze* after I'd travelled about eight miles from the harbour.

But I did know that the *Seabreeze* was just over three miles due south of Brighton's Palace Pier. So if I could find the pier, I could chart a new course.

I turned the boat around and headed towards the shore.

* * *

Another hour later, the running lights of the *Seabreeze* came into view.

In the last two hundred yards, as I approached, I throttled the engine right back and allowed the boat to drift in towards the *Seabreeze's* stern. The Jacob's ladder hung down from the deck.

I roped the cruiser securely to the ladder and looked up at the *Seabreeze's* rust-grey stern.

I stepped onto the ladder and swarmed up it in true pirate style.

NINETEEN

I clambered silently over the taffrail around the afterdeck of the *Seabreeze*.

My leather shoes let out a little *phut* as I landed on the deck. It reminded me I was still dressed for a day in the newsroom.

I was wearing a blue jacket over one of those striped shirts which had come into fashion. Shirley had bought it for me at a boutique in The Lanes. I had a pair of grey trousers held up by a sturdy brown leather belt.

A true pirate would be sporting a doublet, knee breeches, and a tricorn hat. And let's not forget the parrot on the shoulder.

But I didn't have time to worry about sartorial matters, I sternly reminded myself. I was here to find Shirley and spirit her back to shore.

The deck was lit by a series of dim bulbs behind bulkhead lamps. They were encrusted with salt spray. The deck was slippery with oil spills. Despite a freshening breeze, there was the kind of smell you get when the lavvy is blocked. Evidently, they didn't have anyone to do the cleaning around here.

I stood on the deck and sharpened my ears. The old vessel rocked gently on the sea's swell. The joints in the ship's ancient metal plating creaked as it rose and fell.

But the ship was asleep. Looked as though the radio station didn't broadcast every night.

I glanced at my watch. It was ten past three. That would give me around three hours before the ship's crew came alive again and readied themselves for another day's pop picking. But, in fact, I had much less time. Today, mid-summer's day, would be the longest day of the year. With the shortest night.

To be safe, I needed to find Shirley, get her into Winterbottom's cruiser and be clear of the *Seabreeze* before the sun lit up the eastern horizon. That would happen in little more than half an hour's time.

I couldn't search the whole ship in that time. But I was certain I wouldn't have to.

Shirley would have been spitting with anger when she'd been kidnapped. She'd have had the voyage out to the *Seabreeze* to work out what would likely happen to her. Despite our row, she'd know I'd come after her. Just as I'd come after her on Palace Pier.

She'd leave clues. Not easy. But, perhaps, not too difficult when you're dealing with a pair of lamebrains like Blaster and Knocker. I tried to visualise what would have happened when the pair brought Shirley aboard.

They'd have arrived in the *Seabreeze's* cruiser. One of them would have climbed up the Jacob ladder first. They'd need someone on deck to keep control of Shirley when she came up. The other one would come up the ladder after Shirley.

So there would be thirty seconds when Shirley was alone with either Blaster or Knocker. It would be easier to distract one rather than two. That's when Shirley would have left her clue.

It had to be near where the ladder hung from the taffrail.

I crouched down and looked around the deck. There was a locker – not Davy Jones' I assumed – just to the left of the ladder. It had once been painted grey but was now stained by green sea lichen. I knelt down and took a closer look. The thing had a sloping lid that was secured with a rusty padlock.

Tied around the padlock in a neat bow was a thread of cotton. It looked as though it might have been torn from the edge of a lady's handkerchief. There was some embroidery on one end of it made of brown threads. I'd seen something like it before. On one of Shirley's hankies. I remembered the full embroidery was a little koala bear.

The thread was a clue.

And I knew what it meant.

When she'd walked out on me from Prinny's Pleasure, it was after we'd had a row. She'd accused me of being like a bull, charging forward irrespective of her views. She'd compared me to the Minotaur – half man, half bull – that Theseus slew in the labyrinth. And, in the heat of the moment, I'd told her how Ariadne had used a ball of thread to guide her lover Theseus back to her. She'd know this had a special memory for me. And now the thread was her signal.

Shirley was my Ariadne. But instead of leading me out, she was guiding me in – to the very place where she was being held prisoner.

But where was the next piece of the thread?

I spent a frustrating five minutes in a hunt back and forth across the deck.

No second thread. This was getting me nowhere.

I needed to think.

Shirl would've had limited opportunities to lay her thread

clues. It would have to be at times when both Blaster and Knocker were diverted.

I edged along the deck.

Of course! The doors. Bulkhead doors on ships are much harder to open. They're heavy. They have complex handles and locks. Their hinges are stiff.

That's when Blaster and Knocker would have their eyes off Shirley.

I found the next piece of thread in a crevice next to a bulkhead leading into the passage with the different coloured doors. The thread was wrapped around a loose screw.

I heaved open the bulkhead as quietly as its screeching hinges allowed me and edged inside. I was in the passage Chunky Dunn had originally showed me. It was lit by lights in the ceiling. The place smelt of disinfectant.

I stared along the passage. Couldn't see any more threads.

I crept forward like I was a kid playing grandmother's footsteps. Past the red door. Past the green door. Past the yellow door

I edged around the dog-leg. Towards the black door Dunn wouldn't talk about.

There was another thread looped around the nozzle of a fire extinguisher mounted to the wall.

In my mind, I cheered.

I'm getting closer, Shirl. In minutes you're going to be free.

The black door was at the end of the passage. Beyond it, the passage opened on to the deck. Opposite the black door, an old lifejacket hung from a screw fixed to the wall.

I bent down and examined the door. There was a quarter inch gap under it. A thin thread had been pushed through the gap from behind the door.

I raised my hand to knock lightly on the door.

Clink!

The sound of metal on metal came from the deck.

Like two pieces of metal had knocked together.

I withdrew my hand and my body went rigid.

Someone was moving on the deck. Blaster, possibly. Or Knocker, maybe. Perhaps Turner himself.

My only line of retreat was back down the corridor. But that would mean defeat. If someone came to stand sentry-go outside the door, there'd be no chance of rescuing Shirley.

I looked around for a weapon. But there's never a blunderbuss available when you need one.

I grabbed the lifejacket off the wall and pressed myself into a narrow space beside the door. Whoever was approaching knew how to make a silent approach.

I could almost see them stalking like a cat.

A shadow moved as the figure passed in front of a bulkhead light on the deck.

Two more steps and...

I lunged forward with the lifejacket.

I threw it over the figure's head.

But the figure fought back. Elbowed me in the stomach. Stamped on my foot. Punched me on the chin.

I yelled in pain.

My attacker screamed.

My attacker was a woman. Not Zena Lightheart surely.

A muffled voice under the lifejacket cried: "Colin, you're a real drongo. I already escaped."

Shirley.

She pushed me again and I fell. She tumbled on top of me.

Heavy footsteps pounded in from the deck. Blaster and Knocker loomed over us like a pair of storm clouds.

From the other direction, more measured steps approached.

Shirl and I were tangled up with the lifejacket on the floor.

233

Perry Turner walked up and looked down at us.

"Well, well," he said. "'Journey's end in lovers' meeting.' But I'm afraid that lifejacket won't save you."

* * *

Shirley glared at me and said: "You're a real wallaby's arse, Colin."

I said: "That's anatomically inaccurate and not a nice thing to say to somebody who's come to rescue you."

"Yeah! I'm just as free as the wind." Shirl gestured at the four walls. "And after I thought up that Ariadne's thread trick."

"That was the idea of a genius," I said.

"Yeah! Pity my Theseus wasn't one."

We were locked in a tiny cabin. The one behind the black door. Turner had ordered Blaster and Knocker to hustle us inside. It'd looked like we didn't have much choice. They didn't even let us keep the lifejacket.

I looked around the place. It was furnished like a punishment cell. There was a two-tier hard bunk – one up, one down – like the ones the cons slept on in jail. There was an upright wooden chair and a small table screwed to the floor.

The cell was lined with thick wooden panels. They'd been screwed into a sturdy frame. The whole thing had been painted a dirty green. The place was lit by a light screwed firmly into the ceiling. There was a single window. It would have provided a view – except it was filled with frosted glass.

I said: "You got out of here once before."

"Yeah, outside the window there's a metal grille they pull across and bolt in heavy weather. The dolts had forgotten about it. I just opened the window and climbed out."

I thumbed at the window. "They still haven't fixed it."

But as I spoke, the shadow of the grille appeared behind the frosted glass. We heard bolts being shot into place.

"You were saying?" Shirley said.

I sat down heavily on one of the bunks.

I said: "All we need now is for Crystal Starr to turn up."

Shirley sat on the chair and folded her arms in a schoolmarm manner. "Yeah! Is there anything you want to tell me, lover boy?"

So I told Shirley about the whole Crystal saga.

"Just as well that I came back when I did," Shirl said. "If I'd left it another night, you might have been shopping for a crib and choosing a name for your first born."

"I didn't think you'd be away for two nights," I said.

"Me neither, buster. But the closer you get to being chosen, the longer it takes. They put me up in a swish hotel. All expenses paid."

We had a moment's silence.

I said: "Congratulations, by the way. It's great that you got the part in the film."

"If I ever get on the screen. I wasn't banking on this."

"We need to think of another way out," I said.

"I'm listening, mastermind."

We fell silent again.

Heavy steps pounded along the corridor outside and stopped outside the door.

It opened. Perry Turner stepped into the room. He was followed by Blaster and Knocker.

He said: "We shall decide what to do with you later. For now, all we want is for you to get a good night's sleep."

"In that case, you can move us to a stateroom with butler service, buster," Shirley said.

Turner grinned. "I regret I cannot do that – especially in your case. But I can guarantee you sleep soundly."

Behind Turner, Blaster and Knocker parted to let a fourth figure through. Chunky Dunn.

He was holding a white kidney dish. The kind you see in hospitals. But never with a kidney inside.

This one held something more sinister. A hypodermic syringe.

Turner said: "This will ensure you both sleep soundly until morning. Mr Dunn has kindly agreed to administer the injections." Turner pointed at me. "I think you first."

Blaster and Knocker moved around Turner. They grabbed me and heaved off my jacket. Unbuttoned my shirt sleeve and roughly pulled it up.

Dunn stepped forward. He held up the syringe, depressed the plunger, and a little of the liquid squirted into the air. Then he held my arm.

"Just a little prick," he said.

"Yeah! You are," Shirl said.

I would've laughed but at that point the needle jabbed my arm. I felt something flow into me. And I slumped back on the bunk.

Shirl tried to fight off Blaster and Knocker, but she was never going to win that one. A minute later she slumped on the bunk beside me.

Turner said: "Make yourselves comfortable. Good night, sleep tight, don't let the bed bugs bite."

With a dismissive flick of his wrist, he ordered the others out of the room.

"You will eventually awake," he said. "Unless Dunn has misjudged the strength of the injection."

He grinned, turned, and walked out of the door.

"Well, close it," he said to Knocker. "Do I have to think of everything?"

* * *

Shirl and I sat on the edge of the bunk and stared at one another.

Then we put our arms around each other and had a long smoochy kiss.

"Do you think that will keep us awake?" Shirl said. "If so, I'll have another one."

"I don't feel tired."

"What do you suppose was in that?"

"Some drug to put us to sleep."

"Permanently?"

"I don't think so."

We sat there waiting for the drug to take effect.

"I feel cold," I said.

I rolled down the sleeve of my shirt and reached for my jacket.

Shirl said: "If we had a screwdriver, we could take off one of those wall panels before we fall asleep and escape."

I stood up and moved across to the wall. Each panel was secured by four large slotted screws, one in each corner.

I said: "We'd need a screwdriver with a thick head so that it wouldn't slip out of the wide slot on these screws."

"Yeah! Pity I left my toolbox back in Adelaide."

We fell silent again.

"Penny for your thoughts," Shirl said.

Of course!

I thrust a hand into my jacket's pocket and pulled out a penny.

"How about a penny for our freedom?" I said.

I looked closely at the penny. It was an old one, dated 1918. There was a picture of George the Fifth in profile with his little pointy beard. The coin was worn but still thick enough for what I had in mind.

I said: "I can use the edge of this penny like the head of a screwdriver. We can take out the screws and remove the panel."

"Let's do it before we get all sleepy."

"Yes, I don't feel even a bit tired."

I gripped the penny between my thumb and forefinger, shoved it into the slot of the first screw and turned anticlockwise. The screw wouldn't budge.

"This is going to be tough on the fingers."

"Forget that. What else are you going to do with them?"

A scrap of half-remembered classroom physics came into my mind. "If I press down harder as I turn, I think it increases the force. I think it's called something like taking moments about a point," I said.

"Do it – then in a moment we'll see if there is a point," Shirley said.

I pushed and turned. The screw moved. I turned again, easier this time.

Within a couple of minutes, I had three of the screws out. Only one to go.

Shirl put her hand on my arm. "Wait! Do you hear that?"

"What?"

"That scratching sound."

"Where?"

"Came from the other room. Other side of the wall."

"Probably rats. Old rust bucket like this is bound to have dozens of them."

I went to work on the last screw.

"It's out. We can lift out the panel. But let's do it quietly."

I moved forward.

The panel flew out of the wall. Punched by a tremendous

force from behind. It hit me full in the chest. I stumbled backwards. Knocked over Shirl. We fell on the lower bunk. The joints gave way and the upper bunk collapsed on top of us in a clatter of metal and springs.

It sounded like a revolution in a scrap metal plant.

Shirl and I pushed away the thin mattress which had fallen on top of us.

Grinning through the hole in the opposite wall was the head of Chunky Dunn.

He said: "*Ssssh!* Climb through here and we'll make our getaway."

The door of our cabin flew open. Turner stood there flanked by Blaster and Knocker.

Turner scowled at us, pushed past the collapsed bunks, and walked up to Dunn.

"So we have a traitor in our midst," he said.

"Screw you," Dunn said.

Turner looked at the hole where we'd removed the wall panel.

"There will be no screws where you're going," he said.

TWENTY

Chunky Dunn slumped on a crate of baked beans. Economy size.

We were in the *Seabreeze's* storeroom, a place without windows below deck. We'd been marched there by Blaster and Knocker and locked in, behind a stout metal door. I'd noted on the way in there were solid bolts top and bottom on the outside.

The place was lit by a bare lightbulb hanging from a twisted flex. The room was lined with the kind of metal shelves you see in pictures of warehouses. I walked round the place. The shelves were stacked with tinned food, packets of cereals, jars of jam, tubs of marmalade, bottles of pickled onions, heaps of toilet rolls, cannisters of cleaning powder. There was enough stuff to open a corner shop.

Dunn shifted uncomfortably on the beans.

He said: "I fixed the injections so they wouldn't send you to sleep."

"Why would you do that?" I asked.

Dunn shrugged, "I guess my cover is blown, so I might as well introduce myself."

He climbed off the beans and extended a hand towards me. "Detective Inspector Charles Dunn, Metropolitan Police, Special Branch."

Shirley's eyes popped. "You're a cop?"

Dunn pulled a rueful face. "Working undercover."

"Not anymore," I said.

"I'll find a way to get us out of here."

"This place looks pretty solid."

Dunn said: "I had a plan to get you out of the other room. I figured you could crawl through the wall panels I'd removed and we'd escape in the motor cruiser. I only pushed that panel to test how tightly it had been screwed in. If I'd known you'd already removed the screws, I wouldn't have touched it."

Shirl perched on a bench which ran along the back of the room. "Guess we'll have to hand you a free pass on that one," she said.

I joined Shirl on the bench. Dunn resumed his place on the economy beans.

"Why are you here undercover?" I asked.

"Drugs," Dunn said. "We had our suspicions about the *Seabreeze* soon after it moored outside the three-mile limit. It was a strange choice of mooring. Most of the pirate stations that want to catch advertising for the London market moor somewhere off the Thames estuary. Then there was the fact that Turner had no previous connection with the music industry. Most of the others have been DJs who've broadcast on the BBC or Radio Luxembourg."

"And that was enough to raise your suspicions," I said.

"That, and one other vital fact. When we put the ship under surveillance, we discovered its supply vessel was sailing from France. That made no sense at all. Any one of half a dozen British ports would have been nearer. The Met decided we needed to find out what was going on here. As it happens, I'd had a bit of amateur experience as a DJ on a hospital radio station. So my bosses put me in undercover. I got a job here on the basis that I'd come cheap to get into the music business."

"And you're sure Turner hadn't suspected you were a plant before tonight?" I asked.

Dunn frowned. "I may be new to music, but not to undercover work. My cover was perfect."

"If they got the drugs in on the French ship, how did they get them ashore?"

"We've not cracked that yet. We reckon Blaster and Knocker were usually the mules to transport the stuff ashore. They'd normally do it at night. I'd watch them take the motor cruiser and disappear into the gloom. We'd have teams watching for them onshore, but they never used the same landing spot. There are scores of places along the coast where a small motor cruiser could put in."

"We caught them on Palace Pier."

"We caught them?" Shirley said scornfully. "Other way round. Need any proof. Look to your right. You're keeping company with a pile of OMO. 'Adds brightness to whiteness.' Not in your case, buster."

Dunn said: "Actually, things may be brighter than they look."

"How come?" Shirley asked.

"Blaster and Knocker were on the pier to make a drug drop. Because of the barney with you two, they never made it."

"I made the drop for them – into twenty feet of seawater," Shirley said.

"Now they've got two problems," Dunn said. "How to make the drop to keep their customer happy – and how to deal with us. The fact they have that problem may be keeping us alive."

"For now," I said gloomily.

We fell silent. Somewhere deep in the ship a generator was throbbing. There were no other sounds.

Shirl said: "Where does this Zena Lightheart fit into the picture?"

Dunn said: "She came on board about three weeks after I'd been here. Turner had decided he needed an American voice on the air – trendy, he said. Personally, I didn't see why we couldn't rely on good old Brit voices – don't we have enough accents to keep people happy?"

"And Zena got the job?" I asked.

"Yeah! She came cheap, like me. Seemed to fit in, too. Free and easy. I wouldn't say she's into hard drugs, but I've caught that sweet smell outside her cabin sometimes."

"She smokes weed?"

"And it's not seaweed," Dunn said.

"Do you think she's in on the drug running?" I asked.

"Hard to say. I think she knows about it. I tried to raise the subject of drug culture with her one day – subtle like – but she turned the conversation to something else."

Dunn would have been as subtle as a sledgehammer. But he didn't seem to have aroused any suspicions with Turner until tonight's aborted escape.

Shirley said: "While you two are gassing about what happened, Turner's goons are planning three burials at sea. How are we going to get out of here?"

"Standard police procedure," Dunn said. "Wait for back-up."

"Yeah! I can just see the boys in blue boarding the boat with cutlasses clamped between their teeth," Shirl said. "We've got to get our own ideas."

We looked at one another in silence.

"Colin, what are we going to do?" Shirley pleaded.

I shrugged. "I don't know. But with all these beans we won't go hungry."

"No can opener," Dunn said.

We fell silent again.

It must have been two minutes before Shirley said: "I can feel a draught. Quite a breeze, in fact."

I looked around the room. There was no air conditioning, no gaps in the wall or under the door.

Shirl said: "The draught is coming from behind those crates of mineral water."

Dunn and I moved over and shifted some of the crates off the shelf and onto the floor. We uncovered a tall metal grille about three feet square. Behind it, a wide ventilation shaft receded through the wall and turned a sharp right corner after about six feet. The thing seemed to be lined with galvanised metal.

I said: "We never felt this draught before. Why now?"

Dunn glanced at his watch. "The station is about to go on air in a couple of minutes. That means the ancillary generators in the engine room will have started up. There'll also be the ovens in the kitchen. This vent runs the length of the ship and comes out about six feet above the deck at the stern."

"Then we can take off the grille and crawl through it," Shirl said.

"We haven't anything to take out those screws," Dunn said. "After the racket we made last time, we need to do this super silently."

Our shoulders slumped. A good discovery would go to waste if we couldn't remove the screws.

I said: "Are there any tins of sardines on these shelves?"

"He faces death and thinks of tucker," Shirl said.

"Sardine tins have keys a bit like tiny screwdrivers. I reckon if we can get a couple, we can shift these screws."

We found the sardines between the smoked mackerel and the pilchards.

The grille was fixed to the wall by four small screws with narrow heads. It was a tight fit, but with the sardine key we had the screws off the grille in five minutes.

"I'll lead the way," Dunn said. "I know how this ventilation shaft passes through the ship. "Best if Shirley comes second and Colin brings up the rear."

"And I spend the morning staring at your rear in a tin tunnel," Shirl said.

"Well, I plan to enjoy the view," I said.

"I always expected you were a secret pervert."

"Let's get moving," I said.

Dunn heaved himself up and squeezed into the vent. It was a tight fit for a big man, but he managed to creep along.

It was cold in the vent and the metal was slimy with grease. But that helped us slide over the surface.

It was dark, too, except where side-grilles had been let into walls to suck in air.

We'd slid silently about fifteen feet before Dunn stopped and looked back over his shoulder. "We're just coming up to the galley and the mess. It'll be right underneath us. We need to be quiet. Blaster and Knocker will be chowing down their breakfast at this time."

"I can't see anything," I said. "The vent seems to come to a dead end."

"No, it turns a sharp right-angle, then it's just a few yards to the deck."

We slid forward again.

Shirl whispered: "*Sssh!* What was that sound?"

We all stopped.

Something ahead of us creaked. Then the hinges that held the vent to the wall squealed.

"It's just our movement in the vent. But it creaks when the ship moves, too, so it's normal," Dunn said.

But as we edged up to the corner, the joints in the vent creaked more loudly. Then a screw broke loose.

Ping!

The screw's head shot off and bounced around the vent.

"Move more slowly," Dunn whispered over his shoulder.

But before we had time to do that, another screw broke, then a third.

Ping!

"Jeez!" Shirl said. "This is like being a target in a shooting gallery."

"The screws are breaking at the right-angle turn in the vent," I said. "That's where there's most strain on the joints. Especially now some of the screws have broken."

Ping!

Another screw head bounced around inside the vent.

Clank!

The joint burst open and our section of the vent separated from the right-angle turn. The right-hand section sagged downwards.

A high-pitched squeal echoed off the metal walls.

And a body slid out.

"*Yeeeooow!*" the body shouted as it whizzed past.

But we didn't have time to absorb that. Because now our section of the vent had come loose from its fixings. It tilted forward. With all that grease under us, it was like a ride on the Cresta run.

We shot out into the mess room below.

First Dunn.

Then Shirley.

Last me.

I landed on the floor next to Zena Lightheart.

"Guess my rescue plan went tits up," Zena said.

My gaze searched the room for Shirley. She'd landed on the table where Knocker and Blaster were eating their breakfast.

"Blimey," Knocker screamed. "A girl's just landed in my Rice Krispies. Beats one of those plastic toys."

* * *

Chunky Dunn shot Zena Lightheart a dirty look.

"We could have made it to freedom," he said. "Your extra weight in the vent screwed us."

Zena's eyes flashed angrily. "Who's talking about extra weight, Fatso. Button your lip."

I said: "Let's calm down, shall we? We need to think our way out of this."

The four of us were sitting in a circle on the floor inside an abandoned bunk room. In the days when the ship had ploughed the seas as a freighter, the crew would have hunkered down in here at night. I'd like to have thought of them slinging their hammocks. More likely they slept on metal cots screwed to the walls. They weren't here now. The place was as empty as a pauper's purse.

And I'd have preferred to have thought of a way out.

After we'd shot out in a tangle on the breakfast table, Turner had rushed into the mess brandishing a vicious machine pistol. Thirty bullets in ten seconds and woe betide you if you got in the way of one.

Turner had marshalled us to our feet and herded us in here. And that was bad news, because I couldn't see any way out.

Shirley said: "Jeez, what a farce! And I've got Rice Krispies in my panties."

Zena said: "Cool it, sister. That's the least of our problems."

I said to Zena: "If we're going to get out of here, I think it's time you told us who you are."

Zena stood up, leant against the wall, and exercised her back muscles. It was worth watching. She was wearing a denim romper suit and those soft shoes the Yanks call sneakers. She looked like the kind of girl who was no stranger to sneaking.

She said: "I'm a CIA special agent. Working undercover."

"And no doubt licensed to kill," Dunn said sourly.

"If necessary. And don't rule out I might start with you, smartass."

I asked: "Why are you here? And why did you try to rescue us?"

Zena flexed her shoulders and hips. "Top secret. My orders come direct from the Oval Office."

"Lyndon B Johnson himself?"

"Sure. Mr President. But I guess it doesn't make a bison's fart of difference now we're gonna be fish food. Fact is Turner is a bad guy. A seriously bad guy."

"He's a drug runner," Shirl piped up.

"Yeah! On the side. Like the drugs are his pension fund if his real masters turn awkward."

"Real masters?" I asked. "Awkward?"

"Like they decide who they need to kill. 'Coz when you take your orders direct from the Kremlin, your job security ain't always as reliable as if you're working for Sears Roebuck. And you don't get a gold watch when you retire. It's more like a bullet in the back of the head."

I stared at Shirley speechless. And, by the way, you'll know I'm not usually speechless.

Shirley had lost interest in the Krispies in her panties. "Jeez. Is this some kind of spy ship?"

"Worse than that, sister. This is the front line of the cold war."

I said: "You'll have to explain that."

Zena re-joined the circle and sat down. "Okay. You'll remember how John F Kennedy faced down Nikita Khrushchev in the Cuba crisis four years ago."

"Kennedy forced the Russians to withdraw missiles from Cuba that were aimed at the United States," I said.

"Yeah! The Ruskies thought JFK was bluffing when he threatened to nuke them. But it was they who blinked. Big loss of face for the Communist Party. Left the CP floundering. They thought they were on a level playing field with us Yanks. Thought they could compete. But they came onto the pitch and discovered they didn't have the clout to hit a home run."

"So they looked for other ways to spread the revolution," I said. "By undermining countries in the West."

"Yeah! They knew they couldn't match us on weapons. For all their May Day parades through Red Square, their hardware was the kind of junk you see on backstreet second-hand car lots. So, secretly, in the last few years, they've tried a new strategy. They know they can't beat us on the field of battle or in high diplomacy. But, they think, they can undermine us from within. They think our societies are soft. They think if they press the right buttons, they can undermine our will to resist them, partly by dividing our societies. It's a new take on the cold war – a culture war."

"And they'd do that by turning one group of citizens against another," I said.

"Smart boy," Zena said. "Especially, they want to turn young against old."

"So that the young don't think it's worth fighting for the values the old have bequeathed them – democracy, freedom, justice."

Zena nodded. "It's the reason they've turned a blind eye to Turner's drug running. They think the more drugs the young take, the more degenerate they'll become."

"They may have a point," I said. "But those crusty old colonel types, who down half-a-dozen large whiskies in a saloon bar at night, don't pack a punch anymore."

"So, here's the point," Zena said.

"At last," Dunn grumbled.

Zena ignored him and said: "The big brains in the KGB came up with the bright idea that a pirate radio station could be used to sow division between young and old. The trouble was they needed a Brit to front the scam for them."

"But why Turner?" I asked.

"Turner plays the ageing dope. Hides the fact he was at Cambridge in the nineteen-thirties. Member of the dramatic society with one Guy Burgess."

"The spy who defected to the Soviet Union in 1951."

"Yeah! Although he didn't surface in Moscow until 1956 with his old Cambridge mate, Donald Maclean."

"And were joined by another ex-Cambridge man, Kim Philby in 1963," I said. "People now talk about the Cambridge Spy Ring. They suggest there are other members."

"Too right there are. And Turner is one of them. But he's kept his head down."

"As a sleeper."

"He's wide awake now," Zena said.

"And planning something?" Shirley asked.

"Sure thing, sister. He's planning a big one. Trouble is we don't know what it is."

"Has to be something to do with this beach party he's organised," I said.

"Brilliant," Dunn said. "You should be a detective. I don't buy all this spy crap."

"That's 'coz you ain't been inside the shop," Zena said.

"We do undercover work in Special Branch," he complained. "We were first onto the drugs."

"I'll grant you that one," Zena said. "Now you're behind the curve. But you can still be a hero if you tag along with me."

"Can't wait," Dunn grumbled.

"Just a small matter," Shirl said. "We're stuck in this place that stinks like a dunny. And we've got no way out."

"That's not entirely correct," an unwelcome voice said.

Our heads all swivelled in one direction. Turner silently unlocked the door. He cradled his machine pistol in his left arm. Behind him, Blaster and Knocker also held guns.

"It's exercise time," Turner said.

"Twice round the deck followed by a game of quoits?" I said.

Turner smiled. Like an undertaker viewing a corpse.

"You are, at least, going for a stroll," he said. "In the old tradition of pirate ships, you are all going to walk the plank."

TWENTY-ONE

Turner hustled us outside and lined us up along the ship's rail.

He covered us with his machine pistol. Knocker and Blaster had guns trained on us, too.

I glanced at my watch. It was just past eight. The sun was low on the horizon but this was Midsummer's Day. The sun wouldn't set until around ten and there'd be a faint glow in the sky to the west even at midnight.

Three miles landward, Turner's beach party was due to start in less than two hours.

I said: "Instead of wasting our time, shouldn't you be ashore, ready to welcome The Rolling Stones."

Turner grinned. "I plan to do so. I look forward to meeting Mick Jagger again."

"You knew him before?"

"I was his tutor when he was a student at the London School of Economics."

That had my attention.

"You were a professor?" I asked.

Turner frowned. "A humble lecturer. Appointed after I left

Cambridge. I'd completed a doctorate in economic history, you know. My thesis on nineteenth-century railway timetables was published to acclaim."

I said: "And all these years later, the applause is still ringing in your ears. But you resent that you're still a humble lecturer. No professorship for you. That must hurt."

"Academia is a jungle and my true worth was never realised. But I will make my mark on the world tonight. My name will be famous. I will become a hero."

"Of the Soviet Union, no doubt."

"Where else? I've hidden my political views for years, the better to serve my masters."

"The commies," Shirley spat out.

"Do not be disrespectful or you will walk the plank first."

"You're not really going through with that nonsense?" I asked.

Turner waved his pistol to direct our attention further along the deck. The gangplank had been moved aside so that there was a clear space in the deck rail. A six-foot plank had been lashed into place by thick ropes.

Turner said: "As you have to die, it's fitting that you should die the pirates' way."

I said: "Pirates didn't walk the plank. It was reserved for mutineers. And, even then, captains were wary of using it because they could be tried for murder back on dry land."

Dunn piped up. "If you don't mind, Perry, I'll sit this one out. I was never a very good swimmer."

"Shut your face, yellow belly," Zena said. "It's not optional."

Turner gazed wistfully out to sea like he was on a Mediterranean cruise.

He turned back to us. "Life is a performance. Until now, I

have performed in the shadows. But, tonight, I become a star. And your role in walking the plank will make me one."

"We'll swim to shore, then come back, rip your balls off, and shove them down your filthy throat," Shirley said.

Turner laughed. "Very colourful. I must remember to include the threat in my article."

"What article?" I asked. "I'm the reporter around here."

"Not for this publication," Turner said. "The *KGB Journal* has a strictly limited circulation. But I'm convinced my contribution will stand out. I shall call the article 'Useful idiots' in honour of Vladimir Lenin who coined the phrase."

Blaster nudged Knocker. "He got that from that Hungarian piece that was on board earlier today."

"Yeah! She was a bundle of laughs – I don't think," Knocker said.

Turner waved at Blaster and Knocker. "You two talk too much." He gestured towards Shirley and me. "Keep these useful idiots covered while I'm gone," he ordered.

"Are Blaster and me useful?" Knocker asked.

"No, just idiots," I said.

"Even half of it's a win in my book," Blaster said.

"What's happened to Magda Groff?" I asked Knocker.

"The Hungarian piece took the cruiser and went ashore."

Turner raised his eyebrows. He turned to Knocker: "Keep that flappy mouth shut while I'm gone."

He marched down the deck, and disappeared through a door.

"The guy's mad," Shirl said. "He's got a 'roo loose in the top paddock."

"He's got the guns, sister," Zena said. "What are you gonna do about that?"

We fell silent.

Blaster said: "I'm looking forward to the Stones' concert. Groovy!"

We all turned to look at him.

"Yeah! Should go with a bang, eh, Blaster?" Knocker said.

They both laughed. But the laughter died when a voice said: "I've already told you. Shut it."

Turner had reappeared silently on deck. We gawped at him.

He was wearing a fancy blue doublet with gold braiding and a tricorn hat. He had a thick leather belt strapped around his waist. The belt suspended a scabbard from his left side. The scabbard held a cutlass. One of those blades with a broad curving end. Not so good for stabbing someone. Great for carving the Sunday roast. The cutlass' hilt stuck a good four inches out of the scabbard.

Turner cradled the machine pistol in his left arm. But now he held a camera in his right. It was one of those big nineteen-thirties jobs you see in Hollywood films about Al Capone. It had handles on both sides and a flash gun like a searchlight screwed on the back.

I said: "What is this? A fancy dress show?"

Turner glared at me. "Don't be offended. But why should you be? Shortly, you'll be dead. The costume... It is just me showing my fellow CP members that espionage can be fun. I intend to take photographs of you all walking the plank. I shall enter the pictures for the KGB's Most Inventive Killing of the Year award. The winner receives a week's all-expenses-paid holiday in Sochi on the Black Sea. I'll be a shoo-in."

"And the losers spend the rest of their lives in a Siberian labour camp," I said.

"Happily, you won't be around to see my victory."

Zena pushed forward and pointed at Shirley and me. She glared at Turner and said: "Listen, comrade, these two guys are civilians. Leave them out of the killing. Me and Dunn are the pros around here."

"I'm also quite happy to take a pass on this one," Dunn said.

"Zip it up," Zena said.

"We're wasting time," Turner said.

He strode up to me. "You will walk the plank first. Don't fall off too soon. I need a good picture of me menacing you with the cutlass."

"You won't be able to do that and snap the camera," I said.

"Knocker, hold this camera and take the shot," Turner said.

"I already got a pistol in one hand," Knocker said.

"Give it to Blaster."

Knocker handed the gun over. Blaster held it in his left hand. He already had his own gun in his right.

"I need both hands free to swing the cutlass," Turner said. "Blaster, hold my machine pistol."

"I already got two guns. Ain't got three hands," Blaster said.

"Then improvise with the two you've got," Turner snapped.

Blaster moved towards Turner with his arms outstretched to receive the machine pistol."

Out of the corner of my eye, I saw Shirley and Zena crowding in behind him.

Turner dropped the machine pistol onto Blaster's outstretched arms.

Blaster yelled. "*Owww*, that pistol's hurting my arm."

Shirley kicked him hard on the ankle. He staggered sideways and dropped the lot. They clattered to the deck. Blaster tripped over the machine pistol and sprawled across the other guns.

I moved in tight on Turner and grabbed the hilt of the

cutlass. I yanked it from the scabbard with such force Turner staggered sideways.

Zena lifted an elbow and crashed it into his mouth. Blood spurted from his lips and he spat out a couple of teeth.

I took a swing at him with the cutlass and caught his right arm. I'd slashed through the doublet and drawn blood. He yelled in pain and cradled his right arm with his left hand.

Zena pivoted around and kicked Blaster in the ribs. He screamed and rolled off the guns. Shirley swooped down and grabbed the machine pistol.

Zena snatched up one of the other pistols. But Blaster was still lying on the final gun.

He rummaged under himself and pulled it out. We all heard the click as he released the safety catch.

He levelled the gun at me and squeezed the trigger.

But Turner was already charging to knock me to the deck. He barged me out of the way. And took the bullet in the forehead. It exited the back of his head and zinged off the deck rail.

Useful idiot. Yes, as far as I was concerned, he'd played that role to perfection.

Zena stamped on Blaster's wrist and he dropped the gun. I leant down and seized it.

Turner lay on the deck. His eyes had the stare of a dead man. The tricorn hat had fallen by his side.

Something clicked. A bright magnesium light illuminated the deck. Knocker had just taken a picture.

Zena covered him with a gun. "Drop your weapon," she said.

Knocker let go the camera and it crashed to the deck. The flash gear broke loose and rolled away.

"The boss ain't gonna like that," he said.

"The boss is dead," I said.

* * *

Turner lay on the deck with a crimson halo of blood around his head.

He didn't look like an angel.

I said: "Turner dead is the last thing we needed to happen."

"I don't buy that," Zena said. "Another dead traitor. Saves a lotta hangman's rope."

"Turner is the one man around here who knew the whole spy set-up. Now we'll never hear it from his lips."

Zena waved a hand at Knocker and Blaster. "These two guys will tell us everything we need to know."

"I don't know nothing," Knocker said.

"I know even less than that," Blaster said.

"You can't have less than nothing."

Blaster scowled at Knocker.

Zena turned to Dunn. "We can beat the crap outta these two guys. They'll squeal like little piglets."

Dunn said: "Beating the crap out of people is not something we encourage at Scotland Yard. Unless we can keep the bruises hidden."

He aimed a kick at Blaster but missed. "Consider that a down payment on what's to come."

Blaster said: "I'm shaking in my boots – I don't think."

"You will, scumbag," Zena said. "I can do things with a piece of wire, a fifteen-volt battery, and a bent paper clip that will bring the tears to your eyes."

"I ain't afraid of the electric chair."

"After what I've got in mind, you won't wanna sit down."

Blaster turned to Knocker: "I don't know what the hell she's going on about."

I said: "We're missing the point – and wasting time. You'll have time to roll up Turner's spy network in the days ahead.

We need to stop whatever atrocity he had planned for tonight – at the beach party."

Shirley said: "But how do we know what it is?"

Zena said: "I can beat the truth out of these two."

"I'll second that," Dunn said.

"Shut up," Zena said.

I said: "These two dumbos won't harbour the big secrets. We're more likely to find the truth going through Turner's papers."

"Do I look like a filing clerk?" Zena said.

"You look like you've lost the plot," Shirley said.

"Okay, sister. Here's the deal. Dunn and I will bust the truth outta this pair while you and your smartass boyfriend sit down for a nice read. Whoever gets to the truth first, picks up the medals when they're handed out."

"If we don't go to work now, there won't be medals for anyone," I said.

"Do we get a medal?" Knocker asked.

"No, you get your ass tanned," Zena said. "Hey, Dunn, help me bundle these guys inside and tie them up."

* * *

Shirley and I hustled over to Turner's office – the room where I'd interviewed him days earlier.

We barged inside and looked around. The same old Cliff Richard cut-out leant against the two champagne crates in the corner of the room.

The same old manila files on Turner's desk. The same old tower of wire baskets overflowing with papers. The same old filing cabinets along the wall.

This wasn't going to be easy.

I took a closer look at Turner's desk than I could when I'd

interviewed him. He had one of those large leather blotters. He'd made notes on the blotting paper.

Chunky to run extra session.

Supply ship due Monday.

White: CP will fix it.

Champers to shore with Groff.

I was thinking about that when Shirley said: "A bureaucrat could get off on all this paperwork."

I said: "Just as well that we're not. But we can never read all these papers in time. We need to think about what might be important."

"How can we know what was important to a slimeball like Turner? He probably spent his days reading the best bits of *Das Kapital*."

"There are no best bits in *Das Kapital*. Besides, he wouldn't be seen within a million miles of a copy. It would raise some suspicions immediately."

"He didn't seem shy about playing that *Midnight in Moscow* number. Smoochy!"

I moved towards Shirl.

She wagged a finger at me. "When I'm in the mood – and when we've got the time."

I said: "That could be it. When I mentioned *Midnight in Moscow*, he denied playing it. Denied that the station even had the disc. Yet I definitely heard it. Alone in bed at the Widow's."

"And with only your teddy bear to cuddle."

"Forget that."

"Yeah! But why was Turner so touchy about the number?"

"I think it must have been a call sign. Remember, if Turner was linked to the Cambridge Spy Ring, he'd be in deep. Deeper than deep. He couldn't risk being seen with lesser agents on shore. I reckon that when he wanted to send a message, he used his radio show. What could be more natural than playing a popular Kenny Ball number? Not a hint of suspicion."

Shirl slumped into Turner's chair. "I don't see how that could work. The number could alert all his agents that something was up, but they wouldn't know which agent he wanted to contact."

"Unless there was a second record played immediately after *Midnight in Moscow*. And the second disc would make it clear which agent Turner wanted to contact – but also let the other agents know there was dirty business afoot."

"Like it had a special meaning of its own?" Shirl thumped the desk in frustration. "There's no way we'll ever find what those second discs were."

We fell silent.

I paced across the room and looked out of the window. In the distance, I could make out a glow on the horizon where Brighton's seafront illuminations had just come on.

It looked as though Zena and Dunn may have chosen the better option. Perhaps they could beat the truth out of Knocker and Blaster.

But perhaps not...

I turned sharply and grinned at Shirley.

Shirl pouted. "I wish you'd bottle that smug grin every time you have a great idea. What is it this time?"

"We can find out which disc Turner spun after *Midnight in Moscow*," I said.

"Yeah! And we can get a list of what he had for breakfast, too."

"Radio stations keep a playlist for the Performing Rights Society."

"And who are they when they're at home?"

"They collect royalties on behalf of song writers. The writers and composers are entitled to a small payment every time one of their numbers is aired on radio. Stations have to submit lists to the Society. Even the pirate stations do it because they need co-operation from the music publishers and performers."

I waved a hand around the room. "Look at these heaps of paperwork. Like a good red, Turner is a born bureaucrat. He'll have copies of his playlist somewhere. We can..."

But I didn't have time to finish the sentence. Because Shirl was already rifling through the manila files on Turner's desk.

I started on the filing cabinets.

We found the file ten minutes later. A thick lever-arch job with day-by-day playlists for the past two months. It was divided into three sections – one each for Turner, Dunn and Zena. I levered up the mechanism and grabbed Turner's playlists.

"Now we have to run through these lists. We need to look for every time *Midnight in Moscow* is played. Then we must note every disc that's played immediately after it."

"Better make it the next two discs. In case, the next disc is a cut-out," Shirley said.

"I can see you're a natural at espionage."

"You'd betta believe it."

I said: "Let's start two months back and work our way forward."

The first page or two included standard numbers, mostly from recent hit parades. The Kinks' *Dedicated Follower of Fashion*. The Trogs' *Wild Thing*. Elvis Presley's *Frankie and Johnny*. No sign of Kenny Ball's number.

But we found it on the third page.

Shirley said: "Look, the number Turner played next was *My Ship is Comin' In*. The Walker Brothers. I dig them. And the number after that was Gene Pitney's *Princess in Rags*."

We made a note and continued the search. By the time

we'd reached the last page, we'd found nine more plays of *Midnight in Moscow*. They'd all be aired late at night – around eleven o'clock, which was when I'd heard it. Perhaps that was the time agents were told to listen out to hear whether Turner wanted to get in touch.

Midnight in Moscow had been followed five times by *My Ship is Comin' In*, but four times by Crispian St Peters' *You Were on My Mind*. On every occasion the second disc after Kenny Ball was different so we eliminated that.

We slumped down on chairs.

I said: "There are only two numbers played after Kenny Ball."

"So there are two guys Turner contacted."

"I think one of the guys was a gal."

"That Magda Groff you told me about?"

I nodded. "Turner seems to have had a quirky sense of humour. *The Ship is Comin' In* number would be when the drugs were delivered from France."

"But who was supposed to hear it?"

"I don't think it was Groff. She didn't strike me as someone in a drugs racket. I think her number was *You Were on My Mind*. Again, Turner's warped sense of humour in play. I think it was a signal she had to leave a report hidden in the Hungarian dictionary at the library. I'm sure Knocker collected a message from Groff the day I saw them. He'd probably concealed it in the copy of *Chitty Chitty Bang Bang* he was carrying."

I thought about that for a moment. Then I said: "We know Turner has planned an atrocity for tonight. But we don't know what it is – and who will make it happen."

"We should head back to land," Shirley said. "Perhaps your old mate Ted Wilson can rustle up some cops to help."

"Some help! Tomkins won't be interested in our theory. But you're right, the answer to this lies on shore."

"Great," Shirl said. "We'll go back in Winterbottom's cruiser – and I'm taking a bottle of champagne from that crate over there for us to drink on the way."

Shirl crossed the room and opened the lid on the crate.

I saw her jaw drop as she stared inside. "It's empty."

"Turner told me he was sending the champers to The Rolling Stones."

"It's not that. There's a weird message inside the crate."

I crossed the room. Looked in the crate.

A bright red label fixed inside the lid read: "Met sex in bottles."

I felt a cold chill inside me. Like the outside of my body had stayed on the ship and the inside had teleported itself to Greenland.

I now knew what atrocity Turner had planned.

"What does this weird message mean?" Shirley asked.

"It's a message from Turner," I said.

"Who to?"

"To himself. An *aide-mémoire*. A message to be very careful indeed with the contents of the crate. Because the bottles don't contain champagne. "Met sex" is an anagram. He wouldn't have wanted the real word there in case someone saw it by accident."

"I don't get it," Shirl said.

"Met sex is an anagram for Semtex. A deadly explosive."

We fell silent.

I stood up, walked back and forth across the cabin. I tried to make sense of it all. Kicked the leg of Turner's desk in frustration.

One of the manila files slipped to the floor. I picked it up, flipped open the cover.

265

Stared at the playlist inside.

Shirl looked at me with alarmed eyes. "What is it?"

"The record line-up for late tonight."

"But the station's off air."

"Turner never planned it to be. He thought he'd still be broadcasting at midnight - when the Stones' concert ends."

"And he planned to play *Midnight in Moscow*?" Shirley asked.

"Yes."

"Followed by *You Were on My Mind* or *My Ship is Comin' In*."

"Neither," I said.

"What, then?"

"A Seekers' number."

"Which one?"

"*The Carnival is Over*."

TWENTY-TWO

"*The Carnival is Over* has only one meaning," I said.

"What's that?" Shirley asked.

"That Turner planned to blow up the Rolling Stones as they finished their concert at midnight. It would have been his final musical message. His nasty way of gloating to his KGB bosses."

We were in Winterbottom's motor cruiser racing across the sea towards Brighton. We'd left Zena and Dunn on board to keep watch on Knocker and Blaster. By now, I suspected, they'd discovered the two dimwits knew nothing.

The wind rushed by us in a roar. The boat bounced on the swell. I wrestled to keep the wheel steady so we stayed on course.

The Carnival is Over had been like a flashlight which strobed across a landscape. It was like a sunburst in my brain. For a brief instance I could see how all the pieces of the devilish plot linked together.

I shouted above the noise. "I remember seeing the cases of champagne in Turner's office when I interviewed him. They were supposed to be hidden. But that life-sized cardboard cut-out of Cliff Richard slipped sideways when I bumped into it. Turner tried to laugh it off. Said they were a gift for the Stones to drink after the show."

"But the champagne crates really held Semtex," Shirley yelled back.

"That's clear now. And it's also clear why Turner stored them in his own office. He couldn't risk anyone else treating them roughly. Especially not oafs like Knocker and Blaster. It could've been a risky job even delivering them ashore."

"How did he do that?"

"We know Groff had been on board. And there was that note on Turner's blotter: *Champers to shore with Groff.* She'll carry written authority from Turner to stash it wherever she wants. Besides, who's going to be suspicious of champagne?"

Shirl hollered above the wind: "Yeah! Makes sense. As Turner was organising the event, he'll have given her a pass to access all the backstage areas."

I said: "There's something else. Groff had left a soiled sandal at Lady White's. It had tar on it. She'd have picked that up from the beach when she was doing her reconnaissance for a hiding place for the bomb. And there's another point I've just remembered. Mrs Saunders at the Woodingdean grocers had heard that Groff had studied in Moscow. I bet that's where she was recruited by the Soviet secret service."

Sea spray splashed over the prow of the cruiser. The lights of the seafront illuminations looked closer now. The black outlines of Brighton's two piers were fringed with white light.

"Another point has just occurred to me," I said. "The *Seabreeze's* cruiser wasn't tied up alongside. Groff must've hidden it ashore somewhere so she can make her way back to the mother ship after the explosion. My guess is that Turner planned to sail the *Seabreeze* off into the moonlight after tonight's horror. He had no intention of going ashore to meet his old student."

"So no more Radio *Seabreeze*?"

"And no more Rolling Stones unless we can find a way to stop the explosion."

"You think the Semtex is on an automatic timer?" Shirley asked.

"No. That wouldn't be reliable. It'll be detonated from a safe distance by Magda Groff. I must admit I was puzzled when I found a modern television with one of those ultrasonic remote-controllers in her room. She's doctored the bomb with the remote-control gear and the receptor unit from inside the TV. All she has to do is press a button – and boom! She's in total control. Even if the cops decided to clear the area – she could press the button before anyone gets to safety."

"So we have to find Groff and grab the remote-controller?" Shirley said.

I glanced at my watch.

"And if our timings are right, we have fifty minutes to do it."

* * *

The Stones were into their set with *Lady Jane* when I ran the cruiser up onto the shingle.

We leapt out of the boat and stared at the crowd. They thronged the beach shoulder-to-shoulder. They swayed to the beat. They stood ten-deep along the promenade. They lined the railings of Palace Pier. They stomped their feet on the boards to the rhythm of the music.

The night throbbed with the sound of the beat.

Mick Jagger's voice cut through the air like a blunt knife ripping fine silk.

Shirley stood on tiptoes and searched the beach. "I can't see anyone waving a remote-controller around."

"You wouldn't."

"But I can see a police trailer parked up by the steps to the prom."

"We'll make our way up there. At least it'll give us a better view."

Our feet crunched on the shingle as we elbowed our way through the crowd.

Jagger finished his number and the audience roared its approval. They waved their arms in the air and applauded. Girls climbed on their boyfriends' shoulders for a better view. Others jumped up and down like they were on pogo sticks.

On stage, Jagger nodded with a sly grin to the other Stones. And they started on *Paint it Black*.

A uniformed plod was standing at the door of the police trailer.

I walked up and said: "Is Tomkins inside?"

The plod said: "Might be."

"Has he put cotton wool in his ears yet?"

The plod looked interested. "The chief super don't like rock?"

"He's strictly a *Bel Canto* man."

"Is she the Super's fancy piece on the side?"

I winked. "Don't let on. And, by the way, would you like Shirley here to keep you company while I go in?"

Ouch! I felt a sharp kick on the ankle.

I glanced at Shirl. She glared at me.

I opened the trailer door and stepped inside.

Tomkins was bent over a street map of Brighton. He had half a dozen Dinky vehicles on the map. There was a smart Lagonda. A Tamplins beer delivery lorry. A milk-float. A Mini Minor. Tomkins was pushing a Royal Mail van with a ruler.

He moved it from the seafront up West Street into Queens Road.

Ted Wilson and a uniformed cop watched him. Ted's eyes registered disbelief. The plod was grinning.

Tomkins said: "So Foxtrot Uniform Kilo will move northwards to protect routes to the railway station, while Bravo Uniform Mike patrols the Old Steine." He pointed his ruler at the milk-float.

Ted said: "What about the seafront? That's where everybody is."

"Precisely why we should re-group away from the masses."

I said: "Excuse me butting in General Montgomery, but what happens if the stage on the beach blows up with the Rolling Stones on it."

"Then our eardrums get a well-earned rest," Tomkins snapped. "And Montgomery was a field-marshal."

I said: "This is serious."

I stood right in front of Tomkins and gave it to him straight. I told him what had happened on the *Seabreeze*. I told him what would happen on shore. What would happen in less than an hour. I couldn't have been more forceful. Or more urgent.

Tomkins heard me out with a bored look on his face.

He said: "You've tried some stunts in your time, Crampton, but this is about the most far-fetched. Who'd want to blow up the Rolling Stones?"

"Apart from you?"

I laid it on the line about the plot to turn young against old. To create a civil war of the generations.

I said: "Nothing could set young people more on fire than killing the band they revere as the symbol of a new order. Especially if the atrocity could be blamed on ageing prigs like the National Purity Army. There'll be bloodshed in the streets."

Tomkins laughed. "You'll be telling me next that Karl Marx has gone into hiding in Highgate."

"He has – in a manner of speaking."

Tomkins eyes flashed. "What? Do the Met know about this?" he snapped at Ted.

"I expect so since he's been buried in the cemetery there since 1883," I said. "But let's get back to what's happening now. You need to clear the area."

"Can't do that. I haven't the manpower. Nobody would move. There'd be a stampede."

"They can't stay where they are and stampede at the same time."

"Either way, there'd be a panic. Now, let me get back to proper police work. Where's that milk-float gone?"

Ted said: "Colin's story could be true."

Tomkins glared at Ted. "Why don't you do something useful? Like arresting someone for sticking their chewing gum on a lamp post?"

Ted stroked his beard angrily and stomped out of the trailer.

I followed him. Shirley hurried up to me.

"Got nowhere with Tomkins," I said.

"What did you expect?"

Ted joined us and said: "If you're right about this, Tomkins will be fired."

I said: "Much good that will do us. We'll all be dead."

Shirley said: "We need to find Groff and get that remote-controller off her."

Ted pointed left. "I'll search this way." He marched off.

I watched his retreating back and said: "He's going the wrong way."

"Then why didn't you stop him?"

"Because he'd give us away. Remember Groff only has to

press the button on the remote-controller and the bomb blasts."

"And, anyway, how do you know he's going the wrong way?"

"Because Groff will need to be near enough for the ultrasonic signal to reach the bomb's trigger. Those TV remote controls don't send signals long distances. I reckon twenty yards maximum. If we assume the bomb is somewhere near the stage, Groff will be close by when she triggers it."

"She might die herself?" Shirley said.

"All the better to become a martyr to the cause. But I think she'll have chosen somewhere with enough cover to keep herself safe. She must have planned a route out."

I pointed along the beach. Behind the stage, a VIP area had been cordoned off behind a six-feet high fence. Beyond the fence, there were trailers and vans. There was a large marquee. There was a chow wagon with tables, and chairs with comfy cushions, in front of it. There were heavy duty generators throbbing on their wheels. There was a row of temporary toilets like sanitary sentry boxes.

I said: "I reckon she's in there. We need to get in there, too."

I nodded towards the VIP area's main gate. Two burly guards stood outside. Their arms were folded in a way that said "Don't even try to get past us".

Shirley said: "It won't be easy getting past them. Those guys don't look like they'd fall over easily."

We watched as a couple of girls with autograph books tried to blag their way inside. The guards planted themselves in front of the gate and shook their heads.

"I have an idea," Shirl said. "Wait here."

Shirl darted away towards the souvenir shops underneath the prom. She was soon lost in the crowd.

I prowled up to the fence, grabbed the wire mesh, and

looked in. I searched in the shadows. Backstage types scurried around. They carried pieces of stage equipment, lighting rigs, loudspeakers.

The air pulsed with the music. Jagger was into *Get Off of My Cloud*. The crowd roared out the lyrics with him. Nobody much was taking any notice of the backstage crew.

But the crew were sure busy. They moved like people who had urgent business. Who knew they had to do something fast. They bustled and they hustled.

And then I caught a movement out of the corner of my eye. A slower movement than the rest. Less direct. More furtive.

Magda Groff.

She looked around her, like she sensed a threat. She moved cautiously towards a large grey van twenty yards from the back of the stage. Leant against it like she was waiting for something.

She was wearing jeans and a light linen jacket. It had fancy lapels in some kind of psychedelic material. It had deep pockets. It was the kind of gear a Stones' groupie would kit herself out in. The kind that wouldn't make Groff look out of place backstage at a rock concert.

I watched her closely. Groff didn't have the remote-controller in her hand. It couldn't fit into her jeans. Must be in one of the jacket pockets.

Her body lounged against the lorry. But I could tell that every nerve in her was alert to danger.

I realised I'd broken out in a sweat. I could feel it running down my neck and soaking into my shirt. My mind was racing. I couldn't think of a way to get the remote-controller away from her before she pressed the button.

Couldn't think how anyone could do it.

As soon as she sensed a threat, she'd press the button.

Boom!

And hundreds would die.

A tragedy was minutes away, and I could do nothing to stop it.

A familiar voice said: "Hey, Mr Crampton."

I spun around. Ted Wilson was standing there with his hand firmly on the left arm of Pete the Pickpocket.

Pete said: "It's me, Mr Crampton."

Ted said: "Just caught this tea-leaf dipping the crowd up by the pier."

Pete said: "It's a fit-up, Mr Crampton. You know me. As honest as the day is long. Twenty-three hours, isn't it?"

I said: "Ted, don't react, but that woman in the linen jacket over by the van is Magda Groff."

Ted's head swivelled like his neck rested on a pivot.

"I said, 'Don't react'."

Ted let his body hang loose. He let go of Pete's arm. "She's the one with the bomb?" he asked

"Not the bomb, but the device that sets it off," I said.

I turned to Pete. "I need your help."

Pete grinned like a jury had just handed him a not guilty verdict. "Told you there'd be a time when you needed my help. Back in Sally's tearoom."

"This time, you'll serve your country."

"I ain't joining the army. I ain't got the hands for peeling potatoes. And all that square bashing will be bad on my feet."

"You don't have to join anything," I said. "Can you see that woman over there?"

"The one with the face like a wet washday?"

"Yes, the one who's tense and nervous. The one who's fidgeting because she's got a device that sets off a bomb in her pocket."

Pete pressed his face against the wire mesh. "What kind of device?"

275

"A television remote-controller."

"Rather have the TV set. I could flog that to Frankie the Fence for thirty quid. Controller ain't got no value without the TV."

"I want you to pick her pocket and bring me that controller."

"Sorry, Mr Crampton, but I couldn't do that with the cops watching." He nodded towards Ted. "Pardoning your presence, superintendent."

"Inspector," Ted said sourly.

I said: "This is the deal, Pete. If you can pick that woman's pocket and get the controller, the *Chronicle* will pay you five hundred pounds. And Ted will turn a blind eye."

Pete glanced at Ted.

Ted nodded – reluctantly.

Pete said: "Straight up? A monkey for a job I could do with my eyes closed. And the fuzz keeping schtum. No offence, chief constable."

Ted growled.

I said to Pete: "You will keep your eyes open and under no circumstances will you press any buttons on the controller."

"Got that, Mr Crampton. But what you ain't figured out is that we're out here and she's in there – behind the fence. You'll need a cop to make those gorillas on the gate stand aside."

"We can't do that. If they think the cops are involved, they'll start all kinds of trouble and Groff will fade into the night. Or press that button early."

"I'll get you in," Shirley said.

She'd just pushed her way back through the crowd.

"Who's the bird?" Pete said.

"Do I look like a seagull?" Shirl said.

"Er, no. But I just thought..."

"Let me do the thinking," Shirl said. "Now what's the plan?"

We stood in a huddle and I explained the plan. Shirley would get us through the gates. Pete would pick Groff's pocket. He'd hand the remote controller to me for safe keeping. And Ted would step in and arrest Groff.

I looked up anxiously. The pulse of the beat had stopped. The crowd had fallen silent.

Over by the grey van, Groff looked hard towards the backstage area.

From the stage, I heard Mick Jagger bellow. "It's been a great night, Brighton. But it's not over yet. We have one last number. *I Can't Get No Satisfaction.*"

The crowd's loudest roar of the night filled the night sky.

I said: "We have one more problem. This number lasts three minutes and forty seconds. After that, the bomb goes off."

For no more than a second, we exchanged worried looks. Then we hurried towards the gate.

A big bloke with a barrel chest and a whiskery chin – think Desperate Dan from *The Dandy* – stepped in front of us. He was one of the guards we'd already eyeballed. He had a blue jacket with brass buttons which strained at their fastenings. He wore a blue cap with a shiny peak.

He snapped: "Performers, crew and VIP guests only."

Shirley stepped in front of us. She'd undone the top button on her blouse.

She said in a husky whisper: "Excuse me, handsome, I've got something Keith will need urgently after the show."

"Who?" Desperate Dan said.

"Keith Richards."

"What so urgent that he needs it now?"

Shirl lowered her eyelids, bowed her head. Looked like a

nun who'd just been propositioned. Who was torn between the offer and taking her vows.

"What's so important he needs it now?" she said in a soft seductive voice. "Why, me of course."

Dan's cheeks flushed so red I thought he was going to burst a blood vessel.

"Keith gets very excited after a performance," Shirl added.

"How do I know you're not one of those autograph hunters?"

"Because of this." Shirl produced a bright red purse from her handbag. So that's why she'd slipped away early. She must've bought it from one of the souvenir shops on the seafront. The price tag still hung from it. She quickly covered it with her hand.

"What's in there?" Dan asked.

"His condoms. Would you like to check them?"

"That won't be necessary, miss."

"So can I go in?"

Dan looked around for help. There wasn't any.

"Guess so." He pointed at Ted, Pete and me. "But who are these men?"

Shirl raised her hand and stroked Dan's cheek. "Silly boy. They carry Keith to his trailer after I've finished with him."

Dan's jaw dropped and his eyes popped.

We hustled past him into the compound.

We skirted round the edge of a coach to get out of view.

I grabbed Pete the Pickpocket's arm: "I can still see Groff over by that grey van."

"Got her," he said. "Leave it to me."

A group of technical guys trailing wires and a keyboard hurried by. Pete tagged in behind them and disappeared from view.

Jagger was belting out *No Satisfaction* at full volume. The lyrics bounced off the surface of the vehicles. The sound hit us with the force of a hurricane.

Ted bellowed: "I've lost sight of Pete. I hope he doesn't run out on us."

I shouted: "He won't want to miss out on that five hundred quid."

"You have permission to make that offer?"

"If the *Chronicle* doesn't want the story, I can sell the first-hand account of how a street thief saved the world's most famous group for thousands."

"Only if Pete does it. Sounds like the music is ending."

Ted was right. Jagger was building to his finale.

"Groff will press the button when the music fades," I yelled.

My heart was beating faster than a Charlie Watts' drum riff.

Then the Stones played the final thunderous E-major chords and the last notes of *No Satisfaction* boomed across the beach.

There was a huge shout from the crowd.

Then Jagger shouted: "Yeah! We wanted to give you an encore, too."

My heartbeat moved closer to normal.

"We've got, perhaps, three more minutes," I said to Ted. "Where is Pete?"

I glanced across to the grey van. Groff wasn't lounging against the side now. She was alert. Her gaze darted from side to side. She shifted from leg to leg. Her arms hung by her side, but her fists clenched and un-clenched with tension.

And then Pete appeared from behind the truck.

He was carrying a pile of seat cushions. He'd taken them from the chairs by the chow wagon. The pile was so high he could barely see in front of him.

But he headed straight towards Groff. She had her back to him. She stared at the stage like she expected it to fly away.

Three feet from her, Pete tripped over a power cable.

The cushions flew in the air. Bounced on the floor. Fell all around Groff.

She spun round. Her face was contorted with anger. But she controlled herself.

Pete threw open his arms in the apology gesture that's understood the world over. He bent down. Started to pick the cushions up. But Groff couldn't move because Pete was in the way and there were cushions around her feet.

On stage the final crashing chords of the *No Satisfaction* encore boomed out for the last time.

In ten seconds, there would be silence.

This time permanently.

Groff glanced anxiously towards the stage. She needed to move closer to press the controller. To be sure the ultrasonic beam would reach the bomb.

The faster Pete was out of the way, the faster she could move.

She bent down, lifted up some of the cushions, put them on Pete's pile.

Two more cushions to go.

The last chord died.

The crowd went wild.

Groff pushed Pete aside and hurried towards the stage.

One, two, three, four steps. She was close enough now.

She reached inside her right-hand jacket pocket. Her hand lingered there for a second.

She stopped. Reached inside her left-hand pocket.

Put both hands in her pockets. Rummaged furiously in the jacket.

Patted herself down.

Realised what had happened. Turned around.

But Pete had vanished.

She moved back towards the van.

Ted stepped round the side.

She looked at him like she knew what he was going to do. That she accepted it as her fate.

Ted grabbed her arm, twisted it behind her back, and handcuffed her.

Pete reappeared at my side. He handed me the controller.

I levered off the back flap and removed the batteries.

Shirley and I stepped towards Ted and Groff.

Ted said: "The Semtex is in a champagne crate under the stage. We'll contact the army bomb disposal unit to deal with it."

Ted gripped Groff's arm as she struggled in the handcuffs.

Groff's face was contorted with hate. "You think you've won. But this is not the end."

I looked Groff full in the face.

"In your case, Mick Jagger was right," I said. "You won't get no satisfaction."

I could swear her crafty eyes twinkled.

And then a huge explosion rent the air.

The midnight fireworks had started.

TWENTY-THREE

Frank Figgis lit up a *Romeo y Julieta* cigar and relaxed as he savoured the first puff.

He said: "First time His Holiness has offered me one of his finest."

Figgis made a perfect O with his lips and formed a smoke ring. It drifted slowly towards the ceiling.

He said: "You haven't got one as I told His Holiness you don't smoke. I couldn't believe it when you rang me at home with the news last night. I was in bed. Your call woke Mrs Figgis. She got a bit over-excited, too. We, er... didn't get much sleep after that."

I grinned. "So no more visits to the Continentale cinema?"

"I thought we'd agreed you weren't going to mention that."

It was the following morning. We were in Figgis' office. A proof of the midday edition's front page had just come up from the compositors' hall. The splash headline in the paper's largest type read:

THE CHRONICLE SAVES THE STONES

Underneath was a huge picture of Mick Jagger and Keith

Richards. They were holding a grinning Pete the Pickpocket on their shoulders.

We had pictures of a coastguard cutter escorting the *Seabreeze* into Shoreham harbour. And more snaps of Chunky Dunn and Zena Lightheart leading the handcuffed Blaster and Knocker down the gangway onto the dock.

I said: "I spoke to Ted Wilson a few minutes ago. The lights were burning all night at the cop shop. Apparently, it was the first time they hadn't had a nocturnal poker school in the lost property depositary for months. Big wigs from the security services in London crawling all over the place."

"Did Wilson mention any new angle we can use?"

I said: "It seems the spooks have been interrogating Magda Groff. We already knew she came to Britain after the Hungarian uprising. She posed as a refugee but, in reality, was a top KGB agent. It was the perfect way to infiltrate the country. She wormed her way into Lady White's household by pretending to be interested in her purity campaign. All the while, she urged White to become more and more extreme. It was all part of the Soviet's plans to divide British society – the young against the old. The atrocity she'd planned for last night would have set fire to years of simmering resentments – especially if it could be blamed on White's purity headbangers. But it looks as though Groff got careless and White became suspicious – which is why she had to be killed."

"Work that into the copy you've already delivered and we'll run with it in the second edition."

"And it turns out that the security services already had suspicions about the National Purity Army which is why they'd been watching White's house. When I was spotted following Groff, they naturally wanted to know who I was."

Figgis took another puff of his cigar. The piquant aroma of fine Havana tobacco leaf didn't quite mask the acrid whiff of Woodbines that hung about in the corners like a furtive rat.

Figgis said: "I'm worried that other hacks will be hanging around the cop shop and worm details we haven't got out of that idiot Tomkins."

I said: "I wouldn't worry about that too much. The spooks have closed the place as tight as a..."

"Duck's arsehole."

I frowned. "I was about to say 'as His Holiness' wallet'."

"Yeah! He blanched a bit when I told him we'd guaranteed Pete a monkey. He wanted to know whether it was a protected species. He didn't relax when I told him it was five hundred smackers. He calmed down when I told him we'd make ten times that from syndication fees."

"And, of course, you mentioned my own five-hundred pound bonus."

"What!" Figgis leaned forward so fast the ash fell off the end of his cigar.

"And while he's at it, you can ask him to make out another cheque for the same amount to Miss Shirley Goldsmith."

"He'll never buy it."

"He will when you explain that the *Sunday Mirror* has offered her as much on account of she's appearing in the next James Bond film. They'll go for the real-life heroics story."

Figgis hunched his shoulders and went into one of his grumps. But he made a note on his pad.

He said: "So what are you going to spend your fortune on?"

I winked: "I've had an idea about that."

"Not cigarettes, whisky and wild, wild women?"

"Don't smoke, prefer gin, and I already have the last one – I think."

We fell silent.

Figgis puffed on his cigar.

I thought about the worry that was nagging at the back of my mind.

I said: "We started this story with Winterbottom's murder and we still haven't solved it. We don't know who killed Lady White either."

"Surely the Groff woman," Figgis said.

"Not according to Ted Wilson. She strongly denies both killings. Claims White was still alive when she left her house yesterday afternoon. Apparently, two neighbours saw Groff lugging a heavy suitcase up to the bus stop in Woodingdean about the time she claims."

"As the *modus operandi* of Winterbottom's killing was the same, that makes her an unlikely suspect."

I nodded. "I had suspicions about Groff when I saw her at Woodingdean library. They turned to certainty when I saw that note on Turner's desk blotter: 'White: CP will fix it.' CP had to mean the Communist Party. And Groff was clearly a card-carrying *apparatchik*."

"I guess you're right," Figgis said. "CP couldn't be anything else. Presumably, the killer of both Winterbottom and White is some highly-trained Communist Party assassin."

"Or someone who's initials are CP. Like Charlie Parker," I said.

"What about that Puttock?" Figgis said.

"He's disappeared, which is suspicious, but his first name is Jeremiah. So JP, not CP."

"Too bad. At least we got one name to match."

I sat there and stared at the wall behind Figgis' desk. My heart was doing a quickstep. I could feel that flush round my neck which always came when the light shone in my brain.

"What did you just say?" I asked.

"I said, we got one initial matched to one name."

CP. Of course! It didn't stand for the Communist Party. It

stood for something else. In fact, someone else. But not in the way initials usually work. Not one initial, one name. This was two initials, one name.

I stood up and headed for the door.

"Where are you going?" Figgis demanded. "We haven't finished our talk yet."

I turned at the door. "Best hold the front page for the second edition. I now know who killed Winterbottom and White. And I can prove it. Have the comps standing by for my copy."

I went out and closed the door behind me.

* * *

Thirty minutes later I walked into the Clancy club.

Simkins, the club steward, was behind the bar polishing a beer glass.

I said: "You better buff up another half-dozen of those. Three car-loads of rozzers will be along in a bit and they're a thirsty lot."

Simkins dropped the glass, wrapped the tea-towel nervously round his hand, and said: "What business would the roz... the local police want with a respectable person like me?"

I ignored that and said: "It's early, so I take it there's only one other person in the club."

"Er..."

"And he'll be in his private room."

"He said definitely no visitors. On pain of death."

"As it happens, that's just what I want to talk to him about."

"Visitors?"

"No, death."

Simkins gulped. A big theatrical one. Like they do in the

repertory when the actor wants to make sure the punters in the back row know he's supposed to be shocked.

I said: "You look like you've just swallowed a frog. Pull yourself together and get me a gin and tonic."

"One ice cube and two slices of lemon?"

"You're recovering fast. And with a memory like that you'll find a new job in a top bar in Brighton with no trouble. After my meeting with your member, you'll need it."

I took my drink and bounced into the private room.

Crouchpenny was standing in front of a filing cabinet. He rummaged inside and pulled out a sheaf of papers. Took one glance at them and ripped them into pieces. From the pile on the floor, it looked as though he'd been at work for some time.

He looked up as I came in. His face contorted like he'd just had a severe attack of heartburn.

I said: "There are guys at the cops' forensic lab who are expert at putting ripped-up documents back together again. It's a bit like doing a jigsaw puzzle with the added pleasure that somebody goes to prison at the end of it."

Crouchpenny swallowed something invisible in his mouth – perhaps it was his pride – and said: "I hope you're not implying I'm a criminal."

I said: "Not implying. Just stating a fact, CP."

"What did you just call me?"

"CP."

"The name's Manfred Crouchpenny."

"That's what fooled me. Your initials should be MC. But I'd seen the initials CP and I assumed they belonged to someone with a name like Charlie Parker."

"I don't know any Charlie Parker."

"Me neither. But we're missing the point. In the CP initials I've seen, the C stands for Crouch and the P for penny. And I'd bet a pound to a penny I'm right."

Crouchpenny moved to his reinforced sofa and sank wearily onto it. He shifted uncomfortably and his stomach rippled like a wave rolling up a long beach.

He said: "The only point I'm interested in is having you thrown out. Butt and Thumper will be here any minute. Then you'll end up in the street with both ankles unfit for service."

"I'm afraid you're on your own today. Butt and Thumper won't be joining you."

"Then they're fired."

"I think they already resigned."

"What are you talking about?" Crouchpenny snarled.

"Before I came here, I called my old friend Detective Inspector Ted Wilson at Brighton police. He has an all-points bulletin out looking for two men driving a converted hearse. They won't be hard to find."

"What's this all about?"

"It's about murder," I said.

Crouchpenny's eyes bubbled with fury like lava pools. He tried to lever himself off the sofa. His fleshy chest formed into a huge cleavage as he leaned forward. There were middle-aged women in Florida who paid plastic surgeons big money to create an effect like that.

Crouchpenny flopped back on the sofa with the effort.

He said: "I'm a respected businessman, not a killer."

"Seven days ago, your gormless assistant Butt drove you to Embassy Court. You entered by the backstairs so you wouldn't be seen by the hall porter. Then you killed Claude Winterbottom by bludgeoning him to death. You used Thumper's teak cosh. The one with the leather strap. After you'd used it, you wiped off the blood with Winterbottom's handkerchief which you left next to his body. Knowing your devious mind, I suspect you used a borrowed weapon so that if it was ever linked to the crime, the owner rather than you would be suspected as the killer."

Crouchpenny's lips twisted into a sly grin. "You should junk crime stories and stick to fairy tales. What motive could I have for killing a broken-down investment consultant?"

"How about the fact he'd swindled you out of five thousand pounds?"

"That was a business transaction. Big-time players like me can take a hit like that and come out smiling."

"That's not the impression you gave in your threatening letter to Winterbottom."

"Yeah! Well, perhaps I was irked by the toe-rag. Doesn't mean I killed him."

"No, you were too cautious to plan that yourself. But then someone suggested an ingenious double bluff. What if you killed Winterbottom using a distinctive *modus operandi* and soon after killed someone else – someone you had no connection to - with the same MO? Even if the cops suspected you of the first killing, they wouldn't be able to place you close to the second. And they'd have to look for a new suspect. They'd develop a new line of enquiry which would take the heat off you. As it happens, the cops never suspected you anyway because they never saw your threatening letter."

"Never had any heat on me. And, anyway, who's this genius of the double bluff supposed to be?" Crouchpenny asked.

"I'll come back to that in a minute. Let's deal with the second killing first."

"I never did a second killing 'coz I never did a first one."

I said: "Two days ago, Butt drove you to the home of Lady Millicent White where you killed her. Again, you bludgeoned her to death. But this time you wiped the cosh on an anti-macassar from the back of a chair. Magda Groff, White's *au pair*, had been warned in advance what was going to happen, and had made herself scarce so you had a free run."

"And then I went and played with the pixies."

"No, you reported back to the genius of the double bluff."

"Albert Einstein."

"No, Perry Turner."

The muscles in Crouchpenny's flabby jaw tightened. "I know no Turner."

"But I think you do. When investigators show your bar steward Simkins a picture of Turner, I think he'll confirm that he's met you here on several occasions. Incidentally, Simkins is looking for another job."

"Even suppose I met Turner for a friendly drink, doesn't mean he asked me to kill someone. Or that I'd do it. I'll explain that to the cops."

"It won't be the cops who interrogate you. Because Turner was a spy and he wanted you to kill Lady White because she'd become suspicious about a Russian agent. Yes, the very same Magda Groff. I don't know why White had developed a suspicion, but perhaps it had something to do with a television set that Groff had dismantled in her room. Or perhaps Groff has just been careless. In any event, Groff felt the heat and asked for Turner's help – and Turner had you do the dirty business. So you'll be questioned by the security services. You won't have your solicitor present and there'll be no cup of tea and a bun if it all gets a bit too heavy for you."

Crouchpenny leant back on the sofa. His face was white and he was breathing heavily.

"Look, supposing I do a deal on what I knew about Turner?"

"Ah, we're getting to the truth. I suppose you're going to tell me about the fact that for months now, you've been distributing the drugs Turner smuggles ashore. I'm guessing that when Winterbottom scammed you for five big ones, it emptied your personal piggy-bank. You needed to find a way to make some quick money. Your snouts on the criminal grapevine told you that a new guy in town was developing a drugs racket but needed help with distribution. But you'd got in deeper than you thought. When Turner needed some seriously heavy help – killing Winterbottom and White – he had you right where he needed you. Can't have been easy for a guy who previously ran his own rackets to take Turner's orders."

"I can name the dealers I passed the drugs on to."

"Except you haven't done it personally. Butt and Thumper were the errand boys and what could be more innocent than driving around in a converted hearse. Who would think they were delivering illegal drugs?"

"Did one of them squeal? I'll wring his neck."

"No, not intentionally. But when I met them at Digby's garden centre, Thumper carelessly mentioned they'd had deliveries to make on the way back. Deliveries to people who paid up promptly. At the time, I didn't know what those deliveries were, but it's all become clear."

"I'll turn Queen's evidence on the drug business and get a light sentence – could be as low as two years - and get back to my life." He scowled at me. "You'll need to watch your back when that happens."

"That's not much of a threat, Crouchpenny. Because you're going away for murder."

"You can't prove that I was at Winterbottom's and White's gaffs at the time of the killings," Crouchpenny wailed.

"No, but you can."

"Now you're getting desperate."

"Do you remember what happened after you'd killed White? Butt drove you back to the Clancy club. After he'd dropped you, he returned to the Easy Loans office and left the journey chit with your secretary Vicky. Just like he did after your visit to Embassy Court. You'll know that each chit contains details of the date, time and destination of the journey. Your orders, to stop private journeys at your expense. Vicky is a good secretary. She's filed the chits away, just like you told her to so you can claim tax relief on the journeys. You may gouge every penny you can out of your unfortunate clients, but when it comes to spending your own money, you're the original Mr Tightwad."

Crouchpenny heaved himself to his feet. He lumbered across the room to the table which held the telephone.

He said: "I'm calling Vicky now. I shall order her to destroy those chits."

I said: "By the way, I forgot to tell you. Vicky's resigned."

"What?"

"Yes, I called at the office before I came here and explained what's up. She wasn't as horrified as I'd expected. But then she knows you well. Anyway, I was able to give her a lead on some excellent jobs coming up at other firms. Galley proofs of new jobs due to be advertised in the *Chronicle* over the next couple of days. She plans to follow them up this morning. After she's dropped those chits off at the cop shop, of course."

Crouchpenny stumbled forward. Had to grab the edge of the table to steady himself.

I said: "Look on the bright side. All that terrible prison food. The pounds will literally fall off you."

Crouchpenny opened a drawer on the desk. He pulled out a gun. A vicious-looking Heckler & Koch semi-automatic pistol.

He levelled the gun at me. "Interfering reporters. Don't understand, do you? Poke your nose into someone else's business. Well, poke it into mine, and you get it shot off. If I'm going down for two murders, I might as well make it three. And, anyway, three's my lucky number."

I glanced behind him. "Not today," I said.

Ted Wilson had crept silently into the room. There were two uniformed cops with him. One had a rifle levelled at Crouchpenny's back.

Crouchpenny saw my glance and swung round. For a moment he tensed. Held the Heckler & Koch at arm's length, both hands on the stock. Classic grip to fire a pistol. His finger tightened on the trigger.

Then his arm dropped. He shrugged. He threw the pistol on the floor.

Ted said: "Not sure we've got a cell big enough for this one."

I said: "You could always borrow the elephant house at the zoo."

TWENTY-FOUR

Shirley Goldsmith raised her glass and took a delicate sip of her vodka martini.

She said: "I'm sorry the *Seabreeze* is sunk."

I said: "It's still floating in Shoreham harbour. Just impounded by the security services."

We were in Prinny's Pleasure. It was the evening and we'd both had a busy day. Mine included being nearly shot by the fattest loan shark in the world.

Shirley said: "Yeah! I know the ship was rotten, but I just meant they played some groovy sounds."

"Chunky Dunn and Zena Lightheart have spun their last discs. Ted told me the pair have been whisked off to an MI5 safe house in the country. They'll be living the good life – butler service included – while they're debriefed. The spooks will want to know every detail about how that phoney pirate radio station operated. No such pleasure for those two goons Knocker and Blaster. They've been taken to London, Ted tells me. Wandsworth Prison apparently. Their interrogation won't be quite so polite."

Shirl grinned. "No butler service for those bludgers."

"Meanwhile, Tomkins has drawn the short straw. He has to interview Crouchpenny."

"I thought you said Tomkins can't wait to stick the thumb-screws on real killers."

"Not this one. It turns out when Crouchpenny is nervous he breaks out in a nasty smell. Like a heap of ripe manure. Apparently, it's the only time Tomkins has ever done an interview with the windows open. Ted normally complains about being left with the small fry. But this time, he's happy to interrogate Butt and Thumper. They'll tell Ted everything they know about Crouchpenny to save their own rotten skins."

"So that wraps it up," Shirl said.

"Apart from Jeremiah Puttock, commander of the National Purity Army. It looked as though he'd gone absent without leave, but he turned up late today. It turns out he'd been visiting an ancient aunt in Leominster. He'll be hauling down the colours now that Lady White, who funded his army, is no more."

I pulled out my wallet and took out a cheque. Handed it to Shirley. "By the way, the *Chronicle* is paying you a bonus – for freelance services rendered on the *Seabreeze*."

Shirley's eyes widened as she took in the sum. "Jeez! I'm rich."

"I've got one, too," I said.

Shirl drained the last of her vodka martini. "This calls for another drink."

I signalled to Jeff to bring refills.

We fell silent while Jeff prepared the drinks.

Jeff grinned as he stepped up to the table. Some of the gin and tonic slopped over the top of the glass as he plonked mine down.

He placed Shirl's vodka martini on the table like he was stroking a baby.

"Shaken not stirred," he said. "I don't normally do table service, but when it's a film star I make an exception."

He leaned closer to Shirl. "Especially when it's a Bond girl. You're the most gorgeous I've ever seen. Well, perhaps second most after that Ursula Undress."

"Andress," I said.

"Bless you," he said. "These summer colds make you sneeze."

He handed Shirley a beer mat. "Would you sign it? An autograph to put on the wall with all the other stars."

"You haven't got any stars," she said.

"But I will have when the film comes out."

Shirl handed back the mat. "Another time, perhaps. I'm not a star – yet. Perhaps never. Besides, this mat is soaked with beer."

Jeff pulled a disappointed face and sloped back to the bar.

Shirl stared at her drink, then at me.

"I've got something to tell you," she said.

"It's bad news."

"Depends how you look at it. I've decided not to be in the film."

I reached out for Shirl's hand. Took it and squeezed gently.

"But it's a lifetime's opportunity. You were thrilled. I've never seen you so excited."

"Yeah! I was flattered. My ego sprouted wings and I was flying to the moon. But a girl from the Outback soon comes down to earth. I'm no actress. I simply can't be what I'm not. I can't pretend to be someone else. It's just not me."

"Then be yourself."

"I am myself when I do my modelling. And that's what I

love. I can be what I am and express my feelings through the way I look. Genuine feelings, straight from the heart."

"Cubby Broccoli will be so disappointed. He might turn into a cabbage."

Shirley smiled. "So I'm happy about my decision. I hope you're happy with it, too."

I put my arm around Shirl's shoulder and kissed her cheek. "Delirious. We're good together and nothing can shake that."

"Nothing at all."

"And no one can stand between us," I said.

"Not a soul on this Earth."

The door to the bar opened.

Crystal Starr walked in.

She was wearing jeans and a Sloppy Joe sweater.

She looked around the bar, saw us – not difficult as we were the only customers - and came over.

"Thought I'd find you here."

"I thought you'd be on stage this evening," I said.

"I'm resting."

"You've got the night off?"

"Nah! Resting in the theatre means you ain't got no work."

"You're not in the show anymore?"

"Got fed up with the dirty old groper of a producer. Well, actually he fired me. On account of that night when I burst into tears after my little speech and you stormed out."

"I'm sorry, I don't know how you got the idea into your head that I was your boyfriend."

Crystal snivelled a bit. "I had it all worked out in my mind. You'd be my boyfriend. You'd write nice things about me in your paper. I'd become famous and then we'd get engaged. You put the ring on my finger – and we'd live happily ever after." She took a hanky out of her pocket and blew her nose. "Silly dream. I can see that now."

Shirl leaned forward and patted Crystal's arm. "Don't let it get you down, girl." She nodded towards me. "I get the mixed-up signals from him all the time."

"I am here, you know," I said with as much dignity as I could muster.

Crystal said: "Came round in case you knew of any jobs going. Ingénue willing to travel. Own tits and teeth."

I shook my head. "My world is in newspapers."

"Mine isn't," Shirl said. She opened her handbag, rummaged inside, and pulled out a small notebook and Biro.

"How'd you like to audition for a role in the next James Bond film?" she said.

Crystal gawped. "You serious?"

Shirl tore a leaf out of the book and scribbled a note.

"Here's the name and address of the guy who runs the auditions, Curtis Grainger. He knows me. In this note, I've recommended you for the role. Go and see him tomorrow."

Crystal grabbed the note. "Thanks ever so much."

She shoved the note down her cleavage. "It'll be nice and warm when he reads it. Ta-tah!"

She scampered out of the place like someone who's just opened a new chapter in the book of life.

"That was a wonderful thing to do," I said.

"Yeah! That's me. Saint Shirley of the Movies."

"So life returns to normal," I said.

"And you're not Crystal's boyfriend anymore. You don't need to get engaged to her."

I lifted my glass and had a good pull at the gin and tonic.

I said: "I wouldn't get engaged to Crystal, but I might like it with someone else."

Shirley had a thoughtful sip of her vodka martini. Put down her glass. Narrowed her eyes and gave me her serious look.

"Got anyone in mind, buster?"

"Yes."

I reached inside my jacket pocket. "I've already cashed my bonus cheque," I said. "Some of it went on this."

I pulled out a small box. Opened the box and showed Shirley what was inside.

"Jeez, is that what I think it is?"

"An engagement ring. The big stone is an emerald cut diamond, the jeweller told me. And these smaller diamonds on each side are called shoulder stones. The ring itself is gold. Of course."

Shirley stared at the box. "Of course. It sure is beautiful, but..."

"But what?"

"But I thought we were good as we were. Now that Crystal is out of our hair. Yours especially."

She had another sip of her vodka martini. "I don't know whether I want to get engaged. You know where that leads."

"Up the aisle."

"Yeah! Marriage. For life, buster."

"And you don't want to spend your life with me?"

"When we first met, I told you I was on a journey. I wanted to find my true self. I said I wanted the freedom to move on at any time."

"But you've been in Brighton for four years."

"Perhaps that's long enough."

"And you've made a great name for yourself as a model here."

"Sure, but it's not the only country where models do well. There's America, France, Italy... Maybe it's time to move on."

I reached into my pocket and pulled out two tickets. "I also visited a travel agent this afternoon and booked these. Two tickets to the island of Sicily."

"Wow, you have been a busy boy. Can't have much of that five-hundred stash left."

I grinned. "None of it, but I've saved some other money."

"Ain't you the little miser? But, really, I wasn't expecting this."

I leaned forward and put my arm around Shirley.

"Come with me to Sicily, to a small town called Taormina. It nestles on the cliffs above the Ionian Sea. The sea and the sky are so blue, they look like they've come freshly painted from an artist's brush. There's an ancient Greek amphitheatre. In the evening, as the sun sinks, the last rays fall onto the stage where players would have performed in ages past – tales of love and lovers. How Orpheus travelled down into the Underworld in search of his beloved Eurydice. How the handsome Leander swam the Hellespont to declare his love to Hero, the most beautiful of women."

"More likely to have a naughty," Shirley said.

"I know you're a free spirit. That's what I love about you. But getting engaged won't be like being in a cage. More like setting out on an adventure."

"We have enough of those already."

"Sure. But this will be an adventure of the heart."

Shirley picked up her glass and swirled the last of her drink around it.

"Guess as I'm not going to be James Bond's girl I need to think about my future."

"That's great."

Shirl held up a hand. "Doesn't mean I'm saying yes."

"I understand. But come with me to Taormina. On our first evening, we'll go to the amphitheatre when the sun is setting. I'll get all traditional. I'll go down on one knee and ask you to marry me. Tell me then what you've decided."

Shirley's face lit up with her cheekiest of grins. "Jeez! You paint quite a picture. This I've got to see."

"The amphitheatre at dusk?"

Shirley drained her glass "No, buster. You down on one knee."

* * *

Thank you for reading **The Beach Party Mystery**. If you have a few moments to add a short review on Amazon or Goodreads, I would be very grateful. Reviews are important feedback for authors and I truly appreciate each one.

Don't forget, my free novel **Murder in Capital Letters** is available to all newsletter readers. You can subscribe over on www.headlinehero.co.uk.

Want to know what Colin and Shirley did next?
Then begin reading the first two chapters of **The World Cup Mystery**...

A killing before kick-off... and a crime reporter who must
crack the case before the final whistle

THE
WORLD
CUP
MYSTERY

PETER
BARTRAM

Headline Hero Series Book 9

.

THE WORLD CUP MYSTERY

CHAPTER ONE

Taormina, Sicily. 19 July 1966

The lizard had a mean slit of a mouth and a dark green fretwork pattern down its back, like an artist had painted ribs on the outside of its body.

It sat on a stone step and basked in the last rays of the evening sun.

It flicked an insolent lid over a dark beady eye and stared at us.

"Colin, why is he giving us the evil eye?" my girlfriend Shirley asked.

"He thinks you're sizing him up as a pair of lizard-skin shoes," I said.

"Wouldn't get a sandal strap out of that critter."

"He doesn't know that. He wants to know what's going to happen next."

"That makes two of us," Shirley said.

She was right. Here we were in Taormina, a town perched on the cliffs above the Ionian Sea. Me, Colin Crampton, crime correspondent, Brighton *Evening Chronicle*. Hot-shot reporter and trouble magnet, according to my news editor.

And Shirley Goldsmith, proud citizen of Adelaide, Australia. Have toothbrush, will travel. Photographers' model. Totally gorgeous, whether glimpsed through a camera's viewfinder or across a crowded room.

We were sitting on a step in the town's ancient Greek amphitheatre. A tall bank of stone steps, bleached white in the sun, swept in a long arc behind us. Moss grew in crevices where the stones had crumbled. In ancient days, townspeople would have sat on these steps. They'd have wept over a two-hanky tragedy from Aeschylus, who died when an eagle dropped a tortoise on his head. Didn't even get to write a play about it. Or, perhaps, they'd have laughed themselves silly at a ribald comedy by Aristophanes. He invented the dirty joke and the smutty innuendo. And gave centuries of busybodies something to tut-tut about.

But there was no show tonight.

Only a play we'd make for ourselves.

And I didn't know whether it'd turn out to be a comedy – or a tragedy.

The slanting rays of the sun lit Shirley like a spotlight. Her blonde hair shone like polished gold. Her blue eyes sparkled with fun. Her wild lips parted in pleasure.

She was wearing a yellow shift dress, with black trim. Eight guineas from a boutique in London's Carnaby Street. And who cared if the dressmaker had skimped on the silk so the dress ended four inches above Shirl's knees? Not me.

The lizard scurried closer for a better look.

I couldn't blame him.

Shirley glanced at me and winked. "So, just remind me, big boy, why are we here?"

* * *

Why, indeed?

How do I get myself into these things?

I'd brought Shirley to the most romantic spot I'd ever found on Earth to ask her a question.

Will you marry me?

Shirley had tagged along because she'd promised to answer it.

Yes. Or no.

She hadn't yet decided.

What had become our own Greek drama had started a month earlier. We'd been having a drink in a pub when the subject of love and marriage had come up. When I'm with Shirley, the idea of love is never far from my mind. But marriage? Well, we'd never discussed it.

But it was just after I'd written a story for the *Chronicle* about a pirate radio station. It had turned out to be a front for communist spies. The radio station. Not the *Chronicle*.

Shirl and I had been through a lot together. Not least, escaping narrowly with our lives.

And then I'd passed a jeweller's and seen just the perfect engagement ring in the window. I had it in my pocket now. Gold with a big emerald-cut diamond. Smaller shoulder stones on either side. Impulsively, I'd bought it. And there, in the pub, I'd pulled it out and asked Shirley to marry me.

It wasn't like the last reel in a Hollywood weepie, where the girl falls into the hero's arms. No, Shirley took one look and told me she wasn't sure.

And so, that's why we were in the Greek amphitheatre. We waited for the moment when the shadows lengthen and twilight falls. When the stones darken and the moon casts a silvery light over the Ionian Sea. When the scent of romance is carried on the evening air like fragrant bougainvillaea.

The moment when men are bold and women weaken.

Or, at least, that's what I'd heard. And if I were impressionable, I might have believed it. But anything's worth trying once.

I'd told Shirley I would go down on one knee and ask her to marry me. And she'd promised to give me her final answer then.

* * *

So, here in the amphitheatre, now was the moment.

And it was nothing like I'd heard.

My heart was pumping like a steam engine's piston. My skin felt clammy and hot. My eyes viewed the scene through a kind of mist. And it felt like a herd of wildebeest had started their annual migration in my stomach.

(And where the hell was that damned bougainvillaea scent?)

I was about to learn just how the rest of my life would turn out.

The lizard flicked his tail, like he didn't care.

Shirley grinned. "So, are you going to do it?"

"Do what?"

"The one knee thing."

"Of course."

"Anyway, what's that all about?"

"It's a mediaeval tradition. You know, knights and their ladies. It was a way for the guys in their armour to show how much they honoured their women. You said that's what would get you here. Me down on one knee."

"Yeah! Now I'm not so sure."

"You mean you're not going to accept my proposal?"

"You haven't made it yet."

"But if I do?"

"Having second thoughts?" Shirley asked.

"No. But haven't you made up your mind about your answer?"

"Not yet. I want to see what I feel when you actually ask me the question."

I kicked the dust on the ground. The lizard scurried into a crevice between the stones.

"Now you've frightened the poor critter," Shirley said.

"Too bad. Two's company and three's..."

"A sex orgy. Yeah, I know the joke."

I looked at Shirley. She grinned at me. I raised my gaze to the sea. It was that kind of impossible blue. But where the sun's rays slanted across it, there were streaks of gold. In a few moments, they would be gone as the sun sank below the summit of Mount Etna.

When I'd suggested the trip in the pub, I was convinced the sight of all this beauty would have fired up Shirley's mind.

Now, I wasn't so sure.

I looked back at her. She'd folded the fingers of her hands together. She stared intently at me.

"I'm doing it now," I said.

I took the ring box from my pocket and flipped it open.

I dropped to one knee.

Yeeeeooooow!

The cry came from behind one of the pillars in the amphitheatre's backdrop.

Yeeeeooooow!

It came again. The cry of a soul in pain. Of someone who looks into the future and sees only a black empty space.

The cry echoed off the pillars, bounced off the steps. And then rang in my ears. I shivered. Felt my whole body tense.

I looked at Shirley. Her mouth had dropped open. Fear filled her eyes.

Yeeeeooooow!

The cry came a third time. I sprang to my feet. Shirley jumped up. She shot me an alarmed look.

I closed the ring box and thrust it into my pocket.

Now deep gulping sobs echoed from behind the pillar.

The sobs of a woman.

Shirley and I hurried towards the sound.

The woman behind the pillar was slumped on the ground. Her back rested on the stone. Her knees were pulled up under her chin. Her face was buried in her hands. Each sob was so deep it shook her body. She gulped for air.

She had long raven hair and, as far as we could see, a complexion so white it could have been dusted with flour. She wore a cream blouse which was torn on the right sleeve and a simple fawn skirt. She had a pair of old canvas shoes on her feet. There was a ragged hole in the heel of the left shoe.

Shirley knelt down beside her. Put her arm around the girl's shoulder. Whispered something softly in her ear. I couldn't hear what it was.

But the girl turned, parted her fingers and looked through them at me.

"It's my father," she said in English.

"What about your father?" Shirley asked.

The girl whimpered into her hands. "He died... He's dead."

"We're so sorry," Shirley said.

The girl cupped her hands more tightly around her face. She gulped back another sob.

"I think he's been murdered," she cried.

* * *

As soon as we'd landed at Catania airport earlier that afternoon, I should've known there'd be trouble.

We were held up in a queue at immigration for half an hour while an old guy in front argued about whether he should've had a visa in his passport.

Then, when we went to pick up our luggage, a vanity case Shirley had brought with her had gone walkabout.

I said the case was probably too vain to ride the carousel with the other baggage.

Shirley told me I should take it more seriously. She stomped off to make a complaint to an official in a blue uniform with enough gold braid for a Ruritanian general.

He waved his arms about a bit. Shirley waved her arms and stamped her foot.

And the vanity case finally developed some humility and turned up last on the carousel.

So, by the time we arrived at our hotel in Taormina, it was the middle of the afternoon – and we both felt frazzled. But some sandwiches and a bottle of *Asti Spumante* revived our spirits.

Shirley relaxed in her chair and looked out at the street as a girl on a Lambretta sped by.

"So, when you gonna do the dirty deed?" Shirl asked.

"If you mean the proposal, I don't look on it as a deed and certainly not a dirty one."

Shirley grinned. "Listen to you. Sound like some kind of old fogey."

"I want it to be special. That's why we've come to Taormina."

"Could have done it on the end of Brighton pier," Shirley said.

"Too frivolous."

"Or in the Royal Pavilion gardens."

"Too regal."

"Or high up on that Devil's Dyke hill behind the town."

"Too public."

"You sure are Mister Particular."

"I want to knock you off your feet, so you'll say 'yes'."

"More likely to give you a two-fingered salute if I'm lying on the ground."

I slumped back in my chair.

Shirley was in one of her difficult moods. I put it down to tiredness from the journey. Or perhaps she was nervous about the proposal. Maybe she wouldn't accept.

And where would that leave her? Or me?

We needed a diversion. Something to occupy our minds until evening, when we'd go to the amphitheatre.

"Let's go for a walk," I said.

"Where?"

"The main street here is called the *Corso Umberto*. Apparently, it's got a lot of interesting shops."

Shirley grinned. "Sounds like my kind of street."

"Wow," said Shirley. "Just look at all these flags. They must know you're in town."

We'd climbed the steps to the *Corso Umberto*, a cobbled street flanked by old stone buildings. They crowded together so close, like they wanted to be friends.

The place was strung with red, white and green bunting. Shops sported signs which read: *Forza Italia!*

"All this show is for the World Cup," I said. "Italy are one of the strongest teams. They hope to win it."

"And what do those signs mean?" Shirley asked.

"*Forza Italia!* It's like shouting 'Come on, Italy'. I expect there'll be plenty around town yelling it this evening. Italy play North Korea. They have to beat them to stay in the competition."

"I didn't know you were a football fan."

"I'll be cheering England when they play."

"Hey, what's this over here?"

A shop window had caught Shirl's eye. A jeweller's.

"No girl would think twice of turning down a guy with that in his back pocket," she said.

Shirl had her nose pressed up against the window. Inside, a blue velvet stand revolved slowly. The stand held a gold box with a single ring. A hoop of gold with a rock the size of an asteroid mounted in it.

"There must be a zillion carats in that diamond," Shirley said.

"Any guy with that in his hip pocket would be walking around with a limp," I said. "Could rupture a buttock if he sat down."

"Rock that size - no guy would hold on to that for long. Any gal would have it on her ring finger in a trice."

"I thought size didn't matter to you," I said.

Shirley winked. "What are you talking about now, big boy?"

"The same thing as you, I think."

"Sure, the size of the ring doesn't matter. It's what it stands for that's important. But there's no reason why a girl can't dream."

"You want me to trade in the ring I've bought for another?"

"No, of course not. You couldn't do that here."

I pointed at a sign in the window: *Compriamo buoni gioielli.*

"We buy good jewellery," I translated.

"Yeah! And sell it at twice the price," Shirley said. "I bet the guy who runs this joint is a pirate. You stick with the ring in your pocket."

She tore herself away from the window and twirled around in the street. "I've decided I love this street. I love the cobbles and the grey stone. I love the shadows and the light – and these mysterious alleyways that lead off on both sides. Let's go up that one over there and see where it leads. An adventure."

"We'll be having an adventure in the amphitheatre later," I said.

"That's not an adventure. It's a transaction."

"We don't know where those alleys lead – or who lives up them."

"You think it's the Mafiosi – and you're a scaredy-cat."

"And with good cause where the Mafia is concerned. Let's walk on. I think I can see an ice-cream parlour further up the street."

But before we could move, a woman shot out of the alley we'd looked in.

Her face glistened with sweat and her breast heaved with deep breaths. She was young – barely twenty. She had a trim figure, like an athlete's.

She turned and bent forward to rest her hands on her knees. Took a couple of deep breaths. Straightened up and screamed at someone further down the alley.

"*Mi hai picchiato una volta di troppo. Mai più, Brando.*"

Shirley stared at me and raised an eyebrow.

I translated. "You've beaten me once too often. Never again, Brando."

The woman turned and ran – away down the *Corso Umberto*.

But before she'd covered fifty yards, a burly man shot out of the alley. He was built like an ox with a big head and a mop of jet-black hair. He had dark deep-set eyes. He peeled his lips back in a grin that bared teeth like tombstones.

He opened his mouth and yelled in a deep rumbling voice after the fleeing woman.

"*Torna indietro, Rosina. O non ti batterò. Ti ucciderò.*"

"Her name's Rosina and he wants to kill her," I said.

Shirley's eyes flashed with anger. "I'm going after Rosina," she said. "You stop the brute."

Shirl's shoes clacked on the cobbles as she took off.

I turned towards Brando.

He gave me a look like he wanted to barbecue me and feed me to wild dogs. But he knew I'd understood him. And there were other people in the street giving him the hard eye.

He scanned the street. The kind of look I've seen before.

Are there are any cops about?

I sauntered up to him. Played the lost tourist. "*Puoi indirizzarmi all'ufficio postale?*"

The old can-you-tell-me-the-way-to-the-post-office ploy. Never fails.

He curled his upper lip, all the better to give me a view of his faultless dentistry.

"You are English," he said. He made it sound like a bad habit.

I nodded. "*Sai quanto costa un francobollo per l'Inghilterra?*"

"I do not know – or care – about the cost of your postage stamp to England."

He sucked in his cheeks. Gobbed a huge flob of saliva onto the cobbles. Charming.

I said: "*Pensavo ti fosse permesso uccidere tua moglie solo nel fine settimana in Sicilia.*"

"A proud Sicilian may kill his wife whenever he wishes," Brando snarled. But at least in English. "*Ma forse ti ucciderò invece io,*" he added.

"We rather draw the line at killing anyone in England."

Brando pulled back his shoulders and squared up to me. Looked like the old can-you-tell-me-the-way-to-the-post-office ploy was going to fail me. For the first time.

From the corner of my eye, the curtain at the back of the jeweller's window twitched back. A delicate hand reached in and took the monster diamond from its place on the velvet platform.

"Killing me will have to wait," I waved my hand at the jeweller's window. "I see my purchase is being made up and the armed guard that accompanies me will be in the shop putting it into a locked case."

So there would be no mistake, I added: "*Lo faccio all'interno del negozio in modo che quando esce, sia facile per lui prendere la sua pistola.*"

I added in English. "He likes to keep his gun hand free in case of street trouble."

I looked down the *Corso*. Rosina – and Shirley – had vanished.

"*Troverò Rosina e la ucciderò. E lei, signore,*" Brando snarled.

"You'll never find Rosina," I said. "And, if you come to kill me, try to avoid Sundays. I have the day off."

Brando growled something at me. He turned and stomped into the alley.

I called after him. "If you want to kill me in Brighton, you better do it when Detective Chief Superintendent Alec Tomkins is on duty. Never been known to catch a killer."

I strolled off down the *Corso*. I had a feeling Shirley would not have caught the fleet-footed Rosina. Instead, Shirl would be lying in wait for me in a bar.

I hoped she already had another bottle of *Asti Spumante* on ice.

I badly needed a drink.

THE WORLD CUP MYSTERY
CHAPTER TWO

In the amphitheatre, Shirley and I gawped at each other with open mouths and wild eyes.

Shirley knelt down beside the girl. Reached out a hand for hers.

But the girl buried her face deeper in her hands.

"My father's been murdered," she moaned.

"Come on, give me your hands," Shirley said gently. "Then we can dry your eyes and talk about your troubles."

The girl dropped her hands and looked straight at Shirley.

"No one can solve my troubles," she moaned.

"Strewth!" Shirl sounded like a girl from the Aussie Outback when she was shocked. "It's the girl from the *Corso Umberto*."

"The girl who was running away from that brute of a bully?" I asked. "Is your name Rosina?"

I stooped down to look the girl full in the face. Her eyes were misted with tears.

"Yes, I am Rosina," she said with a spark of fire in her voice. "And the brute is Brando, my husband."

"Did he murder your father?" I asked.

"No. My father is in England. But he is dead. The police tell me on the telephone. I think he is murdered. But the police will not say how he died. Even though I am born in England and have a British passport. They treat me like I am an Italian – like I am a foreigner and a nuisance."

Shirley wrapped her arm around Rosina's shoulders. "Why don't we go and sit on those steps over there? You can tell us all about it."

We helped Rosina to her feet. She walked slowly towards the steps. She sat down on one that caught the last rays of the sun. A dark shadow had descended across most of the amphitheatre – like the show had come to an end.

I felt it was only beginning.

Shirley and I sat on either side of Rosina. Shirley gently stroked Rosina's hands.

I said: "Tell us about your father and how you heard of his death."

Rosina gave me a searching look – like she wasn't sure she wanted to share her dark family secrets with a stranger. Then she shrugged.

"I have no one else who will listen to me. At least, not here. Not Brando. Not his friends. And I have no friends. Brando does not like me to mingle with other people."

"Sounds like a little charmer," Shirley said.

"Brando is a brute," Rosina spat. "He beats me because I want to go to my dead father. He says: 'What's the point?' I tell him I have to know how my father died."

"Who is your father?" I asked.

"His name is Sergio Parisi."

"Italian?" I asked.

"But he lives in England. He owns a small café in Crawley."

"That's near Brighton," I said.

318

"Where we live," Shirley chimed in.

"I know Brighton," Rosina said. "There are many smart cafés and restaurants there. Not like my father's. His is a transport café."

"For working people. Nothing wrong in that," I said.

"Perhaps not for the working people. But my father is not like that. He wants to have money – and there is not much profit in a plate of egg and chips. I know he does other things to make money."

"Illegal things?" I asked.

"I won't say. But it is why he wanted me to marry Brando. He told me Brando came from a good family in Sicily. A family with plenty in the bank. I did not know that the bank was somebody else's and Brando's family planned to rob it. But the police here know when to look the other way. Because Brando's family is... connected."

Shirley and I exchanged worried glances.

"To the Mafia?" I asked.

"You do not speak that word around here. Not if you want to keep five fingers on each hand."

I said: "Do you think your father has been killed by the Mafia? They have connections in Britain."

"I don't know."

"But you want to find out?"

"Yes. But all the policeman would tell me over the phone was that they are looking at all the possibilities."

"Did the policeman give a name?"

"Yes, I wrote it on a piece of paper."

Rosina rummaged in the pocket of her skirt. Pulled out the crumpled paper and read.

"He said he was Detective Chief Superintendent Alec Tomkins. He said he would clear up the case."

I said: "Tomkins couldn't clear up the cups from a kids'

picnic."

"You're saying he's incompetent?"

"I'm saying if he had to put a crook behind bars, he'd first have to find the bars."

Rosina wiped her eyes with the backs of her hands.

She said: "This is why I want to go to England. I need to find out how my father died. I need to arrange his funeral."

"What about your mother?" Shirley asked.

"She died when I was two. She was hit by a lorry while riding her bike. She had bought a chocolate cake for me at the baker's."

I leaned towards Rosina. "Why doesn't Brando want you to go to England?"

"I told him I wanted money to buy a plane ticket, but he said he couldn't spare any. I told him he had much money that he hides from me..."

"And he hit you?" Shirley asked.

"You didn't see that," Rosina said. "Brando lets no one see what he does to me."

"That's what guys like Brando do. Their brains are in their fists."

"Yes, I ran from Brando in anger, vowing I would never return. Even though I snatched my key as I rushed from our apartment. And now I don't know what to do. I have no money – and nowhere to go."

"It's worse than that," I said. "We stopped Brando. He told me he'd find you and kill you. But he'd have said that in anger."

Rosina shook her head furiously. "No, no. no. When Brando says he will kill, he means it." Her voice dropped to a whisper. "I know he has killed for money. I cannot say who paid him."

"The Mafia," I said.

Rosina shot me a worried glance. But she gave the tiniest of nods.

I looked at Shirley. She knew what I was going to say. She nodded, too. But not like Rosina. Not a reluctant crick of the neck. Shirley's was a determined tilt of the head – with one of her flashing smiles as a bonus.

I turned to Rosina. "We could get you to England."

"Sure, we had nothing special planned," Shirley said. "Only a marriage proposal."

"But how can we do that?" Rosina said. "Brando knows I want to get back to England and he will be looking for me – even at the airport. And not just Brando. He has powerful friends, too."

I stood up and looked around the amphitheatre. Eerie pools of darkness had appeared between the pillars of the theatre's backdrop. Between them, the colour of the sea had turned from blue to black. Tiny white flecks showed where waves broke. Above us, bats had started to circle, hunting for food.

I thought about the mission that had brought us here. Wondered whether we would ever return. Wondered whether I would ever get to propose to Shirley. And whether she would ever accept.

I looked at her now. She had her arm around Rosina and was whispering something in her ear. Rosina nodded her head gently. Shirley took Rosina's hand and squeezed it.

Shirl looked up at me. "Well, big brain, what do we do next?"

I pulled back my shoulders like a bloke who knows what he's doing. I could see from her face that it didn't do much for Shirley. But it encouraged me.

"We need a plan," I said. "But first we must get Rosina to a safe place."

* * *

Shirley gave me a hard look and said: "Before you dazzle us with your brilliant battle plan, Clausewitz, perhaps you could tell us where we're going to find the cabbage."

"Cabbage?" I asked.

"Money," she said. "We spent most of our cash on paying for this dump of a room in advance. We're gonna need ready money to buy an air ticket for Rosina."

We were in our room at the *Hotel Bella*. The name may have been chosen by a hotelier with a sharp sense of irony.

On our return from the amphitheatre, Shirley and I had waltzed through reception. We'd made like a couple intent on a night of passionate love-making.

Then we'd scooted round to the back and let Rosina in through a fire exit - while no one was around. We'd ordered room service sandwiches – some kind of fatty meat. Looked like something left over from a dissection class. Rosina had hidden in the loo when the waiter had brought in the food.

"There is another problem," Rosina said softly. She had perched on the bed and rested her back on the headboard. "I do not have my British passport. It is in the top drawer of my dressing table."

I breathed out deeply. Problem. Big problem. In fact, huge problem.

I said: "Let's deal with the problems one at a time. We need money. We don't have enough, but we do have a valuable asset."

I looked at Shirley and raised my eyebrows. I couldn't find a way to put the question into words that wouldn't hurt her feelings.

But she'd picked up the message. "The ring? Yeah! You must've emptied your piggy bank to pay for that. Guess we've got no choice. But where are we gonna find a buyer at this time of the evening?"

I said: "The shops around here stay open until nine, sometimes later. They're shut most of the afternoon. And we know the jeweller's in the *Corso Umberto* buys items."

"The pirate," Shirl said.

"We have no other choice," I said.

Rosina said: "No amount of money will get me a passport in time."

"Where do you live?" I asked.

"Brando and I share an apartment above the *Trattoria Garibaldi* on the road to Castelmola. When we married, he promised me a house on the beach. He was talking sandcastles in the air. Like he usually does, when he's drunk."

"He drinks much?" I asked.

"Every night in the bar at the *Trattoria*. Sometimes at the *Bar Mazzini*, nearby. But you cannot get into my apartment without going through the *Trattoria*. There is a door leading to stairs just inside the *Trattoria's* entrance. Anyone in there could see you. And the bar is crowded every night. Often with Brando's friends."

"I think there might be a way," I said. "Tell me, do the *Trattoria Garibaldi* and the *Bar Mazzini* both have television sets?"

"Of course. All Italian bars have them." She shook her head. "But you can't get my passport by watching television."

"I won't be. Tonight, the bar will be packed with football fans watching the World Cup game between Italy and North Korea."

"Brando will be there," Rosina said.

"Only if the television's on."

"It is always on. Especially for football."

"Somehow I've got a feeling that tonight there's going to be a transmission fault. Just at a crucial point in the game. When the *Garibaldi's* TV goes pop, the whole bar will head down the road to the *Bar Mazzini*. There'll be nobody around to see me enter your apartment. Especially as you'll be lending me your key."

"But why should the TV screen suddenly go black?" Rosina asked.

"Because I'm going to turn it off. Now, I need you to tell me exactly how your apartment is laid out. And where I can find your passport."

Rosina shot Shirley a confused look.

Shirley rolled her eyes. "Tell him what he needs to know, kiddo. But let me give you a piece of advice. If a guy says he wants to propose marriage to you, make sure he hasn't got anything else on that day."

* * *

Find out what happens next...

Get your copy here or visit the URL below:

https://www.headlinehero.co.uk/go/wcm-kindle

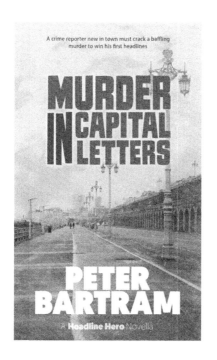

A crime reporter new in town must crack a baffling murder to win his first headlines.

Crime reporter Colin Crampton has been in Brighton only days before he stumbles on the body of a murdered antiques dealer. It's a great story but Colin must face down the cops and rival journos if he's to land his first scoop.

Claim your free copy by visiting the URL below:

https://www.headlinehero.co.uk/murder-in-capital-letters

ACKNOWLEDGMENTS

I've mentioned before that any Crampton of the Chronicle adventure couldn't appear without help from many people. Barnaby Jaco Skinner (Red Nomad Studios) has worked with me from the beginning, typesetting my manuscripts, designing book covers, and creating the wonderful website www.head linehero.co.uk. Members of my Advanced Readers' Team read the manuscript and made many helpful suggestions and corrections. The members of the team who helped are (in alphabetical order) Andrew Grand, Jenny Jones, Doc Kelly, Andy Mayes, Amanda Perrott, Christopher Roden and Gregg Wynia. Thanks to you all! Needless to say, any errors that remain are mine and mine alone.

Finally, a big thankyou to you, the reader, for reading this book. If you've enjoyed it, please recommend it to your friends! In these days of internet sales, online book reviews are very important for authors. So if you have a few minutes to leave one on Amazon and/or Goodreads, I would be very grateful. Thank you.

ABOUT THE AUTHOR

Peter Bartram brings years of experience as a journalist to his Colin Crampton crime mysteries. Peter began his career during a "gap year" between school and university when he worked as a reporter for a local newspaper. After graduating from the London School of Economics, Peter resumed his life as a journalist working for newspapers and magazines in London. He's done most things in journalism – from door-stepping for quotes to writing serious editorials. He's covered stories in locations as different as Buckingham Palace and 700-feet down a coal mine. He's edited newspapers and magazines and written 20 non-fiction books, including some ghost-written.

Peter launched his Crampton series in 2015 with Headline Murder. There are now **15 books** in the series with thousands of readers around the world. Crime book reviewers have variously praised the humorous series as "fast paced", "superbly crafted", "a breath of fresh air", and "a romp of a read". Ordinary readers had awarded the books **more than 2,500 five-star reviews** at the last count. Peter lives in Shoreham-by-sea in the United Kingdom. He is a member of the Society of Authors and the Crime Writers' Association.

Follow Peter Bartram on Facebook at:
www.facebook.com/peterbartramauthor

Follow Peter Bartram on Twitter at: @PeterFBartram

Printed in Great Britain
by Amazon

42995300R00199